The Gringo

Robert Brancatelli

Blumen Publishing
New York

For Arthur Brancatelli
and Josephine Frasula Brancatelli

Yo soy la única persona a la que puede arrimarse, que no lo odia ni sueña con matarlo. Estamos casados hasta que la muerte nos separe.

Mario Vargas Llosa,
La Fiesta del Chivo

I am the only person he can get close to who doesn't hate him or dream about killing him. We're married till death do us part.

The brown boy on the Sarita bicycle cart kept ringing the bell, which only made him want one even more: a creamy *helado* in one of those cones that looks like cardboard but melts like marzipan on your tongue. It had been a while since he'd had one, and in the heat he couldn't stop thinking about the flavors: mango, melon, papaya, zapote, vanilla. Richard loved vanilla, especially pure bean, but the vanilla down here was different from the vanilla back home in Collegeville, Pennsylvania. It was raw, granular, unrefined, as natural and exotic as smoke, but then everything in Guatemala had smoke in it. Not cigarette or cigar smoke, exactly, but what he called "Mayan smoke." It was on his clothes, in his hair, all over his skin. Even his sweat had begun to smell like it. He had noticed it at first in the western highlands on the road to Chichicastenango, the Place of Little Breasts, which the tour guide had explained repeatedly referred to the mountains, not the women. He glanced out the window of the Toyota minivan they were traveling in, and there, beside the urinating *bolo*, or drunk, was a mound of white, smoking ashes. As they drove by, it was like nothing he had ever smelled before: a pine, chicory, Christmas smell that didn't begin or end but just lingered there as if it were part of the landscape. And now it was part of him. He wondered how it would taste with vanilla. *Vain-'ee-ya.*

He had been sitting in the park in the unbearably quaint tourist town of Antigua long enough not to be bothered anymore by the Polaroid men strolling around in blue vests and matching baseball caps, waiting for some unsuspecting couple or European tourist or student with a backpack and nose ring to take their picture for a small fee. Even the shoeshine boys passed him by, not smiling but rushing headlong toward the newcomers that had managed to evade the blue men. They were serious, these little smudges of boys who looked more like midgets than children. In time, he knew they would come back for a handout, which he would end up giving, but not yet. The park was too hot, too crowded, filled with the sounds of bicycle bells, hansom cabs, Gallo beer trucks, eruptive American laughter, the thumping of a cumbia band across the street at the cathedral, and the bleating of those husky Mayan women who had ridden all night long on rickety buses to sell their handmade baskets, shawls, and table runners at a *buen precio*, or at least what they called a good price. Although they appeared on just about every postcard produced by the Guatemalan Institute of Tourism, these women were the worst. Once, he had watched them swarm and then tear apart a hapless tourist like crabs on a wounded seagull, leaving nothing but feathers and beak. All he could hear was the relentless clicking of their tongues. They were the *Señoras del Buen Precio*, and they would do whatever it took to close a sale, which he understood and even respected. They ignored him as they hurried past his bench, looking away and frowning in disapproval.

"Richard, come here! Come quick!"

There was a fountain in the middle of the park, famous according to the glossy tour books, on the other side of which his coworker and friend, CJ, was talking to an old man in a Yankees' baseball cap. The old man held aloft a bundle of shirts wrapped in clear plastic and grinned.

"I need your help," CJ pleaded, making a sweeping motion with his arm.

"No."

"Please, come!"

Richard shook his head, pretending that he couldn't hear, but CJ stood there begging him and swinging his arm in that awkward way of his.

"What is it now?" Richard asked as he approached, annoyed that he had to get up but even more by the cumbia band stuffed in yellow puff shirts with sweat pouring down their faces.

"Twelve new shirts for only a hundred *quetzales*. I ran out, you know. I'm down to my last clean outfit."

Like most things, "clean outfit" was a relative term for CJ, whose idea of dressing up was a pair of old jeans, ragged tennis shoes, and a Jerry Garcia tie three inches wide. In all these years, he still hadn't gotten used to CJ's dress code, or lack thereof. He stared at CJ, the ridiculously bright floral shirts, and the even more ridiculous old man, who hadn't bathed in weeks, maybe longer. He was toothless with greasy fingers the color of cinnamon sticks. He tried not to stare at the fingers, the toothless grin, the old man, and then stared.

"Well?" CJ asked.

"Well what?

"What do you think?

"You don't need my approval."

"No, but I'd like your opinion."

"Sure, go ahead. What's a hundred *quetzales*?"

Good question. As it turned out, it was jail time. Toothless Man had swiped some honcho's dry cleaning from an unlocked minivan behind the Treasury Office. Richard hadn't found out until later in the day, after he had licked most of the smoke out of a *vainilla* ice cream and CJ had been taken into custody by four crisply dressed *agentes* of the *Policía Nacional Civil, Sacatepequez* division.

Apparently, after the deal was done CJ had gone back to the hotel and Richard returned to the park to contemplate the ruin of his life and the grinding of his intestines for an unusually long time. He had picked a bench in the middle of a puddle because it was missing a slat, allowing his tender derrière to sag in the breeze that passed beneath. As if diarrhea weren't enough, he was also in a funk. Traveling did that to him. On the road, he suspended his routine of fiber, pushups, and tomato juice with a shot of vodka and

Worcestershire sauce. At first, not following the regimen produced an uplifting feeling, but then it unleashed unconscious, unpleasant parts of his psyche that his therapist said he repressed. So, he sat there licking, staring, licking, staring, releasing all of that repression. That's when he noticed that the fountain had four mermaids chiseled into its centerpiece. Each one held her breasts in her hands and squirted a stream of dirty water through her nipples. Fascinated, he walked around the fountain to make sure that each one squeezed herself in exactly the same way: the thumb and forefinger on one side of the nipple, the other fingers on the other side. It was a strange pose, especially for a public monument in the middle of a park (you wouldn't find Simón Bolívar doing anything like that), but to his relief all four beauties—eight breasts and forty fingers—were in perfect symmetry. He took comfort in that kind of order, because, after all, the rest of his life had none.

When he returned to their hotel, the three-and-a-half star Posada Oblongada (free cable, Nescafé, Internet, and an oblong courtyard designed for meditative walking exercises—no one seemed to know why), the concierge, a woman with penciled eyebrows and a lascivious look, informed him of CJ's arrest. According to her story, a team of *agentes* had burst into the office, asked for CJ's room number, and then whisked him away in handcuffs to police headquarters. Then they went on a rampage, slicing pillows, chairs, and mattresses in an attempt to find contraband and blanketing the room in goose feathers and footprints. He had to assure the agitated concierge that he would pay for the damages, or, rather, that the law firm would pay.

"Just add it to the bill," he told her calmly.

"But what about my granddaughter? She was very upset by the police with their clubs and thick boots."

"I don't see a granddaughter."

"She's sleeping."

"All right, we'll send you a check for pain and suffering."

"How much?"

"As much as you want."

"When?"

"As soon as we get back. I'll handle it personally. You have my word."

The woman eyed him suspiciously and then shuffled back to her padded stool with the imprint of her buttocks at the front desk. As he left, all he could hear was the sucking of her teeth and the blare of a Columbian soap opera about an anorexic starlet stranded on a Caribbean island with a fisherman with blond hair and blue eyes named Joaquín. It didn't seem to bother the sleeping child, but he stayed till the commercial just to make sure.

Richard hurried to the police station, for some reason also oblongada, in the southwest corner of the plaza directly across from Parque Central, but it took him longer than expected to navigate the maze of dark hallways and guards. He found CJ sitting alone, head in his hands, in the bottom berth of a bunk in a cell that stank of sour milk, wet socks, and sweat. He was annoyed at having to bail him out before his afternoon nap.

"What, no tin cup?" he asked.

"They fingerprinted me and took my passport. Would you talk to the guy in charge and find out what the hell is going on?" CJ asked.

Richard sought out the last guard he had spoken to, a *clase* or private, who led him to the *cabo* or corporeal, who escorted him to the *sargento*.

"It's a clear case of possession with intent to sell. That's why he is being held without bail."

The *sargento* was clean-shaven with chiseled biceps, a pint of mousse in his hair, and Army shoes made of Bakelite.

"But he was going to wear them, not sell them," Richard argued. "Besides, you know he was duped. We both were. We'll pay for them, I promise."

The *sargento* stared at him unmoved, uninterested, and lacquered. "I'm not referring to the shirts," he said.

"You're not?"

"No."

"What, then?"

"The first piece of evidence, which is the shopping bag."

"Shopping bag?"

"Shopping bag."

"I don't understand."

The official paused, shook his head, and disappeared down the hall, heels squeaking all the way. Richard rushed back to CJ's cell.

"You're not in here for laundry," he told him.

"Then what the hell for?"

"Shoplifting."

"Shoplifting?"

"They've got your bag."

"What bag?"

"Look, I'm not doing Abbott and Costello again. Just tell me what happened and I'll try to work something out."

"Well, I did have a Super Selecto bag filled with codeine pills and underwear from when we crossed the border."

"You bought them at the Beethoven Pharmacy in San Salvador?"

CJ nodded.

"So, what's the problem?"

Silence.

"What?"

"I might have left some pot in it, too," CJ confessed.

"How much?"

"A little."

"How much is a little?"

"A lot."

"But I told you not to bring any!"

"I couldn't help it."

"You know, you're nothing but a goddamned pothead."

It was pointless, of course, since calling CJ a pothead was about as meaningful as calling rice white or Mount Everest high or the Titanic a disaster. It may have been true, but it was either so obvious as to be irrelevant, or it didn't even begin to describe the reality. CJ lived for marijuana. He had a plant in his backyard that had taken over the greenhouse he had constructed with scrap lumber and covered with tarp to fool aerial surveillance. It hadn't fooled anyone, of course, including the Jehovah's Witnesses next door, even after he swore to them that it was for his glaucoma, which he didn't have. He also didn't have any fear, which should have given him a huge advantage at the law firm, even as a member of the support staff responsible for the "technology interface," whatever that was. Unfortunately, it also meant that he didn't think about the consequences of traveling through Central America with a shopping bag full of weed.

"So, what do we do now?" CJ asked.

"You got any cash?"

"They took it."

"How much?"

"Twenty bucks."

"Maybe we need to sweeten the pot."

"I used fish fertilizer."

"Don't get cute," Richard said. "Look, I'll go to the ATM around the corner. I'll withdraw as much cash as possible and then bribe the *sargento.*

Before CJ could object, Richard slipped out and made his way past several *agentes.* "I'll be right back. I have something for you," he told them excitedly.

Another bad idea. He had had a string of them lately, from agreeing to come on this miserable trip to drinking the tap water in Santiago Atitlán, where the locals used the picturesque lake at the base of three volcanoes for washing their clothes, pissing, copulating, and dumping their dead when they weren't particularly fond of them, which was more often than he had imagined.

"Can we talk in private?" Richard asked the *sargento* when he returned from wrestling three ATMs at two locations on opposite sides of the park. He was so unnerved he hadn't even checked the squirting *chichis*.

The *sargento* led him to a room with a ceiling about forty feet high and a large, two-way mirror on one wall. He wasn't sure who was watching from the other side, but he was already nervous and out of breath.

"Do you have anything a little more private?"

"This is not a hotel," the man answered humorlessly.

"All right, then, I just wanted to explain things to you. You see, my friend has a little problem smoking dope, but he's an honest guy, and the bag you confiscated is all he has. He doesn't sell the stuff or anything like that. He was just in the wrong place at the wrong time, and, to tell you the truth, he's not very discreet about these things."

Richard paused for a couple of beats and added, "So, I was wondering if I could make a donation to the building fund so that you can do some repairs, maybe get a larger mirror over there, and then let us go back to our hotel. We're leaving Antigua on a shuttle tomorrow morning for a very important meeting in Guatemala City. You won't see us again, believe me."

He held out an ATM envelope filled with freshly inked *quetzales* that nearly ca-cawed and flapped their wings as he fanned through them. It was truly a wonderful sight.

"You shouldn't have done that," the *sargento* said. "You can't bribe your way out. The law is clear about these situations."

"Situations?"

"You'd better leave now before it's too late, especially if you are involved in your friend's crime. You two shared the same room, did you not?"

"We did, but what's that got to do with anything?"

"Quite a bit, I'm afraid."

"Look, I'm not leaving until he's released."

"Then you will join him for dinner."

Suddenly, three guys in bellhop uniforms with epaulettes jumped out from behind the mirror, shoved Richard against the wall, and twisted his arms behind his back. He cursed at them in his best slang, but they led him quietly back to CJ's cell, handling him as delicately as if they were delivering a wedding cake to the banquet hall.

"Nice work," CJ said after they had left. "So what do we do now?"

"I don't know."

"What do you mean you don't know?"

"Well, let's see. How about I'm hungry, tired, and my rectum is on fire? Other than that I'm fine. I also mean that I don't have an answer for everything."

"And all this time I thought you were a know-it-all."

Richard gave him a dirty look and sat down in a grimy plastic chair, rubbing his shoulder, which he swore was dislocated. When he got bored studying the broken tiles on the floor, the chipped bars, and his Cole Haan boots (he should have ignored the salesman and gone with gun smoke), he remembered their first trip down here. CJ had started out as "George" at the airport in San Salvador but then underwent a political transformation that involved several name changes. Soon, "George" begat "Jorge," which begat "Comandante Jorge" (his guerilla period), which begat "CJ" in order to save time, which brought him right back to the Hummer-obsessed rat race he claimed to despise.

Richard agreed with him about the Hummers but not much else; their politics were about as far apart as the way they dressed. CJ lived with his wife and teenage daughter in a gated community in the suburbs, that drab land of pickups, baseball caps, turbo leaf blowers, and back-up beeps. Richard remembered going with them once to the opening of a strip mall, but when a cherry snow cone came sailing out of the crowd and landed on his cashmere Brioni overcoat, he decided enough was enough and he would never stray past the city limits again. Still, he knew he could trust CJ with his life, mainly because he was honest, ruthlessly so, which was a virtue that so far had eluded him. Actually, it had eluded him all of his life, and he didn't expect it to make an appearance anytime soon, but that was another story.

"You still want to do the motorcycle diaries?" he asked CJ.

"Prison diaries, you mean."

"They'll make a movie of us."

"I've seen the prisons down here, Richard. You don't want to know what they're like. And my kid's got an appointment with the orthodontist next Tuesday."

"You'll make it."

"Sure I will."

CJ rummaged through his pockets, pulling out a codeine pill for his arthritic joints. "One pill left," he said, admiring it before swallowing. "My fingers are killing me. Actually, everything's killing me." Then he stretched out on his bunk, which had a stained mattress with gouged out buttons, and closed his eyes.

They waited for more than an hour, CJ lying there and Richard tapping his toes, when suddenly an impossibly thin man in a white shirt and narrow black tie came in accompanied by the *cabo*. He carried a manila folder and spoke English with an accent right out of Central Casting. He was there to discuss the impending arraignment. At first, Richard did not understand him. "Impending," he thought he had said. He, too, wore Bakelite shoes and had a pint of gel in his hair. He remained on the opposite side of the bars as he read the charges against them, which included cocaine trafficking.

"*Cocaine?*"

"Correct."

"But there must be some mistake."

"There is no mistake."

"No, really, you're making a mistake."

"The charges are quite specific. Twelve ounces of marijuana were discovered in the shopping bag, which led to a thorough examination of the hotel room. That's when the agents found two bags of powdered cocaine."

"*Powdered?*"

"Yes."

"That's impossible."

"It's quite possible."

"Are you sure it wasn't talcum powder? My friend's got this rash, you know. That's what the underwear was for. See, he's not used to the humidity and it's been a long time since—"

Thin Man nodded impatiently and continued. "You are scheduled to appear before Judge Antonio Espín Garza next Tuesday. And I have already been informed that the severity of the case does not permit bail. You are facing serious felony charges, which the state will prosecute to the fullest extent. So I suggest you contact your friends at the embassy in Guatemala City once you arrive there."

"But we don't have any friends at the embassy."

"Then make some," he said.

"*Cocaine?*"

"I'm not here to discuss the charges, only the court appearance. Do you have any questions regarding that?"

Richard's bowels started rumbling again. He could feel CJ behind him, rubbing his joints and whimpering.

"All right, then."

"Wait."

"Yes?"

"I want to talk to a lawyer."

"Then I suggest you hire one."

"How do we do that?"

"You will be allowed one phone call and visit in Guatemala City. Once you leave here, however, it's out of my hands."

"When is that?"

"You will have dinner here tonight, and in the morning you will be transported to the federal jail. I'm sorry, but that's all the information I have for you."

Thin Man turned to the *cabo*, who escorted him out of the room, and suddenly they were gone. Richard stood there watching them, and it occurred to him that he should have paid more attention in Criminal Procedure, which had actually been his favorite course in law school—the professor, a Hungarian Jew, was particularly sarcastic—but then he remembered what a distraction that redhead with the long legs in front of him had been. On the discrete recommendation of the professor, she had been given a judicial clerkship and he never saw her again.

"Are you snorting coke?" he asked CJ.

"On my salary?"

"Fair enough. Got a cigarette?"

"You know I quit."

"But I really need one."

"When the waiter comes in with 'dinner,' ask him," CJ said.

"Maybe I will."

Richard sat down again, realizing that the worst part of all of this—other than the cigarette, diarrhea, missed orthodontist appointment, and prison—was having no one to phone, no one to grieve over his disappearance in a bogus Central American drug deal gone sideways. There would be no one to visit him with painted lips, frosted hair, and a box of condoms every month. At least CJ had a family to count on. He had nothing, absolutely nothing.

"What the hell is this cocaine charge, anyway?" CJ asked, panicked. "I mean, who do they think they're kidding? This is a setup."

"Who would set us up? Nobody knows we're in Antigua. How many people even know we're in Guatemala?"

"Well, somebody did this to us. What about that woman in the restaurant last night?"

"The waitress with the mustache?"

"No, the other one."

"The Mayan with the mole?"

"That's the one."

"You think she set us up?"

"No, but I think we should talk to her about getting out. She said she has connections and can get us anything we want."

"Are you out of your mind? We don't need a woman with a mole. We need a lawyer, a very expensive one."

"But I'm telling you it's not a scam. She runs some sort of a business here in Antigua. She was having dinner with that guy, remember?"

Richard did remember him, because they had gotten up at the same time to use the men's room, and the man had politely opened the door for him, allowing him to pass. The guy was tall, thin, and wore a floppy hat with a drawstring tie, which made him seem eccentric and studious. That's what made him stand out: the drawstring hat. He didn't look like a tourist and had a nose that was aquiline, more Roman than *guatemalteco*.

"But I don't understand how she can help us, even if she's telling the truth," Richard said doubtfully.

"I don't know either, but she seemed sincere."

"That's just what we need, sincerity."

CJ poked through his shirt pocket and pulled out a business card encrusted with habanero sauce. He liked his food hot, which was why the waitress had referred to them jokingly as "my Mexicans" to the busboys.

"Here's her number. Get the guard to let us make the phone call, and I'll talk to her."

"How?"

"Just do it."

Richard made a feeble attempt just as the *clase*, a slow-moving youth with stubby fingers, carried in two dinner trays. With a pained expression, he asked to use the bathroom, which was on the other side of a broken-down desk that held their belongings. The youth obliged, and, as they passed the desk, he swiped CJ's cell phone.

"Easy as *pupusa*," he bragged when he got back.

CJ dialed the number and spoke to the woman about their arrest, the cocaine charge, and the cathedral restoration project, which made no sense at all to Richard, unless she was soliciting donations. When CJ started pacing the cell, Richard lost interest and sat down to eat dinner, which consisted of carrots that had been boiled to a slow, agonizing death, hardened rice with red peppers, chicken parts deep-fried in axle grease, and raw sweet bread.

"Mia will be here in a half hour," CJ said.

"Who the hell is Mia?"

"She owns the Mia Maya Travel Agency here in Antigua. She said she knows the *sargento* and his wife. He leaves the jail every night at seven o'clock to have dinner. That's when she'll come over to let us out."

"Let us out?"

"She knows where they keep the keys."

"Let me guess, the desk?"

"Could be."

"You're crazy," Richard told him, holding his stomach. "Goddamn crazy."

It wasn't long before the fried chicken took its revenge, sliding through Richard's intestines like hot grease on Teflon. The van ride to Guatemala City didn't help. He messed his pants twice, with most of it running down his legs into his socks. One of Mia's employees drove them, along with Mia and the guy with the drawstring hat, to the Linea Aurora bus station at 16th Street and Avenida Purgatorio (where else?), where they waited for the 9:00 pm bus to a place called Flores, the capital of El Petén, in the north. Once there, Mia promised to help them get to Belize and a flight to Houston.

Richard wasn't sure how they would get across the border without passports or money, especially with the *policía* in pursuit, but he figured they would deal with that later. At least they were out of jail, even if they had to wait in the grungiest part of town. And it was grungy, filled with adult bookstores, bars, chicken joints, garbage, and mucho traffico. Mia's friend, an archaeologist, was working on a dig close to Flores, but the twin engine Cessna he usually traveled in was being repaired, so he and Mia had to take a commercial bus. He didn't inquire about them, and Mia didn't seem to mind helping two gringos wanted for cocaine trafficking, which made Richard suspicious, but then most things did.

The ride lasted all night long as they descended from the cooler, mountainous region of Antigua into the steaming jungle on winding roads hemmed in by houses, trees, and an occasional *tienda* selling everything from Chinese nail clippers to toasted corn and sliced watermelon. The bus, a double-decker parlor car donated by the Cleveland Ballet, rattled and rolled like a used lawnmower. Richard tried to sleep but was hypnotized by the movie shown on a soiled bed sheet, *The Phantom of the Opera*, and the swaying of the top-heavy bus, which was driven by a tall, sullen Guatemalan in an airline pilot's uniform who looked suicidal. When the movie ended, they handed out little boxes of papaya juice with the thinnest of straws. He fell asleep and dreamt of huge rocks falling like meteors into a bottomless pit, one after the other, with him leaning over the edge and the draft of wind from each rock blowing back in his face until he nearly fell down. Still, he leaned closer and closer; couldn't help himself.

Then someone came up and said, "Richard, wake up."

"What?"

"We've just pulled into Flores. We're meeting some of Chamba's friends here. It's time to get up."

He pretended not to hear but the voice wouldn't let him alone. When he finally opened his eyes, Mia was leaning over him. She had a round face with Frida Kahlo eyebrows and a mole that drifted away from her upper lip, giving her that odd sensuality that comes from imperfection. He was drawn to certain kinds of imperfection; not deformities, but what he liked to think of as "physical endearments," including twitches, birthmarks, uneven eyes, crooked smiles, and noses that fit neither the face nor temperament of the person behind them. Rather than being put off, he found them curious, even arousing. To tell the truth, he was aroused now.

"How long was I asleep?" he asked, catching the light outside, which was a smoldering mixture of brown and green, gray and purple. Steam rose up from the earth as if from some underground boiler room.

"Almost three hours."

"That's all?"

"Well, these seats aren't the most comfortable."

"Who is Chamba?"

"A friend of mine. You've already met him."

"Friend?"

"Yes, that's right."

Aching, he stumbled off the bus into the chilled morning air wrapped in a Linea Aurora travel blanket. CJ stood with a group of gringos near a blue van, holding the Super Selecto bag they had retrieved from the police station. The police had confiscated the marijuana, codeine pills, and cash, leaving CJ's boxers still in their package. Mia introduced them to the group as two clients traveling to Belize, and then he and CJ squeezed into the back of the van. Richard tried to remain inconspicuous but found himself pressed against a woman with the figure of a coat rack and a personality to match. She introduced herself as a "Mayan specialist" from Pennsylvania State University, which made him recall the time he had gotten lucky following a Billy Joel concert at State College with a theatre arts major with unshaved legs and armpit hair. Brenda? Blair? Blythe?

The specialist had short-cropped, gray hair, crooked teeth, and glasses that magnified a pair of hazel eyes. She clutched a cane with a silver jaguar handle between her legs, which looked, he thought, pretty bizarre.

"I've won four Fulbrights for my work in Mayan Studies," she informed him after finishing a discourse on burial rituals that nearly killed him.

"As a matter of fact, some people say I *am* Mayan Studies, but one doesn't go about repeating such things unless one is absolutely confident."

He thought she was joking and started to laugh but everyone else was quiet, so he nodded and feigned a smile. "Absolutely, right."

Then she lectured him about the evils of the conquistadores, Europeans in general, Wall Street in particular, and "patriarchy," which meant men, all of them. When it was obvious that he wasn't going to take the bait, she tried a more direct approach.

"And you are?"

"Richard Mercurius."

"Mercurius?"

"Mercurius."

"That's curious," she said, as if he hadn't heard that one before, although the last time was in the cafeteria in junior high school.

"So, Richard Mercurius, what are you doing here? You're not one of those Adventurer people, are you?"

"No, my friend and I are down here for a client that wants to expand his business into Central America."

"Ah, yes, that nasty CAFTA treaty. I've read all about it. I suppose you business types are going to march through here like Sherman through Atlanta and destroy whatever you—*Good God, what is that smell?*"

Unfortunately, she was referring to him. He had meant to wash up earlier, but he had never felt comfortable in mobile bathrooms, whether on the plane, train, or bus. He found them degrading, even dangerous. All he could think of in response was, "I think that's me. See, I ate a liverwurst sandwich on the bus...."

This wasn't entirely a lie, he thought, since he remembered eating a liverwurst sandwich on the bus during Mrs. Miller's fifth-grade class trip through Perkiomen Valley to study Anabaptist gravesites. He had found death oddly appealing as a child, almost as much as Mrs. Miller, who had breasts that heaved like ocean swells. He had stared at them from the seat behind her, transfixed and seasick with love.

"Liverwurst?"

Cane Lady turned away and lit a cigarette in an act of disgust, but he was used to that kind of treatment at this point in his life.

"Mind if I have one?" he asked boldly.

"Mind? Are you crazy? Anything to get rid of that smell."

He loved the metallic click and butane smell of her lighter, the tingle on the tip of his tongue, the soft pressure of the smoke as it curled its way through his lungs and unraveled out his nose. There was nothing like it, really. He savored the experience, closing his eyes and swaying ever so slightly, and then he threw up. Chamba pulled over hurriedly, Cane Lady pushed him out the door with her jaguar handle as soon as the van stopped, maybe a few seconds before, and CJ jumped out to help him.

"Richard, you're getting worse. We've got to get you to a hospital."

"No way."

"But you're in bad shape."

"Forget it. What do you think will happen when two gringos show up at a hospital, assuming they even have one around here? The cops will find out and haul our asses back to Guatemala City. You want to add fugitive charges to bribing and drug trafficking?"

"No, but what else can we do?"

"We've got to find a way to the Belize airport. I'd rather be seen by someone over there, anyway."

"But I think we should stay with these people for a while."

"I can't do that."

"Why not?"

"They're freaks."

"But they're willing to help us and we've got no money," CJ said. "Besides, I've never seen you this bad, even that time you smoked a joint at my place and ate three mushroom omelets. Remember that?"

CJ was trying to cheer him up, which he often did to help him get through a funk, a hangover, or an eighteen-hour day at the firm. Sometimes, though, Richard found it annoying. Then again, he found most things annoying.

"Just leave me alone and let me die here on the side of the road, will you?"

"Look, we don't have any options, and Mia promised to do whatever she can to get us back home."

"Yeah, I've been meaning to talk to you about that."

"What's wrong now?"

"Don't you think it's a little strange that she was able to salsa her way into that jail and out again without even being stopped? She knew exactly where she was going."

"You're paranoid."

"Sure, but that's not the point."

"Then what is the point?"

Richard couldn't answer. He was bent over with his hands on his knees, trying not to pass out. Not only were the *policía* after them, but he knew what would happen when the client found out that the expert sent down to negotiate the buyout was wanted on a felony drug warrant. Suddenly, his world was turning to shit because of a leathery Mayan and stolen dry cleaning. There was no way he could have predicted this. Hadn't he been through enough already: divorce, homelessness, his father's death? How much more would he have to endure before he got a break? Just one goddamn break. This was supposed to be his year: the Age of Mercurius. Instead, he got a silver jaguar head shoved up his ass, which served as a painful reminder of his first and only colonoscopy.

"Some luck," he said, spitting a long thread of saliva onto the ground.

"Maybe, but it's the only luck we've got right now," CJ replied.

"Right."

By the time they got back to the van, Cane Lady had switched seats, placing herself as far away from him as possible. Richard now sat next to a guy with hair in his ears as thick as Brillo pads who breathed all over his arm. Mia decided that he was too weak to travel and would have to stay at their camp until he recovered. He wasn't sure what she was up to, but he went along with the plan, at least until he felt better and could figure out what to tell the firm. Admittedly, though, he was getting worse.

"Camp" consisted of a bunch of canvas tents and thatched huts at the edge of a national park in Tikal that contained the ruins of an ancient Mayan city. It took forever to get there, and they had to drive on root-infested roads past plazas, temples, and throngs of tourists trekking through the heat. During the ride, Richard found out that the real excavation was taking place at a site called Cival. Chamba said they were making all kinds of discoveries there, like the snake face he found one day after reaching through a crack in a tunnel wall. Chamba had run his fingers along the fangs of a stucco face that measured fifteen feet in length. It was such an important discovery that the Smithsonian decided to pour money into the project and hire a team of archaeologists from around the world to work with him. Mia arranged their travel. She said that Guatemala was big business now ("the next Costa Rica"), and people were coming from all over to see the ruins. Richard said that he was ruined all over from coming here, but nobody thought it was funny. He also found out that Mia spoke Spanish, English, and several Mayan languages, which no doubt helped her business. She was from a poor family in Sololá, somewhere on the other side of that volcanic lake-lá-lá, and had opened her own travel agency after working as a bank teller. That's how she met Chamba, who came in one day to open a checking account and pick up his free calendar. He was from the Motherland, Spain, that land of effete socialism and legal cannabis, but had adapted nicely to the jungle. Money and success will do that for you. Richard, however, never wanted to see this place again.

They put him and CJ into the "infirmary," which overlooked an idyllic little swamp by the name of Laguna del Cocodrilo. It was nothing more than a thatched hut containing two cots, a medicine cabinet filled with cotton balls and dead scorpions, and a crocodile skin hanging from a pole in the corner, head intact. On the wall above the cabinet hung a yellowed photo of a crocodile half submerged in mud with a bird on its head, shitting. Shitting, it seemed, was the Guatemalan motif. They might as well paint it on the tails of their airplanes, he thought.

"Make yourselves comfortable," Mia said as they settled in. "Richard, I'll bring fresh towels and soap for you to wash up and arrange for someone to have a look at you."

"You don't have to do that."

"It's no bother. Besides, I don't get involved in the digs or anything like that, so I have plenty of time."

"Any chance we could use the phone or get access to the Internet?" CJ asked. "We have to contact the office and my phone just went dead."

"I'll see what I can do."

"I'd appreciate that. You've already been a big help."

She flashed a smile of native white that contrasted her eyes, which were *color café*, and Richard wondered whether he was being too hard on her, maybe even too paranoid. It didn't seem possible for a Mercurius, yet something about her made him doubt himself, so he decided to withhold judgment. There was one thing, however, that he had no doubt about: he couldn't stand it down here anymore. Couldn't stand the flies, the smothering heat, the standard issue Rice & Beans, the smoky mangoes, the scaly birds, the plumed serpents, the *helicóptero* insects, the broad-faced stoicism of these people. He didn't trust them. For all of their so-called hospitality (if he overheard one more tourist with a spongy ass and boxy sneakers going on about how wonderful these people were, he'd scream), he'd been hustled here more than anywhere else on the planet, including Market Street in San Francisco. Well, maybe not Market Street.

He still remembered the *señora* in Chichi who followed him down all eighteen of those famous steps at Santo Tomás Church and back to his hotel room with a small girl in tow, because he had made the mistake of telling her how beautiful her *mantel* was, which she practically regarded as an offer of marriage. He ended up buying the tablecloth just so she would leave him alone. He gave her a hundred *quetzal* banknote, and she had to retrieve the change from her bra, turning away from him in the street to do so. He waited patiently as she readjusted the straps, smoothed her blouse, and handed him the change. They parted amicably, he thought, until he heard her cursing at him in K'iche' and covering the girl's ears as they rushed back to the square.

When Mia left, CJ helped him lie down and placed a damp cloth on his forehead. He didn't feel feverish, but he didn't feel normal, either. Something bad was sneaking up on him; he could tell. The heat was unbearable in the hut, which smelt like burnt hay, orange peels, and coffee grounds. It was so hot he expected the place to combust spontaneously.

"You still think she's working us?" CJ asked.

"I don't know. I just think this whole thing is hard to believe."

"Hard to believe? It's a nightmare, but I think you're blaming the wrong person, Richard. Somebody else must be behind this."

"Who?"

"You're the conspiracy theorist. You tell me."

"You think this is a conspiracy?"

"What the hell else could it be?"

Richard thought for a moment, concentrating on his shallow breathing. This was a perfect opportunity to wax paranoiac, but he didn't.

"Well, it would have to be somebody with a motive and the means," he said.

"Somebody at the firm?"

"Could be."

"Eckstrom?"

Eckstrom was the obvious choice. He had joined the firm after Richard but brought enough clients with him to earn a corner office with an antique partner's desk from Colonial Williamsburg. He was the kind of guy who always played home games, never venturing out to talk about anyone else's work, clients, or area of expertise, which allowed him to stay in control. He was, in a word, a prick. Still, he was the obvious choice, which was why Richard rejected him.

"No, he's too wrapped up in himself to put something like this together. Besides, it would take him away from the golf course."

"How about Trudel?"

"The admin?"

"She doesn't like you, you know."

"Why do you say that?"

"She told me."

"Oh."

Trudel was a Danish administrative assistant and part-time aerobics instructor who had an eye for mature executives who needed saving from their destructive vices and even more destructive ex-wives. He spurned her bosom-friendly advances one morning in the coffee room, and ever since then the strudel had been rather stale.

"She's got motive, a lot of it, but she couldn't pull this off."

"Then maybe it's not anybody in house. It could be the client sabotaging their own move down here."

"No, that doesn't make any sense, either. There's got to be somebody else who benefits from seeing us suffer like this."

A long pause followed during which raisin-sized, black flies drifted silently through the heat, and then, as if the entire conversation had been leading up to this one surreal moment, CJ asked, "Your ex-wife?"

"What?"

"Katherine."

"Why her?"

"I don't know. You're always blaming her for something or other."

"That's kind of farfetched, isn't it?" Richard asked.

"You're the one who's always telling me what a bitch she was."

"Hey, they could name a hurricane after her."

"Well, there you go."

"There what I go?"

"Maybe she had something to do with this."

"I doubt it. She got everything she wanted, including the house, cars, and bank accounts. The only reason she'd have to do this would be..."

"What?" CJ asked, waiting.

"Spite."

"Well, there you go again."

"Stop saying that."

"Although she didn't strike me as a vengeful woman."

"Are you out of your mind? Not vengeful? What you don't know about women could fill Crocodile Lagoon, you know that?"

CJ looked hurt for a second and then retreated to his bed. Richard would have done the same thing had the comment been directed at him, except that in his case it was even worse. Forget Katherine. What he didn't know about *himself* could have paved the jungle in parking spaces, which wasn't something to brag about at his age. Then there was that one humiliating fact that made him feel like a loser: he couldn't stop thinking about her, couldn't stop the rush of emotion as he heard her name, couldn't roll the bowling ball off his chest that kept him from breathing, couldn't erase the memories of dancing the rumba at two in the morning and dipping their toes in the Missouri and the time he told her that he was as loyal as a dog and that if she ever wanted to get rid of him, she'd have to shoot him in the head. But he also couldn't shake the feeling of betrayal that still had him in doubt not just about her and her love for him but about everything else.

In the end, she had shot him in the head, heart, and small intestines. That was Katherine for you, his Katherine. Katherine Veronica Muck of the Camden Mucks, which rhymes with sucks but was the last thing she ever consented to do and then only after three cosmos. Now, despite the barrage he had leveled at her of notes, letters, cards, phone calls, emails, text messages, faxes, postcards, poems (poems, for chrissakes—he had to buy a thesaurus!), Katherine Veronica was playing someone else's harmonica.

"You're still searching for yourself," his therapist had informed him two days before leaving for El Salvador.

"No shit, really?"

This from a Jungian analyst with a gray beard and public television coffee mug who thought that the Guaraní running around bare assed with bones through their noses were every bit as sophisticated as the ancient Greeks. The guy had made a small fortune from Richard's misfortune. Katherine was the culprit there. Her longtime therapist, a willowy Filipino and charter member of the Penetrating Gaze Society, had referred him and encouraged him with a straight face (as much as this was possible), "to explore the ambiguity of being male." Richard had no idea what the guy was talking about but soon realized that neither did he.

"I'll figure out who I am three days after I drop dead," he had said in reply, making out another check and wondering how long it would take to fire him. It occurred to him that firing a therapist was at least as hard as getting rid of a real estate agent, especially if you have generous medical insurance.

So now there was nothing for him to do but fall asleep listening to Paleolithic winged things outside the hut. Instead of a window, there was a large, unscreened opening for all manner of reptilian creatures to slither in and observe the new prey. A swamp-green lizard with a tail like a whip scratched its way over the windowsill and back out again. He wasn't sure if it was poisonous, but, true to his nature, he was suspicious. After lying like that in a cot that smelled as if the diggers had taken turns sleeping in it, he had the distinct impression that he was in hell.

He slept fitfully, moving in and out of consciousness with a feverish commentary running through his head that he had no control over. The strangest thing was that his dreams never changed. He had never had happy dreams. Never dreamt of anything like boating on a lake, or a picnic lunch with Brie and *fumé blanc*, or tennis with a young woman in a blonde ponytail and Tiffany bracelet with whom he drinks iced tea afterward under a striped umbrella and watches sweat trickle down her arm to her delicately veined wrist. He was sure that if he ever had a dream like that, he'd trace the tip of his tongue up her salty arm to the hollow of her throat. But his dreams weren't about Tiffany and tennis. They were more like a madman's filled with betrayal, suffering, torture, and, inevitably, the hunt. Whether by one person or a mob with torches, he would be hunted down like a wild pig until just before being caught, killed, or roasted, when he would either escape (somehow exercising creative control over the script), or wake up. The funny thing was that no matter how horrific the dream, he always ended it before it ended him.

In this dream in the middle of the jungle, he and Katherine are driving to the beach in Atlantic City from their home in

Collegeville, which consists of a red brick house on Grinding Mill Way, not far from the neighborhood abattoir where her father works as a cleaner of meat hooks and part-time bookie. Their children, an adorable boy and girl of equal height, are in the backseat shucking raw clams over a tin beach pail and slurping each one with the sound of a hospital ventilator. He drives as Katherine polishes her manicured toenails with a deep red polish the color of communion wine. Her hair is bobbed, revealing a delicate neck and vertebrae. Suddenly, they are transported back to the forties and Hank Williams is playing on the radio. Richard wears a striped suit with wide lapels and a beaver fur fedora, although Katherine hardly notices. She continues polishing her nails, humming to the music and smiling. It is the same smile she uses later on to convince him to go for a swim, which he does, farther out than he has ever gone before.

The water is warm, but there is too much salt in the air. Soon, the air becomes thick with it and he can hardly breathe. Then, as he starts to gag and sink beneath the waves, the salt forms a hand that lifts him in its vaporous fingers and places him back on the beach. But the children of equal height are no longer there, having returned to their grandmother's house in the north. Katherine, too, has vanished. She has run off with her new lover, a pit boss with shiny shoes and a pinkie ring from the remodeled Grinding Mill Hotel and Casino, $9.50 Dinner Buffet, All You Can Eat with Reservations. He is alone with the beach blanket, pail of clams, which looks like worn rubber bands and pieces of chalk in dishwater, and pile of cotton balls that Katherine had hurriedly pulled from between her toes as he swam farther and farther into the salty mist.

He had the same dream so many times he knew it by heart. There were variations, of course, but nothing too difficult to interpret, since she really did leave him on the beach one afternoon after coaxing him into the water. As he had tiptoed in, she hopped out under the pretense of stepping on a crab.

"Damn it!" she yelled, shaking her foot in an exaggerated way and looking over to see if he was watching.

"What is it?"

"Crabs! You'd better watch out. They're all over."

Then she gathered her belongings and said, "I'm going to the bar to order two Bloody Marys and a plate of oysters Rockefeller. I'll be right back, darling. Don't go anywhere."

"I'll be waiting for you, my love."

True to his word, he waited. The next time he saw her was that fateful afternoon on the steps of the county court- house for the divorce proceedings. She had left him with an ocean of debt from the hundred thousand dollar remodeled kitchen (sub-zero, walk-in refrigerator and Miele dishwasher—more than a little ironic, since there were never any dirty dishes to wash), the twelve thousand dollar Sardegna vacation, and the three thousand dollar Birkin handbag, beige and a bit much, even for Katherine. What needed interpretation, though, was his continued obsession with the woman. Despite being abandoned without the proverbial shirt on his back, which friends had pointed out to him in not so subtle ways, he still dreamt of Katherine. In these dreams, she could take the form of a blonde, brunette, Girl Scout, bag lady, lounge singer, stenographer, or Amazon princess. No matter what form she took, he still recognized the woman he was in love with.

"Are you in love with her or a part of yourself that you're missing and that she has come to represent?" his therapist had asked once with a look on his face as if he were peering over the morning newspaper.

Obviously, it was supposed to make him think, but Richard didn't have a clue and blamed law school and his entire profes- sional life for not having prepared him for that kind of question. In fact, it just got in the way and prevented him from doing his job, which was to piss longer and farther than the other guy. He didn't have time to think about how he thought about himself. The whole thing sounded like mental masturbation, anyway.

"How the hell should I know?" he had asked, annoyed.

"I think you do."

"And I think you're an idiot."

"Come now."

As it turned out, the other guy pissed farther than him. It wasn't a pit boss at a third-rate casino that had caught her eye, but the creative writing instructor at a second-rate community college near their happy home. The sensitive soul had written a novel about suburban housewives that *The New York Times* hailed as a "zeitgeist tour de force," which Richard couldn't understand let alone argue with, though he knew enough to cancel his Sunday subscription. What he did understand was that this new love interest offered something that, in Katherine's eyes, had been missing from their marriage from day one (more like Ground Zero): attention. Naturally, that was the one thing he couldn't give her, not with commuting to New York for a client involved in a high-stakes merger. But mergers and acquisitions were too prosaic for Katherine, who sought solace from her existential angst in the ethereal climes of literature, which she pronounced in three syllables, revealing her working class roots in Camden, where her parents ran a dingy but profitable plumbing supply store ("Muck Plumb & Design") before being bought out by a family of Koreans with gobs of cold cash and raw garlic.

The love interest, Nicholas Negroponte, was more than twenty years her junior, a snorkeler of "enormous lung capacity," as Katherine put it later, and good looking enough to make it as a kept man. Maybe he was, maybe he wasn't, but what had finally gotten to Richard was the realization that he would be paying for all of the keeping. As it happened, Negroponte had chosen writing as a way of expressing *his* existential angst, so there was nothing a commuting husband could do once angst met angst that first week of class when Katherine's assignment was to write about her greatest fear. It didn't take her long to figure out that her greatest fear was the life she was already living with a man she already despised. And that, as they say, was that: the end of a not too beautiful romance marred by the fact that sometimes you marry the wrong woman but continue to love her long after the final judgment has left you with a sleeping bag, an office to sleep in, and an oversexed Danish secretary who misplaces legal briefs and would like nothing more than to misplace yours.

The fact that there were no children was a blessing for everyone except his mother, who had declared publicly that the marriage would not make it to Christmas (it was a June wedding), and then, during the rehearsal dinner, offered to raise any offspring her son and "that woman" might produce. It pained her to retire without grandchildren. She had worked at the phone company for thirty years, full-time after her husband's nervous breakdown, which she referred to as "the episode," and longed for the day when she could devote entire afternoons to tea sets, baseball mitts, and soap bubbles, not necessarily in that order.

"Grandchildren are the grand prize," she had told him. "They're what make the rest of the shit you have to go through in life worthwhile."

Actually, he wasn't sure how well she would have done. His own childhood had been nothing to write home about, not with her resentment of his father, his father's depression over a failed career as an inventor, and his younger brother's paranoid schizophrenia, which had been diagnosed only after they found him one morning writing down license plates and muttering to himself about who really killed John Lennon. He didn't think she'd have the stamina to rear more children, even in retirement, to say nothing of having to deal with Katherine, who, despite the veneer of artistic sensitivity, had a set of stucco fangs herself.

In this dream, he looks over at Katherine, who is busy applying lip gloss that matches her blood red nails (she looks like she has just snapped a gazelle's neck), and is enthralled by her slender fingers, the concentration with which she dabs each lip, and the riveted, ice-blue stare into the rearview mirror that she has twisted completely around for a better view of her own beauty. He drives forward without looking back, unable to see where they have been. He should be able to see the heads of the children in the side mirror, but they are at their grandmother's house in the north. He and Katherine are alone in the car, rushing at ninety-eight miles an hour toward the southern beaches. Katherine finishes her lips and informs him that a Cuban is chasing them. She is sure about this, because she saw a swarthy man with a mustache and sunglasses spying on them as they dropped off the children.

"Are you sure?"

"Of course I am. Why wouldn't I be?"

"Well, it's just that you make things up sometimes."

"You should turn there," she says, ignoring him.

"Where?"

"There."

"There?"

"No, not there, there!"

"Oh."

"You just missed it."

"All right, I'll turn around."

"Now we have to go to the next exit."

"It'll be fine, I promise."

"Sure it will."

Then, after another wrong turn and exasperated beyond belief, she yells, "Richard, what is *wrong* with you?"

He doesn't know, but clearly something is wrong. Desperate, he turns westward onto the open highway, where there is room to breathe and seldom a discouraging word, which would have been a welcome change, but instead of cacti and tumbleweed, they pull into a Midwestern town as it begins to rain. The rain turns into a deluge, and the car is pushed back by onrushing water. They take refuge at the World Famous Grinding Mill Memorial and Gift Shop, Visitors Always Welcome, which has an alabaster monument to the war dead made of fingers and nipples, and a changing of the guard ceremony based on Mayan burial rituals. Katherine stays for the ceremony, but he opts for the three o'clock lecture by an octogenarian historian with a plastic daisy in his lapel on the hanging of three Confederate spies from the Alabama 17th Cavalry Regiment during the Civil War.

"It promises to be informative," he tells her.

"Oh, no doubt," she says.

One of Grinding Mill's board members, a stout German *frau* in a flowered dress, knee-high hosiery, and sensible shoes, invites him to a board meeting immediately after the lecture. Since he cannot find Katherine, he accepts. To his surprise, the board members are very welcoming and friendly to him. After the meeting, they sit together at a picnic table and eat a meal of corn on the cob and freshly baked apple pie. Then they begin to leave, one by one. When it is his turn, he thanks them for their hospitality, punches out at the grandfather clock in the office, and rolls his airport luggage through the gravel parking lot to the car.

But then he realizes that he is happy there and has nowhere else to go. Katherine has left him. So he decides to turn around and make this Midwestern town his new home. It is good for his soul. It was also good to have heard the lecture, since now he knows the part played by Grinding Mill in the Not-So-Civil-War. Then the *frau* comments that the lecture was very informative and all that, but now it is time for him to write about his childhood. This has to be done immediately, she insists, while the water is still warm: *während das Wasser immer noch warm ist*. There is no denying her, since she knows too much and might even be related, although the Mercurius family is Hungarian, which she knows perfectly well.

"Where should I start?" he asks.

"How about *your* greatest fear?"

"You mean—?"

"Your father."

"I'd rather not."

"Well, that's the point, isn't it, *mein Schatz*?"

"There's a point?"

"That's for me to know and you to find out."

"All right."

His father, the most bizarre person in his life, was a slight man who wore no more than three pairs of pants the entire time Richard knew him. He spent all of his time in his "laboratory," which was a third-floor room just off the stairs with drywall and a sloping ceiling because it was so close to the roof of the house. As a youth, he had attended a technical school in a small town in Hungary with the hope of becoming an engineer but had to drop out to support his ailing mother and aunt. By the time he returned to his studies, the revolution had forced him to flee (the landlord had caught them listening to Radio Free Europe) with nothing but a woolen overcoat and a suitcase stuffed with algorithmic tables and vacuum tubes. After spending a year in Utrecht, he met Richard's mother, another refugee from a neighboring town in Hungary, who was attracted to the shock of dark hair that hung in a curl on his forehead and that brooding gaze characteristic of all Mercurius men, which some people attributed to Gypsy blood. They married four months later in a civil ceremony and emigrated to the United States so that, in her words, they might "form a more perfect union." Her brother worked at a print shop in Philadelphia and offered his new brother-in-law a job there. For extra income, Richard's father designed tools for a garden supply store in Southern California (his hand-held "Roto-Twister" would have been patented but for a screenplay of the same name). It had started out with weekend projects but eventually took up so much of his time that he had to choose between inventing garden tools and working the four-color press. For the first time in his life, he decided to follow his heart, which proved disastrous. Within a year of quitting the printer's, the supply store was taken over by a big-box retailer in Kansas City with its own research division, which had no need of his services. By the age of fifty-two, he found himself unemployed, without a degree or prospects, and severely depressed.

It could have happened to Richard, too. Katherine was nowhere to be found; not at the changing of the guard, the cluttered counter at the gift shop, the beach, or the oyster bar. Not a trace of the Birkin handbag with gold snaps and lamé interior. Depression would have been understandable given his huge debt, cuckold reputation, and genetic disposition for failure. But sleeping in the office and showering at the club until he couldn't pay his dues anymore were good for him. It made him realize that the birthright his father had left him was not a record of what to stay away from, but what to do when your world turns to shit, whether from illness, Communists, a bully retailer, or toothless Mayans. And what do you do? You stick with it, that's what you do.

His father bounced back, if not financially at least emotionally, by spending the last years of his life working on a mathematical formula to calculate the distance traveled on the runway during takeoff, landing, and taxiing of an aircraft so that this distance could be added to a passenger's frequent flyer miles. His father pitched it in a four-color brochure that his uncle printed for free early one Sunday morning as "The Mercurial Variable." Usually, after waiting all day, he would leave the brochure with a hastily scribbled note with some polite but harried secretary, who would promise to pass it on to Mister So and So, the VP of Such and Such. Naturally, no one ever called back, but he would not give up. Most people thought he was insane, including Richard's mother, who forbade him from talking about it during social events. So, instead, he would turn to his next favorite subjects: the Bush Administration's secret role in the September 11th attacks, or, if the listener seemed too delicate (or horrified), construction of the interstate highway system under President Eisenhower and its use in missile and troop transport. Atomic veterans came in third.

Although Richard's childhood may not have been all soccer matches and father-son brunches with the Hungarian Scouts, it was real. When he wasn't doing homework or chores, he had to look after his brother. This required inventing excuses for Kornél's behavior whenever they went out and he would do something odd like hand out slips of paper to passersby, informing them that if a number appeared in the upper, right-hand corner, they had been selected. Please keep the paper with you at all times. You will be contacted with further instructions. Sometimes, people would curse or threaten harm, and Richard would have to explain that his brother wasn't a wiseass but a little shorthanded in the Mental Department.

He attributed his negotiation skills to these early experiences, but, as a result of having a recluse father and a high-maintenance brother, he was not popular with women, even when he had the time to make time. Besides State College, his romantic life consisted of a schoolboy infatuation with an Italian girl named Laura Fedora (no relation to the hat mogul) with the feet of a goddess and daydreams about a future bride with a long neck and tapered eyebrows who most likely would come from a similarly disturbed background.

He hadn't met Katherine until after law school, when a mutual friend arranged a date for them at a hockey game, explaining with a wink and a nod that "the girl loves blood sports." This was fortunate for her, since two players were ejected for brawling and another got his nose broken.

Afterward, they went for coffee (she insisted on fair trade, although she didn't have that attitude with him), which was when he fell in love with vanilla lattes. He fell in love with Katherine watching her lick foam from the rim of her cup and top of her lip.

"Why don't you go for a swim?" she asks in the dream, leaning forward in her chair at Café Che beneath the photo of a young Patty Hearst, assault rifle in hand. The photo is signed, "Your one and only, Tania."

Katherine wears a bright blue bathing cap with metallic silver spangles, but nobody pays any attention. She coaxes him into the water with a curl of a smile. He feels a tingle in the small of his back and the base of his scrotum.

"Sure," he answers, running into the pounding surf with his heart in his pants. All he can think about is pounding her surf.

But when he gets back to the table, she is gone. There are only empty cups with stained lids and ripped sugar packets. Dejected, he gets in the car and drives back to Collegeville. Once there, he pulls up to the house that he has just bought: a two-story, Tuscan villa with a terra cotta roof, lush but trimmed vegetation, and a circular driveway. He sits at the kitchen table, exhausted from the trip, with Mia across from him. She speaks K'iche' and rubs her official tour guide identification card, which is tied around her neck with red and white bakery string. Then the *frau* enters and serves everyone apple strudel fresh from the oven. As they sit there eating, another woman appears and takes her place at the end of the table, so now they form a triangle with her at the head.

This woman is slender, Filipina, and agent of the month at Grinding Ax Realty, Home of the Grudge Mortgage. In painstaking detail, she explains the complexities of home selection, financing, interest rates, closing costs, and the absolute necessity of encasing the villa in a circus-sized prophylactic to prevent infection from "inappropriate" sexual fantasies left there by the previous owners, a Cuban baseball team. When he inquires about "appropriate" sexual fantasies, she smirks. When he asks about Mayan root infestation, she calls him "stupid." That's when he jumps up and orders her out of the house. She vanishes, her beige handbag disappearing from beside her chair. They run after her, but once again she is nowhere to be found.

Outside, the vegetation is overgrown and wild, having been neglected for years. Night enshrouds them as they stand in the driveway, and he retrieves his father's overcoat, now perforated by moth larvae, for Mia to keep warm. It is a damp cold, a salty cold, and he shivers uncontrollably. It would be nice to feel the warmth of glowing vacuum tubes on his fingers once again. Then there is blackness as the chase begins.

Waking to the sour odor of heat inside the hut, Richard felt weak and drained from his dream. His cot was soaked in sweat, although he was still shaking from the cold, even beneath woolen blankets. An insect buzzed in a holding pattern above his head.

"Am I dead?"

"No, not yet," a voice answered.

"I feel dead."

"You have a bad case of *e-coli*, a bacterial infection."

"How do you know that?"

"I'm the vet from park headquarters," the voice announced.

"Vet?"

"That's right."

"You mean you were in the Army."

"Not exactly."

"Well, no offense, but I want a second opinion."

"All right, you smell."

Richard tried to locate the source of this comedic genius, but all he could see were spots flashing on and off around him. Everything connected to his head, from his hair and eyelashes to the tip of his tongue, was pounding so loudly he could hardly hear.

"I understand you drank the lake water at Santiago Atitlán, which isn't a smart thing to do even for the natives. I've given you an injection of ciprofloxacin, which will get you back on your feet, but you have to take oral medication for the next three days."

"I don't have three days."

"It's important that you make sure the infection is completely gone. I'm leaving Cipro for the *e-coli* and Vicodin for pain."

"Did you say Vicodin?"

"For your headaches. You're weak and dehydrated, so you have to take it easy from here on out. You can't keep running around Guatemala the way you have been."

"I can do that," Richard promised, lying.

"I hope so, for your sake. Otherwise, it's going to get pretty rough."

"Pretty what?"

"Rough."

"Well, that's my middle name."

"Rough?" the voice asked.

"No, pretty."

There was an awkward silence, some throat clearing, and then the disembodied voice took leave of the other people in the room. Richard heard boots on wooden steps, an engine turn over, and a jeep drive away.

"Well, at least I don't have mad cow disease," he told Mia, who stood over him with a concerned look on her face.

"No, just mad human."

"You know, you should try standup."

"Here, drink this water. I also brought some bananas mixed with rice. You have to eat something."

"No, I don't."

"Yes, you do."

"I'd rather not."

"He's giving you a hard time," CJ interrupted from the foot of the bed. "Tell him to shut up and eat the rice."

"Shut up and eat the rice," she repeated.

He obeyed, but not before popping some Vicodin with water. Mia fed him, gently wiping his lips after each spoonful. He kept his eyes on her but she avoided his gaze until the very end. The bananas and rice were sweet but had that smoky flavor that had been following them around ever since they crossed the border. It wasn't in El Salvador but was all over Guatemala. He ate the gruel, shuffled off to the shower, which consisted of a black garden hose hanging from a nail in a cinder block wall, and washed himself clean of the dream he had just had. A hand mirror hung on another wall, and he looked at himself for the first time since leaving the Posada Oblongada. He was oblongada himself: gaunt and pale, with grizzled stubble and a vacant look in his eyes. Not only were the failures beginning to creep up on him just like his father, but he was beginning to look like the old man, which normally would have sent him into a panic, but thanks to the *e-coli* he didn't have the energy. As best he could, he lathered his face with a dirty bar of soap and shaved the stubble with a woman's pink razor that someone had left on an adjacent cinder block wall, but he might as well have rubbed his face on cinder block and rinsed it in battery acid. It felt that way, too.

When he got back to the hut, Mia told them they could take the van to park headquarters to check their e-mail and contact the firm, although Richard had no idea what to tell them in Philadelphia. He put on the khaki outfit she had laid out for him, which was two sizes too big, and they drove off into the jungle. With Richard navigating, they took a couple of wrong turns before coming upon the Great Jaguar Temple, which was a behemoth stone structure with more steps than an Argentine tango. From there, they took a few more wrong turns and ended up in a clearing called, appropriately enough, *Mundo Perdido*, which was filled with big pyramids, little pyramids, and swarms of school kids. These included youth whose families must have inherited silver mines, because they wore traditional garb but used the latest in untraditional cell phones, digital cameras, and iPods. The boys, in mixing bowl haircuts, made obscene gestures and cursed at the girls in Mopan. Richard didn't speak the language, but their meaning was plain enough. The girls, displaying infinitely more tact, ignored them as if they were swamp mosquitoes and pretended to take in the ruins, which they had to access on rope ladders. Already, he was exhausted and soaked with sweat.

"Look, we've got to go back," CJ said. "We're lost."

"No way, just go around *Complejo N* and take this road to park headquarters," Richard said, showing him the map.

"We should go back and pick up the main road from Flores."

"But if we stay on this road, we can cut through the center of the park. It's a direct route to headquarters from there. Just go around *Mundo Perdido* here and take the next right at *Complejo N* there."

"*Complejo N?*"

"Right."

It seemed easy enough. CJ gave in grudgingly, and they drove past abandoned dig sites to a fork in the road that was not on the map. Richard pointed to the right, and they headed toward what he hoped was *Complejo N*, but it was a little more *complejo* than that.

After another half hour of roots, runoff, and encroaching vegetation that looked like the inside of a jungle car wash, CJ told him, "Okay, this is it, Richard. I'm turning around. We've obviously missed the turnoff."

"But it's on the map."

"Maybe it's an old map."

"That can't be. All the hotel ads have Web sites. Hôtel du Soleil '*blends the best of the tropical jungle with first-class amenities, including Jacuzzi, bar, and restaurant in a luxurious setting.*' They even have a 'Tiki-Tikal Room' with live entertainment Friday and Saturday nights. No cover for guests. We can find them at saul-soleil.com."

"You're kidding, right?"

"No, here's another with conference rooms and sauna."

"That's it, Richard. I can't do this anymore."

CJ turned the van around, but the rear dropped two feet into a rut. He floored the gas and an explosion of exhaust, leaves, and mud sunk them even deeper into the rut.

"Goddamn it!" he yelled, getting out and slamming the door.

There was cursing from the back of the van, and then he came up to Richard's window.

"We're knee deep in shit!"

"Tell me about it."

"I'm going to walk back. You stay here with the van and wait for me. I'll get help and pick you up as soon as I can."

"But it'll take forever."

"No, it won't. I'll be right back. Just try to relax, you're delirious. And whatever you do, stay with the van."

"But what if——?"

"Just stay with the van."

CJ started down the path, slipped in the red clay, got up, and slipped again. He was streaked with mud and flailing at the air.

Naturally, this was all Richard's fault. He was a disgrace to Scouts everywhere and would probably be expelled from the Hungarian Scouts' Alumni Association (HUSAA), not that he blamed them. He should have paid more attention during those weekend field trips to Tioga State Forest, the "Grand Canyon of Pennsylvania." After all that camping, hiking, and backpacking, he should have been able to read a map designed by the Guatemalan Ministry of Culture and Sports that looked like the back of a kids' cereal box. It should have come with crayons. Now, there was nothing for him to do but sit there and wait. So he tried the radio, AM and FM, but there was no reception. He tried whistling, but his mouth was too dry from the Vicodin. There he was alone in the middle of a jungle inhabited by wild pigs, boa constrictors, crocodiles, howler monkeys, pumas, ocelots, and man-eating jaguars weighing up to two hundred and fifty pounds. He knew this, because it said so on the side of the map opposite the hotels and restaurants.

"They are the biggest felines in America," he read out loud. "That's perfect, because I'm the biggest coward."

He hummed, but all he could think of was "Material Girl" and a Hungarian lullaby his mother used to sing to him. Then the rains came. CJ still hadn't returned; devoured, he imagined, by a pride or gang or gaggle or whatever the hell they came in of two hundred and fifty pound jaguars. The sky darkened and lightening seared the peaks of the surrounding hills. The temperature plummeted (85°?), so he rolled up the window but noticed water running underneath the van. He opened his door to get out, but the water and mud were already too deep. He closed the door just seconds before the van plunged backward twenty feet down an embankment. He was now looking up through the vine covered branches of a mahogany tree, stuck on a slope that ended another fifty feet in a stream below. All he could do was buckle up and wait for the inevitable. Sure enough, the van continued its descent, picking up momentum as it crashed into the stream below with its rear submerged in muddy water, the back windows smashed, and its grill in the air at a thirty-degree angle.

Comically, he climbed out and grabbed a plastic poncho and two flares from under the front seat. It was raining heavily now, so he put the poncho on and started walking downstream, hoping to find someone who could direct him to park headquarters. He comforted himself with the belief, erroneous or not, that jaguars were not stupid enough to venture out in weather like this, so he was safe for the time being. How long this would last was anybody's guess. Unfortunately, there was no bank to walk on, so he made his way as best he could through sucking mud and tree roots. Then, as his thoughts drifted and he started to forget about the absurdity of the situation, he heard howling downstream. He froze. Monkeys? America's biggest feline?

The howling turned into screeching and he took off running. He remembered competing on the track team in high school, when he was nimble enough to clear hurdles standing still; probably weighed all of 150 pounds. Now, he could barely lift his feet. Someone else should be doing this, he thought, someone with a better shot at survival, or at least a reason for surviving. Sadly, he couldn't think of one. He ran until he couldn't take the stabbing in his chest and the rubbing of the poncho on his jaw anymore, and slowed to a walk. Before stopping, his lungs about to explode, he slipped on a patch of moss and dropped like a rock into the mud. He lay there, not caring if wild monkeys pounced on him and ate him alive. He waited for their hot breath on his neck and their coarse fingers around his throat.

They never came. The screeching ended abruptly, so he picked himself up and started walking again. He tried to remember his Scouting lessons, but they had been replaced long ago by the minutiae of contract law and dark thoughts of revenge. He had to live long enough to get even with an entire cast of characters, including but not limited to Eckstrom of the Corner Office, Trudel the Cold Strudel, his ex-mother-in-law, who had accused him of "instigating those dirty garlic eaters," and whoever planted the cocaine in their room.

"And let's not forget Katherine and her melancholy junior lifeguard," he said aloud just to hear himself.

He followed the stream, hoping to come across a group of American tourists packing insect repellent, mosquito netting, sunscreen, bottled water, salt tablets, and cortisone cream, but he had no idea where he was going. Downstream was better than upstream, since he didn't want to end up in the hills at night, where there were probably so many green-eyed jaguars that the trails were seeped in urine. There was nothing worse than cat urine, except, of course, cat shit. He checked the ground for jaguar droppings and tried to stay aware of his surroundings. At least that's what he did walking to his car at night. He didn't understand why his car was now a university van stuck in a jungle bog, but he was trying not to be paranoid. He was also trying not to pee his pants, but he couldn't hold it any longer. He found a *chicle* tree, peeled off the poncho, dropped his khakis, and peed against the trunk. Then he bent over for more substantial business: the passing of gruel. The relief was as instant as it was amazing. This lasted for a while, accompanied by eruptions of gas. There was nothing like shitting in the rain, especially since his life had become one long abdominal cramp.

This might have been one of the happiest moments of his life; well, if not his entire life, then certainly since eating that ice cream in the park and happier by far than his marriage. It was in the top five for the relief it provided and the transcendent experience of flaunting something that most people would have found appalling. That it may also have contributed to the tropical "biosphere" (he overheard a guy with a pierced eyebrow use that word in a coffeehouse in Antigua) was beside the point. In fact, he wasn't sure it did. He read somewhere that *chicleros* shitting in the woods have wreaked all kinds of havoc on the well water.

Relieved, he scooped up a handful of leaves, wiped himself, and waddled over to the stream as if in a chain gang, praying that he hadn't contracted an incurable strain of rectal-eating virus. Then, as he bent over the water to wash his hands, in a moment he would remember for the rest of his life and that would come to symbolize the absurdity of that life, he looked up to find Mia watching him not more than fifty feet away. She stood there staring at him. He stared back, helpless, unable to move, holding out his smeared hands in a worshipful pose to the Mayan God of Humiliation, who was also the God of Shitting in the Jungle. Apparently, she had witnessed everything, from the unzipping of his khakis, which she had set out so lovingly for him, to his rectal recital.

They were both dumbfounded, not knowing what to do or say. He thought he might look more "masculine" if he angled his body a bit and wiped any excess urine hanging around for auld lang-syne's sake. Sometimes it was the little things that counted (in a manner of speaking). But before he could move, she pointed downstream and said with a smile, "Richard, I think I'll wait for you over there, if you don't mind."

"No, not at all."

He finished washing as best he could and then caught up with her, smelling his hands every few seconds to make sure they were clean. This wasn't difficult to do, since she avoided looking at him. He considered making small talk about travel or the weather or the black market price of stucco snake faces, but it would have sounded ridiculous.

Without looking back, she led him to a path that crossed the stream, where CJ was waiting in an open jeep. He was still covered in mud and hunched over a topographical map, running his finger back and forth over the terrain.

"You found him! How is he?" CJ yelled.

"He's fine," she answered. Then, after a pause, "but he may need another bowl of rice."

"What?"

"You know, for binding."

"Binding what?"

"We'll talk later," Richard told him, climbing into the backseat.

"But—"

"Shut up and drive."

"Nice to see you, too," CJ said. "By the way, you should know I had a chance to check my e-mail."

"And?"

"We've got bigger problems than you smashing a van that doesn't belong to us."

"Like what?"

"Like the fact that somebody's after us."

"Who?"

"I don't know."

"Is it a Cuban with a mustache?"

"I have no idea. I just had an anonymous e-mail waiting for me that said we should have stayed in jail if we know what's good for us."

"Should have stayed home, you mean."

"They mean it, Richard."

"CJ, I'm not feeling too good. Can't we talk about this later?"

"Sure, I just thought you'd want to know that we're being hunted, that's all."

"Of course we are."

Had he been thinking straight, he would have seen this coming. Of course they were being hunted. How could they not be? It fit with everything else that was happening to them. He smelled his fingers again and studied the back of Mia's neck, which was as soft and dimpled as a dinner roll. Was it warm, too, he wondered? He breathed deeply, trying to imagine her smell, but all he got was the pungent odor of wet clay. By the time they reached headquarters, he was so depressed he went straight to bed, dreams or no dreams.

———

CJ left early the next morning to tow the van back to camp, and the vet sent word that Richard was to stay in bed all day (you give a guy a lab coat and he thinks he's your mother). So he lay around in his underwear with nothing better to do than walk figure eights inside the infirmary and think about his miserable existence. He knew that most people would have cringed at the thought of getting caught with their pants down in the jungle, let alone *in flagrante deposito* against a rubber tree, but not him. As a lawyer, he was used to that kind of humiliation. During the course of his career, he had been threatened by opposing counsel, strangled during a deposition, worked to exhaustion by senior partners, and stunned by lazy associates whose idea of legal research was downloading practitioner aids from the Internet. He had spent countless hours reviewing contracts for all kinds of clients, from shampoo manufacturers to hedge fund companies, many of whom were as ungrateful and tactless as they were pigheaded when it came to billable hours. He had been spat on in the street, laughed at in bars, and cursed at on commuter trains. He was even hit with a sandwich bag of monkey blood once by a woman who claimed that his client had no respect for animals (it was a private medical lab and it didn't, although he never found out where she got the blood). Eventually, after years of being overworked, underpaid, and ill-appreciated, his immune system had developed antibodies whose sole purpose was to protect him from shame and humiliation. So, after all the shit (literally) he had endured trying to convince colleagues and clients alike that he was not the anti-Christ, pulling his pants down and shitting in the jungle should have been just another chapter in the Mercurius Family Book of Humor and Humiliation.

And yet, it wasn't. Being an educated man, he had to ask why. The conclusion he came to, in addition to causing Irritable Bowel, had the effect of a psychic earthquake. For the first time in recent memory (granted, his memory wasn't what it once was), he felt ashamed of himself and what he had done. This could have meant one of two things: either he wasn't the lawyer he thought he was, or he was finally losing his mind. Of course, there was a third possibility that he didn't even want to consider but that kept repeating on him like stuffed bell peppers: he was attracted to Mia in some freakish sort of way. That wouldn't have been so bad except that he had given up on relationships (the "R" word) ever since being eviscerated by Katherine and wasn't ready to get mixed up with a woman playing "Me Tarzan, You Jane" with a Spaniard in the jungle. He wasn't even sure how he felt about her, although he knew it took more than horse teeth and espresso eyes to make an "R" work. You needed time, a lot of it: time to study the proposed merger with a magnifying glass and a thick marker for excising objectionable parts of the contract.

Furthermore, while Mia might have made a good point guard in the Tikal Basketball Association (TBA), she was at least a foot shorter than him, which meant that people would gawk as they strolled down the street hand-in-hand, dancing would lead to orthopedic surgery, and lovemaking would require a Rube Goldberg system of pulleys. While he was certainly not averse to flying on the trapeze for a higher purpose, he wasn't thirty anymore, as he had been forced to acknowledge repeatedly on this trip. As if that weren't enough, she was dark, much darker than he would have wanted for a lover, with straight, black hair and a mole that seemed to float around her lip like a fly in a bowl of beef broth. There was just no way it would work.

Then again, it was possible that he was just scared and all this talk about immunization was a bluff. After all, shame had been a silent killer in his family, and he couldn't ignore it anymore. It was the fifth Mercurius standing next to him, his brother, and their squinting parents in those family photos lined up like cherry-framed dominoes on the piano and hanging in the hall. What was he ashamed of? For starters, the fact that they had sent him down here and not Eckstrom; that he had been stupid enough to conspire in his own betrayal with a woman who never loved him; that his father was crazy but had managed to conceal it with disengaging but maniacal charm; that his brother had no one to visit him at the home; that he had failed at everything he set out to do—yes, absolutely everything; that he was reduced to shitting in the jungle with a hit man in pursuit; that Mia was the one who saw him do it; and, finally, that he was in her debt because of it.

With a list like that, he would have to keep his wits about him just to survive. That would be hard, considering he didn't care about anything anymore: not the police, the hit man, or his career, which went into freefall the night they caught him grilling sea bass on a hibachi in his office. It had seemed like a good idea at the time until the sprinklers went off. A drenched Trudel ran to Eckstrom, who made a beeline to Lucien Updike, the dorsal-finned partner who had tried to shame him into taking this trip to prove his loyalty to the firm and his commitment to its bottom line, which meant his nephew's Princeton education (captain of the lacrosse team and pledge master of Betta Getta Keg). He told Updike to stick Princeton in *his* bottom line but went anyway, not because of loyalty to Spinelli, Carter, Updike & Minx, or because the client, Rubber Tree International, needed a "guiding hand," but because CJ had begged him.

Right now, though, he didn't care about any of that. The only thing that mattered was a dry martini with a twist, but good gin was about as rare down here as peanut butter, which they called *crema de cacahuete* and pronounced with a grimace. He suspected they also used it as a binding agent, which brought him right back to shitting in the jungle and Mia. She was younger than him (everyone was these days), not enough to rival the abyss between His Beloved and Lung Lad, but enough to keep things aggravating. He thought about asking to see her naked so at least they'd be even. Who knew, she might even enjoy it.

"I'm supposed to take my clothes off just because you want me to?" he imagined her asking.

"Yes."

"And then we'll be even?"

"In a manner of speaking."

"And what manner is that?"

"If we see each other naked, then we'll be able to trust each other."

"Trust?"

"Now you've got it."

"I see."

So that was it. It was all about trust, or the lack thereof. Admittedly, he used to think mistrust was a character flaw that could be overcome with hard work, diligence, and the American can-do spirit, but then he discovered that he could go to great lengths to extract it from his psyche the way some people had fatty deposits vacuumed out of their thighs, butts, and guts, but it would still be there. Mistrust wasn't a character flaw anymore than alcoholism was, and, like alcoholism, was part of a person's genetic makeup that lay dormant until activated by some traumatic event. As he grew older, he learned to cope with the disease, living peacefully with it but never really gaining the upper hand. Sometimes, not so peacefully.

"Hello, I'm Richard, and I'm a misanthrope."

"Hello, Richard."

This same genetic defect had caused him to mistrust Katherine long before the arrival of Lung Lad in their lives. In fact, it hastened his coming (again, in a manner of speaking), so that CJ was right after all. Richard had blamed Katherine for their problems and expected her to react just as she did, going outside the marriage for what had been lacking inside, which only fueled his paranoia. His therapist had warned him about self-fulfilling prophecies, but it was more important for Richard to be right than happy. It still was, of course, although being on the lam with no money and their fate in the hands of pale-faced academics changed things considerably. Shame and mistrust were giving way to more basic problems like dehydration. He couldn't keep losing fluids like this without replacing them, which must have been a metaphor for their predicament, although he couldn't make the connection just yet. That might change with Mia. He wanted to pursue her, *had* to pursue her, even though he knew he shouldn't, especially with Chamba so close, but when had reality ever stopped him? Or morality, for that matter? What was moral, anyway?

He couldn't take the heat anymore, which felt like a truck tire around his neck. In Guatemala City, it even smelled like that. He had ridden in enough trucks, buses, and taxis to recognize the smell: a mixture of burning rubber, raw exhaust, rain, grime, and rotting garbage. It was different in the jungle, but it didn't feel any better. He decided that he had to do something or he'd go crazy, so he got dressed and went outside. It was ten in the morning and the camp was deserted. The archaeologists had left already for their murals and stelae depicting captured enemy warriors decapitated for losing at *Ulama*, a game of leather-bound hip soccer; the day laborers had gone to their digging and picking.

He found a hoe resting against the steps and dragged it aimlessly through the dirt. Then he saw two laborers mixing cement and talking about measurements for a storage shed they were putting in. He had watched men working down here before and knew that the best of them worked rhythmically with an economy of movement and grace. These two worked that way, keeping their shirts and baseball caps on despite the heat. It was the kind of modesty that completely escaped the tourists, who tramped about the ruins in nothing but bathing suits and flip-flops, many of them branded and pierced like cattle. They seemed oblivious to everything and everyone around them except themselves. He knew he couldn't be too hard on them, though, since he probably would have been doing the same thing if not for his divorce and the subsequent implosion of his career.

"And that's the truth, isn't it?" he muttered, wiping his forehead.

"It sure is!" his therapist shot back.

This time, the voice sounded real and came from behind. He wheeled around but found nothing but air humming with heat and insects. The infirmary sat empty with its window staring back at him, gaping, mocking, filled with nothing.

"So, that's how you get real?" Richard asked.

"It's not the only way, but it may be what you need right now," his therapist answered. "I know it sounds harsh."

"You don't know the meaning of the word," Richard said.

"Come on, now."

"Have you ever been homeless?"

"This isn't about me."

"It's never about you. But you spend all your time trying to pull me in directions I don't want to go."

"That's why you pay me," the therapist said calmly.

"I don't know why I pay you."

"You'd rather hear lies?"

"I'd rather go home."

"I think not."

"How is that?"

"You wouldn't have come here in the first place."

"I came here to help CJ, that's the only reason. I don't care about anything else."

"Sure, that's what you tell yourself, but you don't really care about him. You came here to save your pathetic little job."

"Screw you!"

"There you go being hostile again. What have I told you about channeling your violent outbursts into positive outlets?"

"How's this for a positive outlet?"

Richard got ready to fling the hoe across the yard when he realized that he was arguing with himself. One of the workers stopped mixing cement and leaned on his shovel, staring. Kornél would do this kind of thing, he thought.

"Don't listen to him anymore, Richard," his mother interrupted. "He's a paper asshole. Just get yourself out of the jungle."

He looked up to see his mother peering down from the infirmary window. She wore the *frau's* dress and a pair of black rhinestone glasses that flared up at the corners and looked tiny on her face, which was pink and puffy. She stared at him, squinting, and cleaned the lenses with a Doeskin tissue tucked away in her dress.

"How?"

"You'll find a way," she assured him, exhaling on the lenses until they were squeaky clean.

He hesitated.

"Didn't I tell you to get out of that marriage?"

"Yes."

"And was I right?"

He nodded.

"Well, there you go."

"Have you been talking to CJ?"

"Does it matter?"

"No, I guess not."

She may not have been real, but she was certainly right. Instead of reflecting on the experience of falling into a cesspool, they should be pulling themselves out of it. But crossing the border would be almost impossible now that Homeland Security was building walls from sea to shining sea. Soon, home would look like Northern Ireland or Jerusalem. Ironically, they weren't any different from the twenty million little brown people trying to sneak into the country, well, except for that felony warrant for drug trafficking. He looked over again at the workers and wondered if he should hire a coyote to take them across the border.

"You can hire a rhinoceros," his mother said. "Just get the hell out."

"There's something I have to do first."

"You're a little obsessive, you know that?"

"It's important."

"All right, but make it quick...I'm telling you for your own sake, Richard, make it quick!"

"Yes, mom."

As an avid reader of military history, from Sun Tzu and Julius Caesar to Patton, he knew that the best defense really was an offense, which was why Washington crossed back over the Delaware to give those drunken Hessians at Trenton their due. Caught them with their lederhosen down and their pfeffernusse in the air. With the same determination, he marched to Mia's tent, dragging the hoe behind him. She wasn't there, but he met a boy who told him that she had gone to collect *mimbre* in the jungle. Apparently, she took the wicker back to Sololá where her aunts and cousins made trinkets for tourists that she sold in her travel agency. The whole thing sounded preposterous, but only because that kind of thing was completely beyond him. He wouldn't have had a problem filing a lawsuit on behalf of a client who pricked herself with a wicker knick-knack, evil little things that they were, but beyond that he was useless. His wilderness days were over, not that they ever existed. Teddy Roosevelt was an enigma to him as was the Sierra Club, not to mention triathlons. Eckstrom competed in them (wore periwinkle spandex that matched the color of his hybrid car and clung to him so tight that nothing was left to the imagination), but somehow still thought of himself as an adult.

"Which direction?"

The boy pointed to a path that disappeared in a thicket of ferns and he followed it, thinking that she couldn't have gone very far.

"How hard could this be?"

The boy smiled that smile that seemed to be everywhere yet meant nothing. Richard walked away, knowing that the boy was watching him. Gringos, after all, were fascinating to these people. They were as unpredictable as the rain and bizarre as turkey on Thanksgiving Day. Most Guatemalans treated him and CJ with a mixture of admiration and envy, which explained the aluminum Christmas tree lit with a rotating light in the lobby of their hotel last December. Aluminum trees were not indigenous to the area; neither was snow, which came from an aerosol can and was sprayed on so thick it completely covered the branches.

It was surprisingly cool out of the sun under the canopy, which was dense with mahogany trees, *xate* palms, allspice, and elephantine ceiba trees. After walking a while, he stopped and listened to the quiet. At first, there was nothing, but then he could hear insects buzzing and wood cracking as it baked in the heat. He moved on but soon grew tired and sat down on the root of a ceiba tree to wipe his face. He wasn't sure what he would say to Mia if he found her, but he would probably start with an apology for yesterday. He wasn't sure what was happening to him, but it wasn't schmaltz. Katherine had tried that once by making him out to be her soulmate, whatever that was, but when he laughed in her face, she stormed out of the house in tears and went on the offensive by becoming teacher's pet. Neither was it love at first sight. This wasn't love anymore than what they were doing down here was really business, the bullshit from Lucien Updike notwithstanding. What was left, then? Boredom? He had been bored ever since that winter night in the stacks at the law library when he realized that he was going to graduate, pass the bar exam, and surpass all of his back-stabbing friends in Mergers & Acquisitions at Hot Shot, Big Shot & Toupee. Of course, he didn't believe in any of that anymore, not that he ever did, so Mia might just be a diversion until he found something worth believing in: a pretty wicker picker to while away the hours in this *culo del mundo.*

Above him, tree branches formed a net that caught the ball of the sun and light filtered through, landing softly on the floor of the jungle. He looked around to see if any animals were about when, incredibly, he noticed the object of his desire bending over a pile of *mimbre.* She wore a sleeveless blouse and her arms gleamed with sweat from swinging a machete. His mother had always taught him to respect a girl who could handle a machete, and he could easily fall in love with one that gleamed. So, hopeful, he called out to her, but at the sound of his voice she threw the wicker down and ran off. He was in no mood to chase her, literally or otherwise, but she wore a bright orange babushka that stood out as she bounded gazelle-like down the path.

He started after her, stopping to pick up some wicker that she had dropped at the base of a *ramón* tree, certain that she would thank him for it later. He tried to keep up with the bouncing babushka, but he couldn't see the ground, which was thick with tree roots and vines. Then, just as he was about to give up, he realized that not only had he lost her, but he had lost himself, which was a common occurrence in his life. Instead of the well-marked trail he had started out on, he was now in a *ramón* grove, which was not a punk band from Queens but a tree that thrived near Mayan ceremonial sites (must have been all that human fertilizer). Without meaning to and with the best of intentions, he was lost in the jungle again for the second time in less than twenty-four hours, which may have been a record even for a member of a family not known for its sense of direction, time, or space. But this time there was hope. He had a hoe for protection and the two flares from yesterday, which had fit nicely into his safari pocket.

With his hoe as a cane, he walked through the grove and up a hillock that rose softly like the mound between a woman's legs. It didn't take long to reach the top, and when he got there he saw two thatched huts in a clearing. He imagined Mia in one of them, waiting for him with chilled bottles of Gallo beer and one of those Mayan dishes made from corn meal, pumpkin seeds, and eggs wrapped in banana leaves. What was it called? He tried to remember but couldn't. He had too much on his mind, too much to analyze and consider. He thought about Mia and wondered what it would be like living with her without the pressures of work or clients or being hunted like an escapee from a chain gang. They could live here in the jungle far from Updike and Katherine and anyone else who demanded something from him, whether money or blood. What would that be like? He had never had the luxury of knowing, not in all the years he had worked for the firm, not in all the time before that, when he was supposed to be free and not living like a goddamned slave.

Inspired and horny (well, more horny), he rushed down the hill to the first hut, but she was not there. Neither was she in the second, which oddly enough contained boxes of carob-covered raisins, trail mix, and guava juice in plastic bottles. These were about as out of place as a Zamboni machine, but he helped himself to all of it, amused by the idea of ice hockey in Guatemala. Maybe if he and Mia moved here he would buy a Zamboni and she could decorate it with wicker. He could charge the locals to have their picture taken on it.

After eating his fill of raisins and trail mix, he pissed out the front door, spraying the air as if he were fly-fishing. As he zippered up, he realized he liked being naked in the jungle, even though he was lost.

"Come out with your hands up!"

"*What the——?*"

"Come out with your hands up—and drop your weapon!"

Out of the bush emerged a group of armed gringos in war paint and orange thongs. There were men and women, young and old, scraggily looking and wild eyed, at least a dozen of them. It took some time for the scene to register, and when it did Richard grabbed the hoe to defend himself. For about the second time in his life, he was at a loss for words.

"It's not a weapon, it's a hoe," he said.

"Put the hoe down!"

"Hoedown?"

"Don't get wise!"

He did as they ordered, apologizing for eating their food, but they tied his hands behind his back and threw him down in the mud anyway.

"We weren't expecting anyone to be here, but I'm sure this will earn us extra points," one of them said.

"Points?"

"Shut up!"

The man wore a bright orange Speedo bathing suit and a bark necklace, nothing else. His hair looked as if it had been blow-dried. Unbelievably, a camera crew followed him around, filming his every move.

"Is this him?" he asked, turning to a girl in a bright orange babushka.

The girl bent down and Richard recognized her gleaming arms, but she didn't look anything like Mia. She had a dirty face with bright eyes and a fishhook protruding from her lower lip. She looked him over one side, then the other. When she finally turned away, he saw her dimpled buttocks and a tattoo at the base of her spine that looked like a dragon from the menu of a Chinese restaurant. She still carried the machete, which dangled by her side. He had something she could dangle by her side, he thought.

"That's definitely him."

"What the hell is going on?" Richard demanded.

"We're raiding your camp and you're our prisoner of war," Speedo informed him.

"What are you talking about?"

"The Great Ax War."

"What?"

"The Great Ax War that ended in the defeat of Tikal by Lord Water of Caracol in 562 AD. We are Water Warriors, and you are our prisoner."

Satisfied with this historical sound bite, Speedo joined the others, who began plundering the huts and loading up on trail mix and guava juice. Undaunted, the camera crew followed. It didn't take long for them to destroy this "enemy post," as Richard overheard one of them say (it was from a distance, so they could have been talking about Emily Post, but he doubted it). When they got bored pillaging, they turned their attention back to him.

"So, what should we do with our prisoner?" Speedo asked the others, poking Richard's leg with his homemade spear.

"Hold him ransom," one said.

"Leave him here with a note demanding Team Safari's unconditional surrender. Then they'll have to do whatever we want," another said.

"No, let's take him back to our camp and get as much information out of him as possible," suggested a third.

"That's interesting. The rules don't say anything about interrogation," Speedo mused. "But maybe that's to test us, to see how resourceful we can be."

"Yes, the Adventurer people are very clever," said an older man with glasses and a white goatee who looked like an accountant on vacation, except for the war paint and nipple ring.

They kept this up until most of them just stood around bored, chewing trail mix. Two younger guys started sparring with spears until somebody yelled at them to grow up, which, given the group, seemed pretty unlikely.

Finally, Babushka Girl came forward with her machete, bright eyes twinkling.

"I have an idea. Why don't we get him to be our spy?"

The idea caught on immediately, and they started conferring among themselves. This would have lasted indefinitely had Speedo not found the flares in Richard's pocket. He ordered them set off inside both huts, which caught fire quickly. Soon, white smoke drifted through the air and flames crackled high in the heat, which made Richard nervous.

"So, what do you say? Will you join us?" Speedo asked, bending down next to him.

"Become a Weekend Warrior?"

"That's *Water* Warrior."

This was tricky. Richard figured he was supposed to react with the gratitude one would expect from being accorded such an honor—after all, Speedo's team was doing the raiding—but why not tell them all to piss off, which was his first reaction?

"Would you untie me, please?"

Speedo untied his hands. Richard stood up and surveyed the group, wondering why so many adults wanted to return to their childhood. It would have been embarrassing if it weren't so pathetic. Grown men and women whining because no one loved them the way they deserved to be loved, being incredibly gifted, so they turned their infantile fantasies into reality television for everyone else. Wasn't that why they were down here playing Lord of the Thongs? No doubt, they spent thousands of dollars to come to *Tacky Mundo*, and now they wanted him to spy for them. He would do it, of course, but it would cost them.

"Sure, I'll do it."

"Great!"

"On two conditions."

"What are they?"

"Give me five hundred dollars in cash and take me to park headquarters."

Speedo looked deflated, even hurt. He checked with Goatee Man, who didn't have a clue, either, then back with Richard.

"I don't know," he said haltingly. "That's not the way the game is played. Besides, none of us has any cash."

"How do you know?"

"Those are the rules."

"Ask the camera crew."

"But cash doesn't work down here."

"You'd be surprised," Richard insisted. "Go ahead, give it a try."

"What if we don't have enough?"

"Then we go our separate ways."

To his surprise, Speedo discovered that the camera crew had the money, which he counted out on the ground before handing it to Richard. Then, the transaction complete, they all walked back to their camp, which was more than an hour away. One of the crew, the youngest who doubled as a prop driver, drove Richard back to park headquarters in his pickup, but not before Speedo had "a word" with him. This consisted of his standing six inches from Richard's face and threatening him with legal action if he didn't perform as promised.

"You should know that I'm an account executive on Seventh Avenue and a two-time winner on 'The Adventurers.' And you'd better believe that I will inform the on-location director, who is a friend of mine and has worked for Disney, if you disappear with our money."

"You mean the crew's money."

"The crew's money."

"That thought never even crossed my mind. You can trust me explicitly. As a matter of fact, I'm an officer of the court and bound by the conditions of our verbal contract, which I intend to fulfill to the utmost of my abilities," Richard assured him.

"Good, just make sure you do."

"You have nothing to worry about."

Speedo gave him the same suspicious look the woman at the Posada Oblongada had given him and then walked away. Of course, the moron would never see the money again, and Richard was tempted to tell him.

Then, during the ride back, Richard got the scoop from the prop boy, a Vietnamese kid from Garden Grove, California, whose father, an anti-Communist cinema junkie obsessed with *True Grit* (he wore an eye patch for a year), named his first-born son Wayne. After recounting his drab life in film school at the University of Southern California, Wayne bitched about his job, the pay, "those idiot Orange Avengers," and Speedo, who chased him around every morning to twist his nipples in a game called "Tit Offensive." Richard nodded at the all the appropriate times but was about as interested as a dead man in term life insurance. He would have bailed out if not for the air-conditioning and the tremendous glee he felt for having hustled Hollywood.

"So, why don't you quit?" he asked.

"I've thought about it, but as soon as we wrap up I'm going to Belize to meet my girlfriend, and I need the money," Wayne answered.

"*Really?* How are you getting there?"

"Car."

"When are you leaving?"

"I don't know. As soon as possible, I guess. This is our last segment, 'Final Battle of Caracol: Mayan Armageddon.' Then we're free to leave. They said they don't need the prop guys once shooting ends."

"They don't need the prop guys? That's very interesting," Richard said.

"How come?"

"Well, my partner and I are going to Belize, too. We've been looking for a way to get there as fast as possible."

"Why don't you fly?"

"We'd rather go under the radar, if you know what I mean."

"Any reason?"

"It's complicated."

"Well, I might be interested in helping you. I just lost fifty bucks back there, and I need every penny I can scrape together for the trip."

"What about Mayan Armageddon?"

"They'll get along without me, and I can always get my check before shooting ends. I know the woman who does payroll."

"I bet you do."

"Tell you what," Wayne said. "I'll take you and your boyfriend to Belize City for three hundred bucks."

"*What?*"

"All right, two fifty, but I won't go any lower than that."

"He's my business partner, not my boyfriend."

"Hey, no offense. I just thought that. . .I mean, you said *partner*, which usually means two gay guys, at least with younger people."

"Younger ?"

"You know, younger than you."

They pulled up to park headquarters, which was a baked cabin with a peeling satellite dish and a maintenance yard with a picket fence. A handful of mechanics were working under the hood of a truck.

"Meet me here tomorrow morning at seven o'clock sharp," Richard said, getting out and slamming the door.

"So do we have a deal?" Wayne asked.

"It's a deal."

"Two fifty?"

"Sure, just don't tell anyone. We'll need as much of a head start as possible. I'm sure everyone and his brother will be after us."

"I won't say a word, trust me."

Wayne drove away, tooting his horn and waving. Richard didn't trust anyone, of course, but as the pickup disappeared into the jungle he squeezed the wad of greenbacks in his pocket and felt reassured. It was a strange feeling, to be sure, but a good one. Then, as he walked up the steps he realized he should have reminded Wayne to fill the tank so they could make it to the border. He was old enough to know it was the little things that screwed you.

CJ had been waiting for him to return before going to dinner, which was in a canvas tent on the other side of Crocodile Lagoon. Richard found him sitting on the edge of his cot in the infirmary with his shirt off, dabbing his arms, legs, and chest with cotton balls soaked in calamine lotion and lobbing the used wads at the crocodile skin. They lay in a heap at the foot of the pole. It felt hotter inside the hut than outside.

"It's for the mosquitoes," CJ explained without bothering to look up. "I've got bites all over me. They even got under my clothes. Don't ask me how."

"Well, you look like a leper," Richard said.

"Maybe, but at least I'm not shitting my brains out all over Guatemala."

"Forget the mosquitoes. You'll never guess where I've been."

Richard held up the cash, grinning, hardly able to believe it himself.

"Holy shit! An Indian casino?"

"No, but that's not a bad idea. I should mention it to Mia."

"How much have you got?"

"Five hundred, American. I got it from some studio people filming a reality TV show in the jungle. Can you believe it?"

"What?"

"Remember the Adventurers?"

"That's a strange name."

"No, remember Cane Lady asking us if we were with the Adventurers? I had no idea what she was talking about, but it turns out they're our ticket out of here."

"No kidding, when?"

"First thing in the morning. It's all arranged. I told you you'd make it to that orthodontist appointment. All you need is a little faith."

"No lie?"

"We're as good as sitting at the airport in Belize. The first thing I'm going to do when we get there is order a double martini with a twist."

"Unbelievable," CJ said, getting up and putting his shirt on. "You did it, Richard, you fucking did it! But what's the money for?"

"This is bizarre. I'm being paid to spy on Team Safari, which is a group of gringos running around naked in the jungle going through some kind of mid-life crisis."

"Sounds familiar."

"Not anymore, amigo. We're getting out of here and I'm going to find out who set us up. I'm tired of putting up with people's bullshit."

"That's great to hear, Richard, really, but you should know I got another e-mail today."

"Anonymous?"

"No, not this time. It was a copy of an e-mail Updike sent you about Guatemala City. He's pretty pissed about it. Apparently, everybody was there but us: the team from Rubber Tree, Javier, the factory owner, and that bald guy from corporate lending."

"So, what did he say?"

"He told you to think seriously about what you're doing down here and how it will affect your career and the rest of your life. Then he said you shouldn't have left the jail in Antigua, because that will only make things worse, and that we should turn ourselves in. He said he'd try to find representation for us but he couldn't guarantee anything."

"A legal team? Who would that be, Eckstrom?"

"God, I hope not."

"Right."

"Anything else?"

"No, that was all."

"And nothing about the deal?"

"Nope."

Richard thought for a moment and walked over to the medicine cabinet. Something didn't add up (not that anything did down here), and it bothered hm.

"Finding representation is very noble of him, but it's a crock of horse shit. Something else is going on here. You know that?"

"Like what?"

"I don't know."

"Well, what did you expect him to say? He's not going to ask for your resignation until he knows all the facts. I'm just glad he didn't come out and fire me."

"I wouldn't worry about that now, CJ. He hasn't got the balls to do it. He'd need two other partners to back him up. Besides, that's not what's bothering me."

"What then?"

Richard wiped grime from the glass door and pinched it between his fingers. He studied the dead scorpions inside; their dried-out shells were brittle and translucent, their venom no longer a threat, but something else was there, something familiar. He couldn't name it, but it reminded him of the time he had complained to Katherine about her being restless in bed. Not wanting to be outdone, she immediately accused him of the same thing. That was their reality: a competition bordering on violence, which was what sleeping with her was like: two scorpions in a shoebox, scratching and clawing each other all night long.

"We've got trouble right here in River City," Richard said, looking up.

"What do you mean?"

"Betrayal, that's what I mean, and I was all set to apologize to her. I can't believe how stupid I've been. I almost fell for it again."

"Fell for what?"

"You weren't the only one who got taken on this trip."

"I'm not following you."

"No? Well, see if you can follow this. Here's a question you might want to ask yourself. *How did Updike know we were in jail?*"

"What?"

"You heard me."

CJ started, then stopped. "The police must have picked up some identification in our room and contacted the office in Philadelphia," he said.

"Really? Like what?"

"My ID badge."

"Did you bring it with you?"

"No, I don't think so."

"Then how did he find out?"

"Maybe somebody from the firm called because of the missed meeting and the concierge told them."

"But we didn't tell anybody we were going to Antigua. It was supposed to be a little side trip, remember? Two days' rest and relaxation. You said yourself we earned it, so why not go?"

"Right, I forgot."

"Which means what?"

CJ studied the floor, smearing drops of sweat that fell from his face with his flip-flop. It was painful watching him but even more painful for Richard to realize that he had been duped again, that maybe he wasn't as clever as he had thought. What else had been a complete delusion, he wondered?

"Somebody had to tell him," CJ answered.

"Bingo, which is where this gets creepy, because that means there's somebody down here who knows people up there."

"How could that be?"

"I don't know. It's hard to imagine, but just look at the facts."

"There are facts?"

"There are always facts, whether you like them or not. Here are the basic ones: the dry cleaning led police to our hotel room; when they found pot in the Super Selecto bag, they had probable cause to search the entire room; when they searched the room, they found cocaine; and somebody had to plant it there, because neither one of us did, right?"

CJ didn't say a word but just stood there staring at Richard. "Right."

"Somebody who knows we were in jail for smuggling cocaine told Updike about our arrest and jailbreak."

CJ sat back down again on his cot and, without turning to Richard said, "The guy who sent the first e-mail?"

"That depends."

"On what?"

"On whether it's a guy or not."

"So, we're back to that?"

"We never left it."

"Look, what possible reason could Mia have for setting us up, and how in God's name could she know Updike?"

"Why do you care?"

"I don't, really. It's just an awful accusation and it makes you look crazy."

"Well maybe I am, but facts are facts. I haven't put them all together yet, but when I do, I'll prove it to you. She and Chamba are the only ones who know about our escape, so it has to be one of them. It's as simple as that."

"Why not him?"

"Because he's a professor, that's why. All he cares about are snake faces and footnotes in *The Journal of Mayan Manure*. But Mia's a businesswoman, which means one thing—money. Notice how she cornered the market on the travel arrangements for the Smithsonian? She knows what she's doing. Don't be fooled."

"That's her motive, somebody's paying her off?"

"It wouldn't be the first time somebody sold out."

"Fine, have it your way."

"I don't understand why you're getting so upset," Richard said. "I mean, you just met the woman."

"Forget it. It's nothing."

"It doesn't sound like nothing."

"Well, it is, so just forget it. Why don't you tell me your plan for getting us out of here? I'm more interested in that."

"All right, it's simple. We're meeting this kid tomorrow morning at seven o'clock who's going to drive us in his air-conditioned pickup to Belize."

"Kid?"

"Some college student from film school. We're escaping from Tikal and crossing the border with one of the camera crew from the Adventurers."

"That's it, that's your plan?"

"Didn't I say air-conditioned? What the hell else do you want?"

"Oh, I don't know. A way out of our legal mess would have been nice. You know, something a little more detailed so I can tell my wife I still have a job."

"Let's save that miracle for Belize, shall we."

"We need a miracle?"

"You'll be lucky if you get out of this with that stolen shirt on your back. Damn lucky. Never mind a job."

Richard lay down on his cot and stared at the thatched roof above him, following the dried palm fronds as they converged toward the top. There was a hole at the top for the heat to escape, although it did little good. Some kind of bird, Terradactyl-like, screeched from the treetops nearby.

"Are you all right?" CJ asked after a while.

"Not really."

"When was the last time you ate?"

"I can't remember."

"Then let's get something to eat. Come on, they're serving dinner."

"You go. I'll catch up with you later."

"No, you won't. Besides, Mia will be there. She came by earlier looking for you. She said she had something to tell you."

"Did she have any wicker with her?"

"Wicker with her?"

"It's an inside joke."

"Everything with you is an inside joke, Richard. Let someone in on it once in a while, would you?"

"That would be hard, especially now."

"Look, if you're so convinced she's behind this, why not play along? That way, you can find out what's really going on."

"I already know."

"You do?"

"Sure, it doesn't take a genius to figure it out. Updike and company want me out and this is the best way to do it: set me up on a felony drug charge in Guatemala. They probably thought they'd never hear from me again."

"What about me?" CJ asked.

"I'm sorry to tell you this, but you're collateral damage, part of the cost of doing business. I'm sure they meant no harm."

CJ shook his head doubtfully. "It seems like an awful lot of trouble just to get rid of one lawyer. You must have something on them."

"I've got something on everybody."

"Even me?"

"If I have to keep a file on you, I might as well have one on myself."

"I thought you did."

"Sure I do. It's right here," Richard said, tapping his temple.

When they walked over for dinner, he remembered having a kind of file in his youth that documented his crush on Laura Fedora. He had made regular entries in his journal in the summer of 1976, so that by the end of August, he had amassed a collection of personal observations about love, death, and family that was beyond anything he could have hoped for. It had even inspired him to become a novelist, which never happened, of course, like so many other things in his life. The journal ended tragically, which he should have realized was an omen. And now here was another omen: he felt betrayed and stupid for having fallen for Mia, the little Mayan travel agent with the fly on her face. The thrill he had felt as he rushed down the hill into the clearing was gone. After all he had been through, he was still battling mistrust. Sure, it was true that without all the facts and a signed confession it was possible that she was innocent. At CJ's suggestion, he would play it that way, but he wasn't hopeful. A lifetime of bad experiences had taught him not to be. He wasn't a pessimist. It was just a matter of being realistic and protecting yourself. He had trusted Katherine completely and she played paddle ball with his testicles. And then, thankfully, a reprieve. Mia had already eaten and left the tent. It was time to follow his mother's advice.

Naturally, things turned out to be a little more *complejo* than they had planned. The pickup didn't belong to Wayne but the studio, which took a dim view of their using it for the ride back to El Remate, a town halfway between Tikal and Flores on the eastern shore of Lake Petén Itzá, where Wayne was staying at the aforementioned Hôtel du Soleil, Visitors Mostly Welcome. When the on-location director found out from Speedo, who found out from the goateed CPA, who happened to be at park headquarters the next morning to be treated by the horse doctor for bursitis in his left elbow just as Richard and CJ met Wayne, he went from Beauty to the Beast and called the *policía* on a satellite phone. The police rushed to Tikal, arriving sometime that afternoon, lured not by the theft but the description of the suspects, which matched the photos that had been faxed to them the day before, and rumors of a reward. The information they had was that the fugitives were armed, dangerous, and holding a studio executive hostage. Wayne, the executive, accepted the two hundred and fifty bucks up front and agreed to a hundred dollar "bonus" if he helped them hide out in Belize. The trick was getting to the border without being picked up. To do that, they had to drive back to Wayne's hotel to gather his things and get the car that the hotel owner had generously given him.

Hôtel du Soleil sat on the shore of Lake Petén Itzá like a fat lady at the edge of a pool. She had iron latticework, a red brick porch, and an awning with bright yellow stripes. From the road, it looked like a giant piece of Mary Jane candy. Somebody had the bright idea of dropping crushed oyster shells all over the porch for décor, but they looked like cremated remains. While Wayne went upstairs to pack, Richard and CJ waited in the lobby, which had ceiling fans with fly strips, a checkered green linoleum floor, wicker chairs, and CNN on a television set above the bar. Soon, the owner and his "partner" came over and introduced themselves. Saul was a gracious French Jew in his sixties with a passion for chess and prize fighting whose family came from Morocco. Isabel was a bulimic Argentine in her forties named after Isabel Vargas, the Mexican ranchero singer. Her passion seemed to be acting fifteen and smoking French cigarettes like a fiend.

"I write highly stylized pornographic novels," she told them, lighting a cigarette and drawing in the smoke.

"Really?" Richard asked.

She nodded.

"Say, do you mind if I have one?"

"A copy of my novel?"

"No, a cigarette."

"Help yourself. They're *Gauloises Blondes*."

"Merci."

She smirked and then, uninvited or bored, launched into a description of her current writing project, which was entitled "Deconstructing Daphne" and chronicled the exploits of a savagely beautiful interior designer and live sex performer named Daphne Dauphin (*nom du théâtre*) who performed nightly at "The Gaza Strip" and wrote existential haiku when she wasn't deep in the throes of her work. When Isabel finished, CJ and Richard stared at each other, the floor, and then Saul, who offered them a cocktail from his well-stocked bar as soon as they gave the expected accolades.

"Anything you like," he said. "My compliments."

"Anything?"

"Anything at all. Anyone who can appreciate my Isabel's literary talent deserves a drink. Now, what will it be?"

"Martini."

"Americain?"

"Is there any other?"

"No, of course not," Saul said, smiling.

Dutifully, he descended an old staircase to the cellar in search of a bottle of gin. Richard was so excited he could smell the delicate blend of juniper, angelica, coriander, almonds, orange rind, and licorice. Who in God's name could resist? Isabel lingered like flatulence, eventually making a Gloria Swanson exit stage right to remind Wayne that his athletic gear was drying on the clothesline in the back. Once she left, Richard breathed easier.

"You're still mad about leaving Mia?" he asked CJ.

"I'm not mad. I just don't like the way we did it. We left without telling her and before everyone else was awake. I also think you had it in for her from the beginning, and I don't know why. She wanted to help us out, but you screwed it up with this kid you met in the jungle who doesn't even know what he's getting into."

"I want to get home as soon as possible."

"So do I, but we were safe with the archaeologists. Now we've got them, the police, and half of Hollywood after us."

"I thought you had an orthodontist appointment."

"I'll never get there if I'm in prison. All we had to do was sit tight until you got better. I still think you're delirious."

"I'm fine. I just can't wait around forever. Besides, I don't trust academics. They're too damned uptight. How do you know they wouldn't have turned us in?"

"Who would have done that?"

"The boyfriend."

"What boyfriend?"

"Chamba."

"You're not serious."

"As a heart attack."

"Richard, the guy's gay."

"Are you sure?"

CJ stared at him without answering, which Richard took as pretty sure, a near certainty, even without the guy whistling the entire score of *My Fair Lady*. This was terrific news, but it still left him with the twin dilemmas of commitment (should he or shouldn't he?) and trust (could he or couldn't he?), neither one of which was as certain. So where did that leave him? The same place he was before: lost in Guatemala.

"I just wish we had been decent to Mia, that's all," CJ went on. "She was there when we needed her, and we might need her again."

Richard was about to concede the point when Monsieur returned with a suspicious bottle of Bulgarian vodka, three grimy glasses, and a jar of cocktail olives with a sell-by date of May 15, 2009.

"I'm sorry, but we don't have any gin," he apologized. "Most people here drink Gallo with lemon slices or margaritas, but for my new friends, we will make the martinis with vodka; that is, if you find that acceptable."

Richard stared at him.

"Monsieur?"

"It'll have to do."

"You won't be sorry, my friend."

"That's all I've been since I got here."

"Say again?"

"It's great being here."

Saul went to work immediately, mixing the vodka with vermouth, stirring gently, and plunking in the olives, three to a glass. To top it off, he added little cubes of *e-coli* laced ice and toasted cheerfully, "*A votre sante!*" A Mayan woman with a mouthful of gold-capped teeth and a matching uniform served them cheese, crackers, and an endive salad with vinaigrette dressing. In no time, they were joined by what must have been the entire registered occupancy of the Fat Lady, which Richard was now calling, thanks to the Vicodin and vodka, the "Dussel A." This included a retired physics teacher with a pocket protector and lisp volunteering at a community radio station; two burly lesbians from New Haven adopting a pair of handicapped twins who could have easily slapped Richard around the room without breaking a sweat (the lesbians, not the twins); a gray-bearded "sniffer," or computer geek hired by the Guatemalan government to find flaws in their communications system; an unbearable Bohemian couple that met on the Staten Island Ferry the night of the blackout and were drawn to each other by their mutual love of French film and Kafka; a dude on a surfing expedition to Nicaragua and El Salvador in search of "babes and waves," not necessarily in that order; and two sinewy editors of a rock climbing magazine in Düsseldorf named "Hot Rocks." They had to show him a glossy copy before Richard finally believed them. By the time they finished the icebreakers (arranged by Isabel, who got on famously with the Kafkas), Richard was blitzed and checking out the smaller of the lesbians. Her name was Grace, although she appeared to have little of it.

"Put the local station on, would you?" demanded the sniffer, pointing to his wristwatch and sniffing. "I bought a lottery ticket this afternoon and they're about to announce the numbers. I have a good feeling about this."

The waitress played with the remote and after some time finally succeeded in changing the channel. With everyone watching, a mustached reporter interrupted the final moments of a soap opera about a stranded starlet and her beachcombing lover with late-breaking news about two North Americans wanted in connection with cocaine trafficking, kidnapping, and theft. They were armed, dangerous, and believed to be in the vicinity of Tikal. It was also reported that they were working with elements of the Columbian and Calabrian mafias. Passport photos of the men filled the screen, along with their names (Richard's was spelled "Mercurio") and a toll free number to call should anyone spot these *"bandidos yanquis."*

As luck would have it, *his* luck, the photo was actually realistic, even flattering. He had been so pleased with it that he gave the girl behind the counter at Photo Finish a five-dollar tip. The *coup de grâce*, as Saul du Soleil might have said, was a video of him urinating out of a hut and the announcement of a fifty thousand dollar reward for information leading to their arrest. As far as he could see, the only good news in all of this was that his penis looked ten pounds heavier on television.

"And now, for the winning lottery numbers."

Halfway down the staircase, Wayne stopped and looked at the group, which sat in stunned silence. He carried a duffel bag big enough to hold Jimmy Hoffa, a backpack the size of a rubber raft, and bottles of guava juice that clinked as he moved. Slowly, the guests moved off, most taking their salads with them, Isabel excused herself to attend to something or other, and Wayne squeezed his belongings through the kitchen to the rear of the hotel, knocking over a plaster parrot on a perch, a row of cooking utensils, and a tray of silverware in the process. Richard and CJ followed close behind, but then Saul clutched his chest and dropped to the floor like a sack of yams. Those without salads rushed back, Hans und Fritz administered CPR, and Isabel ordered everyone to remain calm. She had already called for an ambulance from the fire department along with the *policía*. This last point, clearly, was for the benefit of the *bandidos*.

"Wayne, the car. Do you have the car ready?" Richard asked.

"Right over there," he said, pointing to a dilapidated shed made of planks and patches of awning.

"Then let's go!"

They rushed to their getaway car, a 1968 Plymouth Fury III, "butterscotch," according to Wayne, who boasted that it had 383 cubic inches under the hood and a two-barrel carburetor. It had a black vinyl interior, a black Landau roof (what was left of it), and tires with more thread than tread. Wayne told them that in the past month he had put in a new battery and spark plugs, tuned it, adjusted the carburetor, and flushed out the sludge that had been sitting in the tank since a hotel guest had offered it to Saul in lieu of payment sometime during the second Reagan administration. It still took twenty minutes to start, which was just enough time for Isabel to come running after them with Wayne's jock strap and gym shorts in hand.

"It should be okay now," Wayne said as they meandered around the Fat Lady onto the main road to the border.

"The ride could get a little rough, though. You've also got to keep the windows rolled down, because the muffler is missing and carbon monoxide gets inside. Drives like a charm, though, doesn't she?"

"A dreamboat," Richard answered, looking over his shoulder to see if anyone from the hotel was chasing them.

"So, why was Isabel so upset about my laundry?" Wayne asked, priming himself in the rearview mirror.

He was so taken that Richard expected him to twist the mirror around to get a better look at his own masculinity. He had put gel in his hair and shaped it into short spikes, which must have been why it had taken so long to pack. Somehow—maybe the moldy martini, maybe the guilt, maybe he wanted to toy with him—Richard decided to tell the truth, which was a novel approach and required three tries.

"She's upset, because Saul had a heart attack when he found out that the police are after me and CJ."

"Is he all right?"

"He'll be fine. Isabel called an ambulance."

"We should go back and make sure."

"Can't do that, Wayne."

"Why not?"

"We'll get arrested."

Prop Boy got an uncomfortable look on his face and squirmed in his seat, which had exposed springs and curled ribbons of duct tape.

"Why are they after you?"

"Well, a lot of things, really, but mainly drug smuggling and kidnapping."

Another pause during which Richard could see the kid's brain working, conjuring up horrific images.

"Who did you kidnap?"

"Whom."

"Okay, *whom?*"

"You," he told him. "But don't worry. It's all a mistake that we're going to take care of as soon as we get to Belize. That's when you'll get your *bonus.*"

Maybe not the best choice of words. Wayne nearly had a heart attack himself and swerved off the road just as three police cars and an ambulance flew by in the other direction. Richard thought he saw a blue van in the mix but couldn't be sure. When they finally came to a stop, the Fury was turned around, allowing them to view the parade of emergency vehicles rushing past them toward the Fat Lady. As CJ chased down a still spinning hubcap, Richard explained the situation to Wayne, gave him a business card, and assured him that he really was a lawyer (this calmed him down). Wayne swore on his father's eight-millimeter, Bell & Howell movie camera that he wouldn't turn them in if they promised not to steal his car, ravish his girlfriend, Heather Lee, or chop him into stir-fry. Richard considered the request and then agreed to the terms, although he still wanted to meet Heather. To seal the deal, Wayne gave them baseball caps from the trunk stenciled with *Die Abenteurer!*, which were promotional gifts from the editors, who had lobbied Disney Dude for a rock-climbing segment in the show sponsored by "Hot Rocks." Also in the trunk were tiki torches, plumed serpent masks, an empty bottle of Jack Daniels, and a wooden flute used by the Hollywood host of the show, Tray DeLay, at tribal council. Once they got the car started again—"Oh, yeah, I forgot to mention there's a leak in the intake manifold"—they put their caps on and settled back for the long, hot ride to the border.

Outside of El Zapote, a dirty little village named after a fruit tree and one of the flavors of *helado* Richard had tried on their last visit to Guatemala, the Fury unleashed its fury, erupting like a geyser and stranding them in the middle of dirty little nowhere. When the spewing stopped, they took turns blaming each other, stuffing themselves with carob-covered raisins, and chugging warm guava juice. According to Wayne's map, there was nothing but jungle and swamp between them and the border, so the smart thing would have been to walk back to El Zapote to spend the night. Richard pointed out that they would have to abandon the car, with the likelihood that they would find it charred, dismembered, or missing in the morning.

"There are real bandits out there, not just patsies with law degrees and daughters in braces," he told them. "I overheard two women talking about it in the waiting room at Linea Aurora in Guatemala City."

"Whatever, dude," Wayne replied. "People hitchhike here all the time. Busses even come through here, if you can believe that."

"Oh, I believe that. But what you're not going to believe, *dude*, is how far my foot can go up your ass."

"Okay, guys, let's calm down," CJ said. "We've got to figure out how to get out of here."

"Fine."

"Sure, whatever."

They decided to hitchhike back to El Zapote, since no one wanted to walk. With the hood up, the radiator hissing steam, and the three of them stationed at different doors of the car, an hour passed. No one came in the other direction. In fact, no one came in either direction. Another hour passed. Disgusted, Richard got out and walked along the side of the road. He wore his *Abenteurer* cap and a long-sleeved shirt, which protected him from the sun, but the heat was ridiculous. He headed for a leafy mango tree on the other side of a rusted, barbed wire fence, which caught his shirt, ripping a hole in it.

Sitting against the trunk, he saw a dragonfly buzzing nearby. He watched it until it started arguing with him.

"What is *wrong* with you?" it asked.

"What?"

It repeated the question.

"Nothing," he answered, shooing it away.

"Don't lie to your wife."

"If I don't lie *with* her, I must lie *to* her."

"You were always the clever one, weren't you?"

"I get it from you, my love."

Truthfully, CJ had warned him not to let Katherine live "rent free" in his head, but he couldn't resist. The problem was that he secretly believed her. There must have been something wrong with him; otherwise, he wouldn't be in this mess right now, even if it were the result of a well-planned conspiracy. He was as sure of this as he was about not wanting to spend the rest of his life pounding out Guatemalan license plates, which was a distinct possibility. At first, he didn't believe it could happen, being innocent, but then he realized just how naïve that was. Innocence had nothing to do with it. The law was concerned with punishment, and if they could convict two gringos in their crusade against pleasure, thus proving to Washington that they were serious about the War on Drugs, so much the better. The embassy would be pleased, the drug czar would hand out macanudos freshly rolled on the thighs of virgins, and Congress would increase aid in flourishing speeches from the floor of the House. Mia's friend, the *sargento*, would receive a commendation, a big cardboard check for fifty thousand dollars, and a letter suitable for framing from the DEA. He'd even get a front-row seat at their sentencing. As if that weren't enough (apparently, it wasn't), Richard hadn't felt right since he watched Saul take that nosedive in the endive, smashing his martini glass and foaming at the mouth on the cracked linoleum.

"I don't think I've seen anything more pathetic," he said, shaking his head and staring back at the Fury.

What made it pathetic wasn't the attack or the pain Saul must have endured or the dramatic effort to revive him, but the look on his face as he lay there helpless. Richard had seen it a hundred times before, although under different circumstances. It was disappointment. Disappointment in a wasted life, a failed business, a relationship with a vampire (come on, even if Isabel were a nymphomaniac—how good could the sex really be)? It could have been any one of those reasons or none of them. Still, he recognized the look immediately. It was as if Saul were saying, "That's it? Two guys walk into my bar and my life is over? A couple of vodka martinis and a game of Charades and it's time to check out? That sounds like a joke. *C'est assez shitty, no?*"

And it was shitty. Richard knew from experience, because his life wasn't much different. He imagined hitting the floor the same way someday, although with a better drink in his hand. If his mother had taught him anything, it was always to wear clean underwear in case, God forbid, he had to be taken to the emergency room. He added gin to that bit of folk wisdom, because if the drink he was sipping turned out to be his last, he certainly didn't want it to be Bulgarian vodka. Quality gin (grain not cane) was one of the few things he had left in life, since even before their arrest he had to face the excruciating reality that he, like his father, was a failure. Despite all of his hard work, he wasn't an investment genius, a tax wizard, or Johnnie Cochran. He was nobody from nowhere with nothing to look forward to but Sudoku in a Barcalounger and morning walks down the driveway in a pair of fuzzy slippers to pick up shoppers' coupons. It wasn't supposed to end like this, and he had to believe that the only difference between him and

Eckstrom was luck. What else could explain it? That sonofabitch had it, he did not. Eckstrom had a pension, he did not. He did, however, have a penchant for pinot noir and the nape of a woman's neck when her hair was pinned up. Everything else was random, arbitrary, although he wanted the hand of God to reach down and smite his enemies, leaving nothing but the stench of burning flesh and the wailing of orphans.

"That's not too much to ask, is it? A little revenge never hurt anyone."

Then there was Katherine, Queen of the Low Blow. He remembered telling her once to stop berating his mother, since all the woman ever wanted were grandchildren and a vegetable garden with Hungarian peppers. Katherine stared at him in that cruel way of hers and replied, "Well, now, you couldn't give her either one, could you?"

Intuitively, she knew long before the first punch was thrown that marriage is war and love a battlefield. How this came to her at such an early stage of the relationship, he didn't know except that maybe she listened to Pat Benatar while he was at the office. Now, like any fundamental truth, it was so obvious as to appear trite. He decided that the only prerequisite to understanding that marriage is war is a frontal lobe, which made him wonder whether St. Paul even had one. It could have been damaged when the horse threw him on the road to Damascus, but only an idiot would claim that love is patient, kind, and endures forever. He believed that love, if it were anything at all, is violent. Why else were "marital" and "martial" so close? As for not brooding over injuries, not only did Katherine brood, she made up the injuries. He had no doubt that just to have him arrested she would have thrown herself down a flight of stairs, photographed the bruises, and then called Collegeville's finest with some sob story created by her well-lunged boyfriend.

For his part, he had sensed that they were at war but chose to ignore it, hoping that their problems would eventually sort themselves out. It was easy to do, especially in the beginning, but as time went on and the evidence began accumulating like balls of pubic hair in the corners of the bathroom, it was hard to deny. Washing dishes one night while she was out with her "study group," something caught his eye. Certain pieces of silverware—a fork here, a steak knife there—he had never seen before. Not only did they not belong to them, but they didn't even match each other, which was a telltale sign of bachelor's china. He confronted her later that night with the evidence and demanded to know if the owner had ever walked sticky-footed across their floor or sullied the sheets of their bed with his naked buttocks, but all she said was, "You're a sick man and you should be ashamed of yourself!" Of course he felt ashamed, but mainly from having to ask her in the first place.

"If you must know, they belong to Sylvia," she claimed the following morning, once the clamor of battle had ended and there had been enough time to think of an excuse.

"Really? Then why don't we give them back to her? Come on, let's go."

"Now?"

"Why not?"

"She's not home."

"How do you know?"

"She took her kids to that figure skating competition at the mall in King of Prussia. They'll be gone all day."

"That's too bad. I was hoping you could give them some pointers."

"*Me?* On what?"

"How to skate on thin ice."

It took her a second and then she said, "You think you're so smart, don't you? Well, we'll just see about that, mister!"

"Yes, dear."

Not long afterward, he was the one on thin ice. Sadly, he found himself divorced, homeless, and sleeping at a friend's apartment on Chestnut Street in Philadelphia. To add insult to injury, he would roam the streets at night, unable to sleep because of his friend's terrier lapping up water like a diuretic camel. One morning, after walking all night through Center City, gulping bourbon from his silver flask with a quarter moon and dodging the police, he returned to the apartment at dawn. His friend had already left for his job as a patent attorney in the legal department of Phantasy Pharmaceuticals, maker of erectile dysfunction medication "for seniors who love to live and live to love" (it was printed on his notepads and the refrigerator magnet), so he curled up on the couch to enjoy the peace that only true abandonment can give.

As if on cue, the dog started slopping. What made it worse this time was the water bowl sliding across the hardwood floor in the kitchen in a never-ending ritual with each lick of its tongue. Lick of the tongue, slide of the bowl, click of its toenails as it followed the bowl across the floor. Lick, slide, click. Lick, slide, click. Lick, slide, click. Had the beast not belonged to the friend that had introduced him to Katherine with a wink and a nod, he wouldn't have rushed into the kitchen and grabbed his finely crafted German carving knife from the dish rack. But it did. To Richard's surprise, the terror-er waited not with dread but calm resignation, as if accepting its own death. It looked up at him with water dripping from its hairy lower lip, waiting. Richard started to hum, ever so softly, "Three Blind Mice" and raised the knife like Abraham over Isaac. And that's when it hit him—

Suddenly, a mango dropped from the tree and splattered on the ground. Startled, Richard looked up to see where it came from and was hit in the face by another one. He had always thought of mangos as exotic and sweet, a little strange perhaps, pampered maybe, but never evil. This one landed on him like a dead koi, and his nose was bleeding. He wiped the blood on his sleeve and backed slowly away from the tree. He stood near the barbed wire fence, rubbing mango from his face and wondering just how low his life could go. Bitching about it was useless, but what else could he do? Looking around, he saw that the road had turned from blacktop to gravel and formed a long, white scar on the back of the jungle.

To the east lay Belize and soft white beaches; to the west, Hôtel du Soleil and a prison cell. Across the road in the distance a farmer burned garbage, the smoke rising lazily before disappearing in the heat.

He watched the smoke, lost in thought, until he saw a truck snaking its way along the road. CJ and Wayne flagged it down and talked to the driver, who was an old man with thinning hair and glasses. The man walked over to the Fury, and Richard could tell from his angular walk that he was American. The man whipped out a handkerchief, tugged some things under the Fury's massive hood, twisted some other things, and poked a few hoses. Then he dove under the engine. When he came back up, he said something to Wayne, who relayed it to CJ, who motioned for Richard to come back in those sweeping gestures of his.

"Water pump," the man assured Richard in a Mid-Western accent as he climbed into the back of his truck, which was a dark green Willy from the forties with a bulldog front and stubby bed. It was in perfect condition without any dings.

"We can take care of it back at my shop."

"Great, thanks."

The guy was a dead ringer for Barry Goldwater and looked the type that didn't suffer attorneys, whiners, or confidence men gladly. Since Richard was all three, he decided to keep his eyes open and his *boca cerrada*.

They headed back toward El Zapote but then veered off the main road at a sign nailed to a tree that said "Camp Noah and the Rosary Factory." It was only when CJ stuck his head out the window and said that they had been invited to spend the night there that he realized it wasn't a joke. They continued north toward the Nakum ruins past a mosquito-infested lagoon, which put them no closer to the border, but at least they were off the main road. After driving for miles on a rutted path that nearly catapulted him out the back of the truck, to the delight of Wayne in the cab, who kept pointing and laughing, they pulled up to a wooden lodge surrounded by zapote trees with another sign that read "Magis." A large woman in a black dress came mincing out to greet them. She wore black shoes with pointed toes and had a pinched expression on her face. Goldwater told her about the breakdown and she introduced herself as "Rosa Mimosa Madrigal," a Sister of Mercy who worked with Fr. Flaherty "bringing light to the people living in darkness."

Richard figured she was at least two hundred pounds, maybe more.

"Darkness?" he asked.

"Yes," she said painfully.

"Well, sister, we've certainly come to the right place."

"Why is that?"

"Darkness," he repeated.

"I don't understand."

"Here, in my heart. I have a heart of darkness. And now I am in the land of darkness."

She stared at him.

Cynicism is a tree with many branches, from doubt and suspicion to a pessimism that produces the hardened nut of misfortune. Uncle Zoltan, his mother's brother who operated the four-color press at Central Penn Printing, died that way. Feeding pigeons one day during his lunch break at Fairmount Park at the end of April, with his retirement set for June, he choked to death on a peanut shell. Cyan-colored and gasping for air, he collapsed onto the grass amid cooing pigeons and cigarette butts as crew teams glided silently through the chilly water of the Schuylkill River. It was a fitting, if not graceful, end for a man who had been reared on the cynicism of his mother's family, the Szabos, and the state sponsored atheism of Cold War Hungary. Like most cynics, Uncle Zoli expected nothing from other people but everything from himself, so when he couldn't save himself from a degrading death in the grass, he probably thought he deserved it.

"You have only yourself to blame," he had announced the day Richard misplaced a penalty kick in a regional playoff of the Hungarian Scouts, relegating his team to second place. "Always remember that."

"I will, Uncle Zoli."

"And who's to blame for the loss?"

"I am, Uncle Zoli."

"That's correct."

Richard's favorite branch and one he continued to swing from with childish abandon, was sarcasm, which was the tearing of flesh for the purpose of getting a laugh. It didn't matter whose flesh was torn or how deep the tear, as long as it got the hoped for response. In sarcasm, as in other forms of human interaction (humor, sex, standardized test taking), timing was everything. If you botched the delivery, you could lose your audience's trust and become a target yourself, which was to be avoided like falling koi. If you took too long with the setup, people would lose interest and walk away. Sarcasm, then, was not for the faint of heart. Richard learned this over the years, having been roughed up at recess by classmates and told off at fondue parties by colleagues over some insult or off-color remark he had made. But, as he saw it, the problem was almost always with the offended person, who would fail to grasp the essential nature of sarcasm. Although directed at an individual in a highly offensive way, sarcasm was not about the individual at all. It was about the joke, the jibe, the jingle, the gerrymandering of phrases that transcended monkey bars or the latest investigation by the SEC. Ironically, if the offender had not been trained through encounter groups or motivational workshops held in the Monterey Ballroom (act now, space is limited), but was naturally gifted, he might not even be aware of the offense. Such was Richard's case. Ever since he could remember, he had been attacked and derided

for insulting people unwittingly, his claims of innocence notwithstanding. They would still stuff him in a garbage can before lining
up at the bell.

It happened again within minutes of meeting Rosa Mimosa,
who took offense at his referring to the du Soleil as the "Fat Lady,"
even though she knew Saul and despised him for his autographed
picture of Nicholas Sarkozy and comb-over. Richard had noticed
the comb-over but missed the photo.

"I'm so sorry to hear about the heart attack. We'll certainly
pray for him," she said with the sincerity of an Enron defense
attorney.

"How nice of you. I'm sure they'll appreciate that."

"Well, I know Isabel will. She's a very sensitive woman and is
completely dependent on that man."

"I bet she is."

Once inside the lodge, Flaherty offered them warm lemonade that tasted like floor wax and, assuming they were interested,
explained the workings of the rosary factory in detail. As far
as Richard could tell, children came from the neighboring vil-
lages to work from dawn to dusk threading little plastic beads,
stringing little plastic crucifixes, and cramming little plastic
rosaries into little plastic packets made in China. Then, once a
month, Flaherty drove the rosaries to the border, where he was
met by an exporter who took them to Belize City for shipment
to shrines throughout North America. His next trip was in a day
or two. The whole thing sounded made up even if covered under
CAFTA.

"We include cards explaining where the money goes and providing biographical information about the children. The cards list
their names, ages, and where they come from. People really love that
sort of thing, you know, the human touch."

"Oh, you can't beat it," Richard agreed.

"They do their work in what we call the 'factory,' which is
next to the Magis. Most of the money goes to feed and clothe

the children, whose only recourse would be a gang or the military, which down here is the same thing, except in the military they wear fatigues and fly around in Apache helicopters provided by the US."

"What happens to the rest of the money?"

"We save it for those kids who go on to high school and college."

"But you must put some of the profit back into overhead like your salary, the rosary beads, electricity, things like that," Richard said.

"Salary? No, no, that comes from the province. I'm a priest from the Missouri Province of Jesuits, which funds Camp Noah. I also teach at our business school in Belmopan, which trains young people to be entrepreneurs, so we make money that way. I probably should have retired years ago, but I stay mainly to irritate the faculty. They're a bunch of pompous idiots."

He paused to pat down wisps of white hair that were floating from one side of his head to the other.

"Anyway, I opened the Rosary Factory ten years ago to give the people here a chance to improve their lives. We started with a micro loan from the government and focused on sales to the US, which is where most of our shipments still go. Today, though, we get donations from all kinds of people who want to support our work. The factory has grown so much we were even featured in *The End Times*. Ever hear of it?"

"Sorry."

"It's a newspaper from some evangelical group in Oklahoma City. They really liked the idea of combining factory work with religious education."

He looked at Richard, waiting for a reaction. "Didn't realize this was all part of our ongoing catechesis, did you?"

"Got me there."

"Sister here does a terrific job recruiting and catechizing the youth. Rose, why don't you tell them about it?"

"Now?"

"There's no time like the present."

With an expression that could only have come from a buildup of intestinal gas, Rosa Mimosa obliged. As she described her ministry, Richard discovered that she was a woman of little humor and even less mercy. She was also a hypocrite. Normally, he would have been the last one to cast stones at the glass hut of hypocrisy, but hers was a mighty fortress, a two-faced temple painted with Marxist rhetoric about the "local means of production" on one side and a Disney sweatshop on the other. He had never heard of using slave labor for religious education, but maybe this was a new technique. If so, it was an illegal one, but reporting her wasn't an option. Besides, as he saw it, the children had nothing better to do, the rosaries had to be produced, and the world certainly needed more light. Who would argue with that? It was just that this woman wasn't the one to do it. Still, had he let CJ do the talking, as originally planned, they wouldn't have had any problems. He just couldn't let Rosa Mimosa's diatribe on the "Capitalist Empire in Central America" hang over the dinner table like a fat curveball without swinging at it. He felt it his duty to invoke the Fat Lady again, declaring how much he admired Saul for his hospitality but disliked Isabel for her pretension and vindictiveness.

"She even likes that butthead, Zidane," he added in his closing remarks, still smarting from the memory of his penalty kick.

"Oh!" the nun said, sputtering.

The bombshell hit during dinner, which consisted of fried plantains, Rice & Beans, shredded meat that looked like cheesesteak, and chipped coffee mugs filled with boiling water (something about internal body temperature and the external Celsius—Flaherty had it all worked out). Apparently, archaeologists from Cival stopped by Camp Noah regularly to buy supplies and hire workers for their excavation. Sister had even befriended one of them, a "specialist" in Mayan rites of passage involving bloodletting and menstruation. Richard nearly messed his pants again. There could be only one person with that kind of encyclopedic knowledge and scientific detachment concerning ritualized torture, but when asked if this scholar was a nasty-looking woman with a silver-headed cane, Rosa Mimosa glared at him without responding.

"As a matter of fact, she is," Flaherty said. "But I'm afraid you're out of luck. They were here yesterday and won't be back for some time."

"Oh, that's a shame. When it comes to bloodletting, I'm all ears."

This wasn't good. The fact that Cane Lady, Isabel, and Rosa Mimosa (the Three Witches of Tikal) knew each other was too much to bear. It would only be a matter of time before they figured out they could kill two birds with one mango— revenge and the reward money—by turning him and CJ over to the police. Richard also couldn't believe that in a universe of otherwise random events in which decent people suffered and life was anything but perfect, producing grotesque abnormalities on a daily, even hourly, basis, a pattern had suddenly emerged in which the elemental forces of nature had conspired for one purpose and one purpose only: to screw him over. How could this have happened to a well-mannered kid who excelled at calling out "Olly, Olly Oxen Free" while playing in the neighborhood park with his friends?

"Olly who?" Flaherty asked, interrupting one of his after dinner stories about nothing in particular.

"Nothing. Please go on."

And he did. The priest told them how God came to him in a dream every night for forty nights and ordered him to build a camp with a replica of Noah's ark, so that one day plaid-clad tourists from the banks of the Wabash would have an alternative to the pyramids of the ancient Maya, where so much innocent blood had been spilt. He had plans for a "Golgotha Theme Park" that would offer, among other things, a Good Friday miniature golf course and crucifixion ride in which "the earth quakes, rocks split, tombs open, and the bodies of the saints are raised." There would also be a *pupusa* stand and free rosary beads.

"It's all a matter of deciding what you want," he explained. "By that I mean, once you have a goal in sight, the means of achieving it are almost incidental. You can be as creative as your imagination will let you. Our goal is for people to understand that everything in life is related to their faith, even leisure activities."

Richard had to ponder this, since, despite a rigorous education at St. Rita of Cascia High School in Philadelphia, it seemed that nothing had been related to his faith since his first erection, which was early on, of course. He was pretty sure about that.

"There must be a lot about religion I don't understand," he confessed. "It's just way over my head."

"So stretch your neck," Flaherty shot back.

"All right."

The priest stared at him intently, and this dreadful silence filled the room. Then he leaned forward with one of the most serious expressions Richard had ever seen and put his hand on his knee. Richard was so nervous he farted. It was high-pitched and dry.

"So?" Flaherty asked.

"So?" Richard repeated.

"So, what do you want?"

"I don't understand."

"Yes, you do."

"I do?"

"What do you want, Richard?"

And there it was: the question that had been haunting him most of his life, long before coming down here, before the divorce, before law school, before his father's breakdown, ever since he found out that babies are *not* produced by the gaseous intermingling of male and female bodies lying next to one another under the bed sheets, which was a theory he had worked out after considerable calculation. Upon hearing the brutal truth (fifth grade in the schoolyard), he was so disgusted that he punched the kid who told him and accused God of being either incompetent or unimaginative. He had been trying to return to that Gaseous Age of Innocence ever since, without success. "What do you want, Richard?" Not, what is wrong with you or why are you so difficult, but what do you want? Could it be any clearer than that? It was the simplest thing in the world, which must be why it had escaped him all these years. Amazingly, it had taken a Barry Goldwater look-alike in the jungle to wake him up.

"Well?" Flaherty pressed.

"What do I want?"

"Stop stalling and answer the question."

"I don't know."

"I thought so. I could tell."

"How?"

"You're too restless, too distracted. It's as if you can't enjoy anything or be present to anyone, because you don't know who you are."

"You got all that from one question?"

"It's a gift."

"What if I told you I know exactly what I want?" Richard insisted.

"You'd be lying."

"But *you* know?"

"I didn't say that. The only thing I know is that your car needs a water pump. Beyond that, it's guesswork."

"Well, my whole life is guesswork," Richard mumbled.

"So tell me what's going on."

"The truth?"

Flaherty stared, tight-lipped, but just as Richard was about to tell him, he realized he had no idea who this guy really was or what he was doing down here. The theme park was frightening enough, and he couldn't believe anybody would actually live like this, even a priest.

"Don't worry. You can trust me," Flaherty assured him.

"Okay, here goes. I hear voices."

"Voices?"

"Voices."

"Whose?"

"My mother and father."

"Anyone else?"

"My therapist and ex-wife."

"What do they say?"

"Well, my ex-wife thinks there's something wrong with me, my therapist thinks I don't want to face what's wrong with me, and my father thinks I was born that way."

"And your mother?"

"She just told me to get out of the jungle."

The priest nodded knowingly and said, "That's what 'Tikal' means, you know, the 'Place of Voices,' but you need to be careful. It's no accident that those particular voices came to you. They mean something."

"Really, what?"

"It's not up to me to tell you, but I can give you a piece of advice."

"Just as long as it's not a piece of your mind."

"What?"

"Forget it."

Flaherty leaned forward and whispered, "It wasn't the airplanes that killed Kong. It was Beauty that killed the Beast."

"*What?*"

"It's my favorite line from the movies. I have the original on VHS and watch it every so often in my office."

"VHS?"

"We're a little behind here in El Zapote."

"But you're kidding, right?"

"Son, I never kid about transcendental truth."

Then he went on about the "inner beast" and how everyone blames their misfortunes on other people, circumstances, or fate, but in the end we are each responsible for what happens to us, barring things like natural disasters, terrorist attacks, and the Holocaust. Richard thought that he could have added peanut shells, cocaine charges, and being taken prisoner by the Orange Avengers, but he wasn't about to quibble over morality and suffering with a guy who kept a dog-eared copy of *The Spirit of Medieval Philosophy* in a bowl of rotting zapotes on his kitchen table. Flaherty claimed that the airplanes wouldn't have killed the gorilla had he not obsessed over Fay Wray in white chiffon and lace (how could he not, the poor bastard?), so it was something in Kong's psyche that lured him to his death, not Navy biplanes firing machine guns.

Richard wasn't sure whether gorillas had psyches, but he said that Kong wouldn't have met Fay without the promoter, whose lust for money and fame rivaled Ahab's obsession with that other white beauty. In fact, Kong wouldn't have been in New York at all if not for the same unscrupulous character. But Flaherty brushed him off, insisting that Adam blamed Eve for eating the apple ("which is from Milton, by the way, not Genesis"), who in turn blamed the serpent, and that obsession leads to obsession and vanity to vanity, with all of it ending in a header off the broadcast deck of the Empire State Building.

"Damn uplifting if you ask me," Richard said.

"The point is, make sure you don't do the same thing."

"Kill myself?"

"No, no, don't blame the airplanes for your downfall."

There was a pause and then, turning on his heels as he headed off to his bedroom, Flaherty added, "Get it?"

"Got it."

"Good night, then."

Later that night with the lights out, crickets pulsating in the heat, and CJ snoring like an outboard motor, Richard thought that maybe he was beginning to get it after all. Asking what he wanted wasn't a cynical question. It was a declaration of hope, which was one branch you wouldn't find anywhere on the Mercurius family tree. It was in another garden entirely.

In this dream, he walks down a tunnel with caged lights on the ceiling and water trickling down the walls. The tunnel runs underneath the Magis, deep in the Mayan earth, and has a damp, musty smell. From time to time, the floor heaves in waves beneath his feet, and it takes all of his concentration to get to the door at the end of the tunnel. He is naked except for a pair of hiking boots, unlaced, and a silk boxing robe with a hood. Rosa Mimosa is in the Magis above, chasing him, but she has turned into a rat, her nose twitching as she sniffs the corners of rooms and mothball-scented closets in search of the tunnel entrance. Once she finds it, she scampers after him, but he reaches the door just ahead of her and closes it as she expands into an enormous bulk of fur, teeth, and tail. On the other side of the door is an arena with a boxing ring and a cheering crowd. The scene is in black and white like those televised Friday night fights in the fifties sponsored by Ballantine Beer ("Take a ring, and then another ring, and another ring, and you've got three rings: Ballantine"). He walks past row after row of seats to the ring, where CJ and Mia wait for him. CJ hands him a pair of recently purchased boxing trunks from Super Selecto. He slips into them, takes off the robe, and moves toward his opponent, Nick the Snorkeler, who has "Enormous Lung Capacity" embroidered on his trunks (it is also painted on his tour bus in the parking lot).

Richard throws everything he can think of at him—jabs, hooks, uppercuts, combinations, even a kick to the shins when he wasn't looking—but the Snorkeler remains just out of reach. At the bell, the Snork returns to his corner, where Katherine sponges him off with estate bottled pinot noir while reciting dirty limericks ending in "Hells, Bells, Cock-le-Shells."

The second and third rounds are as frustrating as the first, but in the fourth Richard gets tired and drops his left, allowing Snork to clobber him with a mango that he had hidden in his glove. Mia summons the ringside doctor, who gives him a codeine pill dissolved in warm vodka. The vodka has lint floating in it, reminding him of the snow globe he bought once in the Empire State Building, which had a fluorescent King Kong swinging his fist in the air at tiny airplanes. It was a gag gift for Katherine, who, true to form, gagged.

"You've got to take it easy. This kind of running around can kill you," the doctor cautions. "But don't be koi about it, either. Go for the knockout."

"Right, the knockout."

To his amazement, in the fifth round he knocks out his opponent, but it isn't the Snorkeler anymore who lies on the canvas as limp as cold asparagus. It's his father. Richard stands over the body, stunned. Then he sulks back to his corner, which now has a pot plant in it as big as a bamboo tree, a rat gnawing the root, and a macaw perched on the top rope. As he collapses on the stool, CJ tells him that his father has died and that a rumor is going around about the cause of death.

"What is it?" Richard asks, horrified.

"You won't like it."

"Tell me."

"Fluoride deficiency. They're doing the lab work right now."

"He warned me about fluoride, you know. He said to watch out for the toothpaste my mother buys, because it's part of a government conspiracy."

"Which conspiracy?"

"The mind control conspiracy financed by the fluoride lobby."

"But he had too little," CJ says.

"That's what they want you to believe."

"Why would they want me to believe that?"

"I don't know, but he wanted me to use baking soda instead of toothpaste, but not too much. It wears down the enamel."

Just then footsteps echo behind the door and Flaherty enters the arena wearing clerical black. He bobs and weaves through the crowd, snagging a bag of roasted peanuts from a distracted *señora* who sells them at double the official *buen precio*. He pulls the cord down for the microphone, which is an elongated lizard tail, and makes the announcement.

"Ladies and gentlemen, may I have your attention, please. We have a unanimous decision at two minutes and ten seconds into the fifth round of our title bout."

The crowd roars, and from the ring Richard can make out Babushka Girl (her babushka is bright orange—the only color in the arena), jumping up and down in her seat. The hook in her lip is attached by fishing line to a pulley in the ceiling, which excites him no end.

"Ladies and gentlemen, please...order...order...We need order...The judges have rendered their decision."

He waits until everyone is quiet, turning to all four sides of the ring and holding up a scorecard laminated in candle wax from Santo Tomás Church in Chichi, which refers to the mountains, not the women.

"The winner by unwarranted, unprovoked, unjustified patricide, and still searching for his soul in the junkyard of his mind—which just went platinum on the country charts—*Ree-Chard Muuuur-cuuuur-ee-us!*"

He holds the *Mur-cur* as if Richard just scored a winning goal, and the crowd goes wild. Quite pleased with himself, Flaherty lets go of the mike and gobbles up a handful of roasted peanuts. Mia puts a banana leaf on Richard's head, and he takes a victory lap around the ring, holding his gloves up and goading the crowd.

"Peanuts?" Flaherty asks as he passes by.

"No, I never touch them."

"Well, you certainly touched him," the priest says, nodding toward his father's body, which now has a puddle of drool next to its mouth.

"I never laid a hand on him!"

"You don't say?"

"Well, maybe, but it was an accident. I had no idea he would be here, no idea he was going to die, and no idea this trip would turn out like this."

"You didn't?"

"Of course not."

"I think you did."

"Why would I lie?"

"You're pathological."

"Am not."

"Then you've got a lousy memory."

"Could be. I can't remember."

"Just remember what I said about the airplanes," Flaherty warns, popping the now empty bag of peanuts.

With that, he steps nimbly between the ropes and disappears. Richard takes the banana leaf off and retreats to his corner. CJ and Mia are gone, and the pot plant is now ripped up and lies on the canvas with dirt strewn everywhere. The crowd has turned hostile. It has morphed into an army of archaeologists wearing drawstring hats and carrying spoons, scrapers, picks, trowels, and measuring tape. They assemble in front of Cane Lady and march in place, the noise growing louder and louder as they stomp their feet. The blare of wooden flutes and conches fills the air as a band fitted with plumed serpent masks joins in. Then Cane Lady raises her cane, twirling it in a figure eight above her head, and orders them to take the ring.

"Spare no one!" she yells. "And show little to no mercy!"

Screeching, the macaw flaps away, but not before dropping a pile of hot ammoniated shit onto the canvas. Richard unties his gloves with his teeth and grabs the lizard tail microphone, swinging to the far end of the arena. Then he jumps down, throws open the door, and bolts it behind him, running back up the tunnel to the Magis. Despite the bolt, however, the archaeologists swarm the tunnel like a column of khaki-colored army ants. They carry tiki torches and hack the walls with their picks. He knows that if they capture him, they will offer him as a sacrifice to the Mayan God of Sarcasm, whose picture he saw in a bookstore in Antigua. The god had no flesh on his skull and will say to him, "You are caught in our snare, white man. Relax and let your flesh be peeled from your bones." And Richard will answer, "Piss off, bonehead!" This will infuriate the sarcastic god, who will order the army to wrap him up in measuring tape and entomb him behind a wall of the tunnel, where he will rot until some lisping Spaniard and his boyfriend discover him in a thousand years. By then, he should look like a bundle of old tobacco leaves stuffed into a pair of hiking boots.

He reaches the foyer of the Magis, which has a carved mahogany staircase, black and white photos of the Cuban baseball team that ran Camp Noah during its heyday in the forties, and half a dozen Chagall stained-glass windows of biblical scenes. He stands on the trap door that leads to the tunnel. He locked it with a gold padlock and covered it with a rug that smells like anchovies, confident that this will repel the rampaging archaeologists. But since he hasn't been right about anything thus far, he doubts this will be any different.

"Why are you over there?" Flaherty asks.

The priest is standing tiptoe on the porch, peering through the eyes of a stained-glass Moses, who kneels before the burning bush in astonishment.

"What do you mean?"

"They're not coming through that door."

"Then where?"

"Come look. But first take your shoes off. This is holy ground."

Richard takes his boots off and goes out to the porch. Flaherty points toward the rosary factory, which is an ark filled with all kinds of animals, clean and unclean, male and female, seven pairs of everything that slides and glides and creeps and leaps upon the earth. The archaeologists emerge through a trap door in the floor, which is covered in oyster shells. Rosa Mimosa organizes them into catechetical teams whose mission is to hunt down the American imperialists "like the swine that they are" and collect the five million dollar reward, which she promises to spend on plantains for everyone. The operation is well organized and financed, as if someone else is behind it. Richard is suspicious but doesn't let that get in the way of his stupidity, which he prefers to think of as bravura.

"If you think you're going to see any of those plantains, I've got some Iraqi oil bonds for you!" he yells at them.

This sends them into a delirium, and they rush into formation again to the din of flutes and conches. They march toward the Magis with Rosa Mimosa in the lead dressed in a flowing black cape with a rat tail a hundred feet long.

"Time to get away," Flaherty says.

"Any ideas?"

"Not me. You're the one with the escape clause, which is another line from one of my favorite movies."

"Which one?"

"That's for me to know and you to find out."

He vanishes again, leaving a warm-up robe behind him. Richard is pissed at being left behind so he throws a rock at the burning bush, which shatters and sets fire to the porch. The fire keeps the troops at bay long enough for him to escape barefoot into the jungle by swinging on Babushka Girl's fishing line, which doesn't hurt her and has great tensile strength. So do her lips, which he kisses, avoiding the fishhook and patting her firm derrière. They ride into the jungle on a black motorcycle with red trim. It's a brand new, 750-horsepower Bravura as pretty and quick as a red-winged blackbird skimming over the Pennsylvania hills in May, which sounds like Rodgers and Hart, but she has no idea what he is talking about.

"Don't worry, most people don't," he tells her.

They stop at a clearing behind the Magis, and he discovers that it is not Babushka Girl but Mia who has been riding behind him. She removes her helmet and black Mayan hair unfurls down her back.

"So, what do you want, Richard?" she asks, peering into a wicker picnic basket.

"I've always been fond of drumsticks."

"Spicy?"

"Is there any other kind?"

"Not in my book."

She feeds him, rolling a drumstick over and over against his lips, now pursed, and drying the grease with her hair. He likes being with her but knows she has betrayed him.

"I'm not sure what to do about that," he says.

"Try writing home and ask what they think. They must be worried sick about you, anyway," she says, taking a red notebook out of the wicker basket.

"No, I don't think so. It's been too long since I moved out of Philly and there's no one left who would know me."

"No one?"

"Well, there was that kid in the fifth grade who told me about intercourse. He called it 'sticking it in.' I heard he moved to Schwenksville, opened a bratwurst factory, and married a chubby woman with lupus whose mother was on the borough council, but I don't think he would remember me."

"Anyone else?"

"Not really."

"You don't like being forgotten, do you?"

"How did you know?"

"That's all you talk about."

"No, I don't like it. Why would I? I want to be remembered by everybody, even the people chasing us. I'm not going to let the past die, even if it exists in my mind but no one else's."

"Sound familiar?" she asks.

"I don't know what you're talking about."

"Of course you do. You're probably working on your own version of the Mercurial Variable right now."

"Maybe I am, maybe I'm not."

"That's for you to know and me to find out?"

"You read my mind."

"That's very mature of you," she says, making a notation in her notebook and checking off something before turning the page.

"What are you writing?"

"Nothing."

"Tell me."

"It's nothing."

"Oh, yeah, well how's this for nothing?"

He jumps onto the motorcycle, dances on the seat, and kick starts it with his bare foot. Then he rips through the jungle, riding deeper and deeper through the brush into the darkness. The smell of her hair fills his nostrils, mixing with the raw earth of the jungle.

"I want to have sex with you," he tells her.

"That's very mature," she says, making another notation and closing the book.

"No, really...*I love you.*"

The next morning, he woke to the smell of Mayan smoke and the sound of Fr. Flaherty working on the Fury with furor. According to Wayne, who sat on his bed eating watermelon and spitting the seeds on the floor, the priest rose early, towed the car back to camp (rousting a *bolo* and his three-legged dog from the backseat), and plugged a leak in the water pump with rosary packets. Richard didn't believe it, so he rushed to the window to have a look. Chickens were pecking around the yard, which had puddles from a morning rain, and the fruit of the zapote trees looked moist and dark in the dim light. Below, a handful of men in black kimonos and red bandanas burned copal and danced around a fire. The Fury was at the factory, a *stalag*-looking building, and Flaherty was underneath, hacking, sawing, and banging away like a madman. He was surrounded by shoeless children, their little toes pointing upward in a semicircle, and wire coat hangers dangled from the driver's door. Just beneath the bedroom window and so close to the Magis that he almost missed it, was the infamous blue van with smashed windows and dented rear door. Richard's heart started racing, although he didn't see any police cars or swat team with thick boots.

"Wayne, where's CJ?"

"How should I know?"

"Well, goddamn it, find him!"

Wayne gobbled the last of his watermelon and left. Richard put his pants on along with the *Abenteurer* cap and a red t-shirt with a stenciled Che Guevara on the front that he found in the closet. Then he raced downstairs, expecting the worst, but to his surprise the Magis was deserted. He wasn't sure what to make of the van being there; he just hoped Rosa Mimosa hadn't snitched on them yet. Relieved, he went to the kitchen for something to eat but was stunned to find Mia sitting at the table, chewing a stick of black licorice and fanning herself with *The Spirit of Medieval Philosophy.* Her hair was braided around her head like a loaf of Easter bread, and it looked as though she had plucked her eyebrows and put blush on her cheeks.

"So you are alive. We thought the police picked you up and you weren't able to contact us," she said in a voice that sounded deeper than he remembered.

"Look, Mia, I'm sorry about that."

"You are?"

"Sure."

"Then why didn't you tell us you were leaving?"

"I don't know. I guess I didn't think I'd ever see you again."

She gave him an odd look and put the book down. "The *sargento* asked me to turn myself in for questioning."

"But you didn't do anything."

"They know how you escaped from jail, so now I'm an accomplice, but that's not what I wanted to tell you. I didn't even know you'd be here. I only found out when I saw CJ."

"So what are you doing here, then?"

"Believe it or not, I came with Millicent to pick up some batteries and evaporated milk for Cival. They forgot them the other day."

"Millicent?"

"The woman you threw up on."

"Oh, my God, where is she?"

"I left her outside with Sister. They were having a very serious discussion."

"Does she know about me and CJ?"

"Richard, the whole world knows about you and CJ. You've been all over the news. You even made the front page of the newspaper. There's a copy in the van if you'd like to see it."

"That's all right, thank you."

"I just don't understand why you left. Chamba and I were doing everything we could to help you. You were safe with us."

"That's what CJ says."

"Maybe you should listen to him for a change."

"Yeah, he says that, too."

Richard sat down at the table, his head pounding again. He could hear chanting from the Mayans and wondered how long it would be before he lost it. Three, four minutes?

"Mia, there's something that's been on my mind for a while now. I'd like to ask you something, but don't get upset."

"Go on."

He paused for a moment. "Why did you help us?"

"Why?"

"I'd like to know."

She bit off a piece of licorice and shrugged as if the question came out of nowhere. "CJ asked me."

"That's it, that's the reason?"

"It was for me."

"Well, it's funny you should say that, because that's the reason I came on this trip," he said. "CJ asked me."

"See, it's simple, then."

"What about the cocaine charge?"

"I never believed that."

"Why not?"

"Well, for one thing, Richard, you don't look like a criminal. Second, tourists are set up here all the time. I don't even pay attention to it anymore unless they're my clients. But, more important, you make me laugh. You're a funny guy."

"Really?"

"I think humor is very important in a relationship, don't you agree? And as much as I like my friends, the archaeologists, they can be boring at times. I've never told them that, not even Chamba, but it's true."

"*Relationship?*"

"But now you tell me something," she said. Then, not waiting for his answer, "Why did you really leave?"

"You want the truth?"

"Only if it's not a lie."

"I was afraid."

"Of what?"

"Exposing myself."

"Well, you certainly got over that in a hurry."

"Good one... I told you you should do standup."

She smiled, which he took as an invitation to sit down, but just then Rosa Mimosa and Cane Lady came into the kitchen. The former looked like the cat that swallowed the plumed serpent (two of them, roasted in virgin olive oil with scalloped potatoes), and the latter was positively gloating.

"Well, if it isn't our fine feathered friend," Cane Lady sneered. "Sister here has been telling me all about your exploits. Seems you're quite the celebrity. So, tell me, what are you going to do now, rob us?"

"No, I'm not a criminal."

"You're not? What would you call yourself, then?"

"Framed."

"And I suppose that poor boy you kidnapped is just along for the ride?"

"Kidnapped? We're paying him."

"Well, that's an interesting variation on a theme: a paid kidnap victim. This may be a first for the FBI." Then, turning to Mia, she said, "I never would have thought you capable of such a thing, my dear."

"Capable of what?"

"The word, I believe, is 'collusion.'"

"I don't know what you're talking about."

"That's a lie. He's probably paying you, too. You really are a pair, both of you. I can't wait for the trial."

"What trial?"

"The one they'll have after your arrest by a team of FBI agents from the Guatemala City field office, which should be any moment now. They're on their way, you know."

"I don't get it," Richard said, relieved that Mia was not involved with Cane Lady. At least it looked that way.

"Get what?"

"Why you're doing this. What's in it for you, the reward money?"

"Oh no, it's much more than that, although Sister and I were just discussing how to divide the fifty thousand dollars."

"What, then?"

"Can't you guess?"

Richard shook his head. The hazel eyes constricted as Cane Lady leaned forward on her cane with all one hundred and five pounds, and he swore that he would remember her answer till the day he died, maybe even a day or two after.

"Revenge, my darling boy," she answered reptilian-like. "Revenge."

He figured this had to be as significant as jungle voices, gorilla psyches, and asking him what he wanted in life, but revenge had always been *his* motive, *his* modus operandi, *his* raison d'être, *his* be all and end all. How could this gnarled academic who walked like Richard III claim it for herself just as he reached the lowest point in his already miserable existence? He deserved a revenge that was not shared. At least give me that, God, he thought.

"Cat got your tongue?" Cane Lady asked.

"You know, Millicent," he said, recovering, "I haven't known you very long, but I can tell you're a vicious woman, the kind that enjoys watching other people suffer. Maybe that's why nobody else can stand you."

She sputtered, trying to respond, but he was too quick. He prided himself on being the quickest wit around. He still remembered as a kid the first time someone had said, "Watch Mercurius. He's sneaky fast." He was destined for law school and things offensive from then on. It had been a magical moment worthy of the family scrapbook.

"Except for Sister here, who has a crush on you. And I don't have to tell you that's a mighty big crush."

There was a collective, politically correct gasp that delighted him no end, but before anyone could react, Flaherty came bounding into the kitchen. Wayne, CJ, and a little girl of about seven in a soiled pink dress followed him.

"You're ready to go," Flaherty announced. "I attached a muffler from an old Ford that was lying around, which will keep you from getting asphyxiated, but it's not soldered on so it doesn't exactly fix the problem."

"Thanks, I appreciate it."

"Now, where did you say you were headed?"

"Mexico."

Then Richard thanked him, offered to pay for the repairs, and, once the offer was declined, promised to remember all of them in their prayers, which they were saying even now as they fled to the Fury.

"Remember Saint Paul," Richard yelled over his shoulder. "Let your praying be ceaseless."

He caught Rosa Mimosa rolling her eyes and pulling the priest aside to tell him the truth about his guests. Flaherty must not have understood, because as they bolted past him he asked, "Don't you want to pack a lunch? We made fresh lemonade."

"No, thanks, got drumsticks."

"Oh, that's great," he said. "Rose, they have drumsticks."

Still, this was getting monotonous, this rushing out of town at the last minute one step ahead of the guys in hydrogenated pomade and sunglasses. What made this escape a little more interesting was that Wayne had to go back for his CDs and "facial stuff," bitching the entire time that he hadn't had breakfast yet. Richard ran out with CJ, jumped behind the wheel, and waited for their studio executive, who came barreling out of the Magis with his duffel bag and backpack as Cane Lady took a couple of whacks at him as if he were running a gauntlet. Unfortunately, Richard had to turn the car around, which meant passing by the front of the Magis the same way the president's limousine had to turn onto Elm Street at the Texas School Book Depository. This felt just as ominous, especially when everyone lined up to watch: Flaherty, Rosa Mimosa, Cane Lady, twelve barefoot children, the drunk with his three-legged dog, and the Mayans in black kimonos who, without missing a beat, continued dancing. As they came around, Mia ran up and jumped into the backseat, all elbows and leather sandals, the licorice stick drooping from her mouth. Richard floored the gas, and the muffler that Flaherty had secured with coat hangers and prayers exploded like gunfire. The chickens squawked and the onlookers scattered in all directions, including the grassy knoll.

"Buckle up, everyone. It's going to be a bumpy ride!"

As he turned onto the path that led to the main road, he did all he could to keep his hands on the wheel and his head from slamming the roof, since they were bouncing around like bobble-heads. At this speed, it was obvious that the Fury was missing shocks, struts, and anything else having to do with suspension. The engine sounded fine, though, and they were racing on the slick red clay of the jungle thanks to those 383 cubic inches and a two-barrel carburetor. He decided that if the Fury made it to the border, he'd get over the bouncing. He might even get over "butterscotch," although he'd have to talk to Wayne about a paint job.

What he wouldn't get over was the fact that life was now mirroring his dreams. Despite the fact that there was no army of archaeologists in hot pursuit, his life had taken on an uncanny resemblance to his dream world, which his therapist had warned him about and said would only get worse. He had been after Richard to write down his dreams, or at least talk about them, but Richard would have no part of it. Now, of course, he wished he had. He might have been able to make sense out of what was going on. He might even have been able to react with something other than disbelief at the scene that unfolded before them as the Fury reached a slight rise in the road. It was so startling that he had to ask CJ to confirm it, which he did. About a mile in front of them, four Chevy Suburbans were lumbering toward Camp Noah, their lights flashing and sirens wailing. These weren't the vehicles used by the local *policía*. These were Americans: buzzed, buffed, post 9-11 patriots in no mood for bullshit from a wiseguy in a German baseball cap and a Communist t-shirt. Before he could say a word, Mia, who also spotted them, reached over and tapped him on the shoulder.

"Stop the car!" she yelled.

"Are you crazy?"

"Well, what else are you going to do?"

"I thought I'd ram them."

"No, you have to turn around. I know another road on the other side of the Magis. They'll never be able to follow us. It's too narrow."

"Narrow? What the hell do you call this? We're not exactly on the autobahn."

"Have you got a better idea?"

He hit the brakes and the car slid another twenty feet before stopping. As he backed up, he saw the little girl in the pink dress in the backseat, the three-legged dog, Mia, and Wayne. He threw the car into drive again and headed back toward the Magis. Their arrival there brought everyone out again, except this time they were traveling too fast and clipped the Willy, crushing a fender and peeling the front bumper from the chassis as if they were opening a can of smoked oysters. The impact sent them toward the Magis, where the Fury spun around in a circle, splattering Rosa Mimosa and Cane Lady with mud. On Mia's direction, he drove to the rear, where they picked up another path that was so tight he remembered having better luck cramming a grapefruit down a garbage disposal.

Somehow, though, they managed to escape without getting stuck, hitting a tree, or landing in a ditch. Riding through the jungle with Mia at his back was a little strange, particularly since in the rush he had forgotten his Cole Haan boots and was barefoot, but this wasn't the time to be analyzing his dreams. With any luck, they'd be back on the road from El Zapote to the border. The only problem was that they were going nowhere faster than you can say, he believed the word was, "collision."

In the Mercurial dance of life, you moved one step forward and two back, which meant that in order to get anywhere you had to wait for your turn in the line of dance. Otherwise, you'd get trampled. Their turn may not have been fancy, but it was definite: the plastic seal holding even though they were plowing through some of the thickest wicker yet. There were also no bloodhounds on their trail or helicopters throbbing overhead. Richard knew they were lucky, although just a few days ago he would have thought the whole thing crazy. Now, he wasn't sure about anything, including what to do with the little girl and a dog that hadn't been bathed in God knew how long, making it impossible to breathe even in something as cavernous as a Plymouth.

"There's nobody behind us. Pull over for a second, would you?" CJ said.

He stopped the car and CJ got out to relieve himself on a rock with pictograph graffiti. Wayne followed, grumbling about breakfast and rubbing the back of his head from the thumping he had gotten from Cane Lady. Mia said that the girl lived in a nearby village and knew of another path that led south to the main road.

"It doesn't take us back to Camp Noah?"

"She says no."

"Can the car get through?"

"I think so."

"All right, we'll drop her off and then head for the main road. They think we're going to Mexico anyway, so we shouldn't have any trouble with the police."

"But what about Millicent? I told her you were going to Belize."

"You don't think she bought Mexico?"

"Richard, she may be vicious but she's not stupid. If you were going to Mexico, why were you headed east?"

"Good point."

"Getting out of the country may not be as easy as you think."

"So far, nothing's been easy."

"Well, you haven't helped, you know."

"I never do. It's part of my problem."

"I can help you with that," she said, "but first let's clean up this mess. I have to get back to my business in Antigua. Otherwise, I'll end up losing everything."

Mia may have been lying, but she was right about one thing: they'd need a miracle to get out of Guatemala, since what had started out as petty theft had become an international incident involving the cast, crew, and management of "The Adventurers," their own law firm, the FBI, a team of archaeologists, and an unknown hit man. Had he been alive to remind him, Uncle Zoli would have blamed him for all of it, although the more Richard thought about it, the more he was convinced beyond a pubic hair of doubt that he was dealing with two conspiracies, not one. The first involved the Three Witches of Tikal, high-ranking government officials, and the Guatemalan Institute of Tourism. They wanted publicity and the reward money, which was straightforward enough, and he could even respect Cane Lady's desire for revenge. He didn't like it, but he understood it.

The second was much more diabolical and involved Mia, Updike, and Eckstrom, who apparently wasn't content with a corner office. The sonofabitch wanted every office, and he had a plan to do just that. As for Mia, the fact that he had been betrayed by a pair of java eyes and a Meet Me Behind the Temple smile hurt him beyond belief, particularly since he had made that mistake before. Had he learned nothing in his half century on the planet? If he had a hundred lives to live, would he end up being abandoned in all of them? Wasn't there one scenario where the girl either didn't leave or came back to him in tears?

Their jaunt through the jungle lasted more than an hour and was filled with mud moguls, brush, and, to his amazement, tree frogs. At one point, he sideswiped a tree and they came cascading down onto the windshield like giant wads of snot, smearing the glass and sliding off into the brush. The dog barked, the little girl laughed (and the dish ran away with the spoon?), and Wayne recorded the scene on his digital video camera, which he had taken out as soon as he had returned to the car. Every two minutes he asked Richard to stop so that he could get out to video the frogs up close, but Richard ignored him and ordered the windows rolled up, even though it meant an agonizing death by carbon monoxide poisoning. He explained that it was better than being mauled by jaguars, mountain lions, dinosaurs, or whatever the hell else was out there. Meanwhile, Mia and the girl amused themselves by dueling with sticks of licorice, playing patty-cake, and petting the three-legged mongrel, which was trembling with excitement from the frog attack (or lack of air).

"Where in God's name are we?" Richard demanded after a long silence, searching for Wayne's map in the glove compartment.

"Somewhere in the jungle southeast of Tikal," CJ answered.

"That's a relief. I thought we were lost."

"Well, what did you expect? There aren't any highway signs out here."

"Highway signs? There's nothing out here."

"Take a pill."

"Good idea."

Richard took his pills out but found only two at the bottom of the plastic vial. He looked over at CJ.

"So much for honesty," he said.

"What do you mean?"

"You haven't complained once about your arthritis since jail. Why is that?"

"Father Flaherty prayed over me," CJ answered.

"Don't hand me that bullshit. You've been pilfering my pills, stealing from your own friend. What the hell is that?"

"Watch your mouth. There's a child present."

"There's a thief present, you mean."

"All right, I didn't know what else to do," CJ confessed. "I ran out and my fingers were killing me."

"You should have asked me."

"You would have given me some?"

"No, but you could have told the horse doctor that you have arthritis and need medication. How about telling the truth for once?"

CJ turned toward him. "You're lecturing me about telling the truth? You wouldn't know it if it dropped out of a tree like one of these goddamn frogs and hit you in the face."

"Hey, calm down, there's a child present."

"Sorry."

Richard swallowed the two pills that were left and drove on. For a long time no one spoke. Wayne filmed the occasional frog that plopped onto the hood of the car before bouncing off, dazed, into the brush.

"There, up ahead," Mia said finally. "There's a village to the right of that tamarindo tree. That's hers."

Richard turned at a huge tree with scrotum-looking fruit into a clearing with huts and a stone wall. Adjacent to the wall was a shack in the Mopan style of limestone and thatch with a hand-painted sign that read, *Casa de Artesanías*. A second sign promoted herbal cures for everything that ails you, from bunions and worms to troublesome in-laws. What ones weren't? he thought. He pulled up to the shack, parked in the shade, and immediately the little girl scrambled over Wayne through the window. Wayne filmed her as she went inside and the dog hopped behind her. As they got out and looked around, Richard noticed that the place seemed unusually tidy, with trimmed grass and recently varnished benches. On the other side of the clearing was a level area with gravel and a third sign that read, "Parking for Eco-tourism."

"How far would you say the main road is from here?" he asked CJ, who was already sorting through rainbow-colored hammocks outside the shack.

"I'm not sure, but it can't be too far. Why?"

"I didn't expect to find a parking lot here."

"No, neither did I."

"This is an eco-tourist spot?"

"I guess so."

"So what's eco-tourism?"

"You know, traveling green, protecting the environment, not leaving a signature, that kind of thing."

"It sounds like a scam."

CJ held up a hammock. "So, what do you think?"

"With your luck, it probably belongs to somebody else."

A diminutive woman in a *huilpil*, or traditional Mayan dress, came out to help, and Richard decided to let CJ negotiate his own *buen precio*, since she probably didn't speak Spanish anyway. The irony was that after all the trips he had taken down here, speaking the mother tongue had gotten him absolutely nowhere.

"Mia, we shouldn't stay long," he told her inside the shack, which had a dirt floor and smelled of hemp and leather.

"That's fine."

There were wooden boxes all over filled with trinkets of all kinds: corncob pipes, combs, flutes, dolls made of corn silk, clay jars, tablecloths, leather belts, course cotton blouses, wallets, pomade, and handmade soap. He started browsing and came across a pair of sandals made from tree bark. He couldn't resist and asked Mia to do the haggling for him.

"Just pay it," she advised him.

"Full price?"

"Yes."

"I don't think I can do that."

"You don't want them to think you're cheap, do you?"

"I am cheap."

She stared at him, waiting.

"Will they take American?"

She checked with a teenage girl, the daughter of the woman outside, who said that they would gladly accept American money.

"I figured as much," he said. "They probably take every American who comes through the door."

Unexpectedly, the girl covered her mouth, giggling.

"She understood me?" he asked Mia.

"No, I don't think so."

"Then what's so funny?"

"She's laughing at you, because you're walking around barefoot. She's never seen a tourist do that before."

"You mean a gringo."

"A gringo."

"Then tell her if she thinks that's funny, she should try driving around with a three-legged dog in the backseat. Go ahead, tell her."

Mia translated and the girl giggled again. Richard made a show of putting the sandals on and then tipped her a dollar.

"Stop flirting," Mia said. "She'll think you're serious."

"I am serious."

Wayne, who was filming everything, including his own purchase of five packs of chewing gum, three hemp bracelets, and a Mayan backscratcher in the shape of a jaguar claw, announced the arrival of a bus.

"What do you mean, bus?"

"A bus just pulled up right over there," he repeated, pointing to the parking lot.

They ran outside just as a gargantuan bus entered the clearing. It was white with tinted windows and a green kangaroo on each side proclaiming, "Eco-Australia, Go Green!" It ground down its gears, belched, and unleashed a flock of elderly tourists. The men wore pastel *guayaberas* and khaki shorts with dark socks and loafers. The women had slightly better taste; they wore those cotton blouses with tropical birds embroidered on the front that Richard had seen in every tourist spot from San Diego to San Miguel, El Salvador.

"Jesus, are there no mirrors?"

"I don't know about that, but they're headed this way," CJ said, turning back toward the car and opening the door.

"No, not there. It's too risky."

"Where then?"

"Behind the hut."

The four of them raced to the back of the *Casa* as the wave of tourists came forward. The Aussies shouted at each other in that accent that made everything sound like a problem, which Richard found strangely reassuring.

"What do we do now?" CJ asked.

"I'll find the driver and ask him how far it is to the main road," Richard said. "Stay out of sight till I get back."

He found the driver, not Australian, resting under another tamarindo tree and fanning himself with a newspaper that had his and CJ's photos on the front page. He was in an Eco-Australia uniform, which consisted of a short-sleeved, white shirt with green epaulettes, a clip-on tie the color of fennel, and a matching hat with visor. He said that the path widened past the parking lot and that "CA 13" was five miles to the south. Richard thanked him and walked back to the hut, catching himself in a window of the bus. It wasn't pretty. He took his cap off and ran his fingers through his hair, which was disheveled and greasy. Somehow, his t-shirt had gotten torn, he needed a bath, and he hadn't brushed his teeth yet. He couldn't do anything about it now, so he put his cap back on and started to walk away when he realized that he had forgotten to ask about bottled water, since their supply of guava juice, thankfully, had run out.

But the driver was gone. Richard found him on the opposite side of the bus, talking to two FBI agents and a fully clothed Speedo, who was pacing back and forth like a caged puma. A Chevy Suburban was parked alongside the bus, its blue lights flashing mutely. Using a group of elderly ladies that smelled of lilac and zinc ointment as cover, he made his way back to the hut as the two agents and Speedo worked their way through the crowd to the Fury.

"We've got to make a run for it. The FBI is here."

"Where?" CJ asked, panicked.

"The jungle. They'll never find us there."

"No, you don't want to do that," Mia said. "We'd never survive."

"Where then?"

CJ looked at Richard, who looked at Wayne, who was recording all of this for posterity (or their trials).

"Richard, this is serious. Stop posing for the camera," CJ said.

"I'm not posing, I'm thinking."

"And?"

"We'll get on the bus."

"What?"

"We'll board the bus and be stowaways. It's our only way out of here. We'll go one by one, discretely, without making any fuss. Then we'll hide in the bathroom."

"That's crazy."

"As if that matters anymore. Come on, Mia, you're first."

Mia peered around the corner and walked calmly across the clearing to the bus. The door was cracked open and she squeezed through. Then CJ went, but as he reached the door, he slid on the gravel, fell, and cut his elbow. He got up quickly and disappeared inside.

"Wayne, it's your turn."

"Actually, I'd prefer to go last," he said.

"*Prefer?*"

"I want to record you. I've decided to make a video documentary of our trip, and this will be an important part of the Great Escape segment."

"What are you talking about?"

"I realized I could make a bundle of money and a name for myself by filming a documentary on the international drug trade."

"Are you out of your mind? There is no drug trade here, and I don't know if you noticed, but we're not exactly *narcos*."

"Look at it this way. You're using me, so I thought I'd use you."

"How about looking at it *this* way?"

Richard dragged him across the clearing so forcefully that Wayne swallowed his gum. As they boarded, the driver pressed a green air horn, signaling the end of the break. The Aussies swarmed back, filling all but three seats in the back. Inside the bathroom, Richard was pressed against the door but managed to keep it open without the light coming on. When everyone was present and accounted for, the driver put the bus in reverse and started to back out. Suddenly, the bus jerked to a halt, the door opened in a swish of compressed air, and a sun-glassed agent jumped on followed at the heels by Speedo. The agent introduced himself as Special

Agent Brad Something or Other from the Homeland Office of Baseball and Apple Pie, showed his identification card, and asked if anyone had seen two fugitives, one hostage, and an accomplice, the latter being a Mayan woman with an unusually large mole on her cheek. No one responded. There was a cough, then another. Finally, a woman raised her hand and asked him to repeat the question, which he did, rudely. Then he took his glasses off—nervous, electric eyes the color of aftershave scanning the passengers—and walked up the aisle, close enough for Richard to see that he was wearing cowboy boots.

"Brad" looked all of thirty-five and wore stone washed jeans and a linen jacket. Richard wanted to slap him but knew that would have gotten them a direct flight to Guantánamo Bay. Brad stopped three rows short of the bathroom, and Richard wondered if he could hear his heart beating. He remembered that Edgar Allen Poe story from high school about the disembodied heart beating beneath the floorboards. Then, as he held his breath, he felt something strange. He looked down and there, peering out of the bathroom from between his legs, was the three-legged dog. The little girl was on the floor next to him, shushing him to be quiet. All Richard could hear was the panting of the dog and the shushing of the girl.

Sensing something not quite right, Brad leaned forward and listened. But then, miracle of miracles, he wheeled around, apologized for the "inconvenience, folks," and exited the bus in a flash. Speedo nipped at his heels, begging him to go back and check the bathroom, but it was too late. Brad Dude had decided.

To counter their bad taste, God must have blessed Australians with strong bladders, because not one of them got up to use the bathroom during the entire ride to CA 13, which took forever and was mined with sinkholes. Richard marveled at how they could fit such huge buses into backwater places like this, except that he knew that tourists would pay top dollar for anything "indigenous." He had seen them squeeze in just about anywhere to observe a religious ritual, and he knew the locals would do just about anything to invent one, parting Señor Gringo of his Yankee dollar. It was the national pastime here, which meant that you could probably get a degree in it, beginning with the introductory course, "How to Sell Dry Cleaning Without Really Trying," and ending with the ever popular, "Cocaine Setups, a Seminar." As insensitive as it may have been (he was worried), he believed that the reputation these people had for honesty was, quite honestly, a load of horse manure, the result of liberals' lingering infatuation with the Noble Savage and that famously indestructible Anglo-Saxon guilt, which he had never really understood, being neither Anglo-Saxon nor a chump. No matter how much guilt he felt personally, it was a professional liability that he had to repress. That was just a fact of life and something that the junior people at the firm never quite accepted.

Fortunately, fortune was beginning to turn. He knew this, because the bus was beginning to turn, and it was turning in their direction: a wide, low-geared throttle to the left, which even a Hungarian Scouts flunky knew could mean only one thing. They were headed east on CA 13, that gravel highway to heaven, to Belize, to freedom, to that chilled double martini at the airport bar. He was so sure of this that he began composing the legal brief for his lawsuit. As soon as they got back, *he* would be the one to show no mercy, from the gelled *Policía Nacional Civil, Sacatepequez* division, all the way to those Merciless Sisters of Guatemala. Every one of them would suffer his vengeance, his desire to stick that jaguar handle where it would do the most good.

As he turned around to share the wonderful news, he stepped on the dog, which yelped, scaring the girl, who screamed, which startled Wayne, who dropped the camera, which flashed a picture of them in living color. In that instant of apocalyptic light, he could see CJ at the sink tending to his scraped elbow and Mia straddling the toilet bowl, her feet perched precariously on either side, looking like she was about to give birth Apache style.

"How the hell did the dog get in here?" he asked.

"That was me," Mia confessed. "I let them in when you were talking to Wayne. I felt sorry for her."

"How about feeling sorry for me? Look, all I wanted to say is that we're turning onto the main road that leads to the border. So, let's just sit tight and not make a sound."

"You mean we have to stay in here?" CJ asked.

"That's exactly what I mean."

"No way, Richard. We can't stay cooped up like this, not all the way to the border. Besides, have you smelled the dog?"

Actually, in all the excitement, he hadn't. He looked down at the sad-eyed dog, which wagged its crooked tail and stuck out its tongue.

"All right, there are three empty seats directly across from us, but we can't all fit. We'll have to take turns until we get to Belize."

"So let's go," CJ said.

"Fine. Wayne, you take the first shift in the bathroom."

"Yes sir," he said, saluting, his video camera back in action.

With as much grace as the Marx Brothers, Richard, Mia, CJ, the girl, and the dog left the bathroom in a conga line to the seats. Richard was by the window, Mia in between, and CJ by the aisle. The girl sat with Mia and the dog curled up on Richard's footrest, laying its head on his knees. He hadn't noticed before, but it had one brown eye and one blue one, which he found appealing although he wasn't sure which one to look at. By now, most of the other passengers were preoccupied with reading, sleeping, or measuring out pills in what looked like plastic fuse boxes, so no one noticed.

The air-conditioning was on high, and, although he wasn't used to the cold, it felt so good that Richard didn't care anymore about getting caught. He wanted to sleep until the bus arrived not at a spatial destination but a temporal one, back in time to the day before they left on this trip. Back to his first day at the firm, to his wedding, to law school, to his misplaced kick, to his first *in utero* kick. To a time before he had feet even.

He tried to close his eyes and rest but couldn't, which was fine because before too long Mia asked, "What are you thinking about?"

"Nothing."

"Are you sure?"

He shrugged his shoulders.

"If you're worried about the FBI, then you have to set things straight with them, not just get out of the country."

"I know."

"I've been giving it a lot of thought, and I have a plan," she said. "I was going to tell you about it back at the camp."

"Really?"

"Yes, although I'm not sure it will work. Do you want to hear it?"

"Sure," he said, intrigued.

"I'll turn myself in and tell them you were set up by a radical environmental group opposed to globalization. They wanted you out of the way so your client wouldn't build a processing plant here. I'll say they came after you and threatened your life. When you said no, they planted cocaine in your hotel room. That way, it's a political offense and the police will see you as victims instead of criminals. The embassy will get involved, and they'll have no choice but to drop the criminal charges."

He stared at her, more than a little impressed. "Mia, that's brilliant. How did you come up with it?"

"I read it in the newspaper."

"You mean it really happened?"

"Anything can happen here, and it usually does."

"I understand that, but won't you get into even more hot water?"

"I'll say I got involved to help you. I would have done it for any of my clients."

"You would have?"

"No."

"Then why do it for me?"

The question caught her off guard, which gave him enough time to add, "And don't tell me because I'm more interesting than the archaeologists. Nobody told you to jump into the Fury back there. You did that on your own."

He studied her face for a sign of guilt or remorse, but she was having none of it. She looked away, parting the girl's hair from her face. The girl stared at Richard and then whispered something to Mia.

"What did she say?" he asked.

"It's nothing."

"Come on, tell me."

"She says you're a nice man with kind eyes. She's also very thankful that you rescued her from Camp Noah."

"Rosa Mimosa, you mean. So, what's her name?"

"Jacinta."

"Well, Jacinta, you're welcome."

Mia translated, and the girl smiled broadly. The dog whined, and he ran his finger through the furrow between its mismatched eyes.

"So, does this radical environmental group have a name?" he asked.

"*Planeta Libre.*"

"Sounds like a cocktail. Where'd you come up with it?"

"It's an underground newspaper in Mexico. I used to date a guy who wrote for it."

"You don't say? I definitely want to hear about that, but later. Right now, I want you to answer my question."

"Which one was that?"

"Why you came on this little misadventure."

"We talked about that already."

"I'd like to hear it again."

"It's simple," Mia said. "I promised to help you get out of the country, and I keep my word. I also thought that with more people involved, you'd get more publicity, and with more publicity, you'd have a better chance of clearing your name."

"That makes sense."

"I also realized that I have to clear my own name, especially since I've got clients coming here soon."

"That makes even more sense."

"Well, I have to look out for myself," she added. "If I don't, who will?"

"Exactly."

"You really believe that?"

"Are you kidding? I live by it. I even have a bumper sticker that says it."

"You do?"

"No, but I should."

"Well, I'm not so sure."

"Well I am," he said, turning to face her. "I can save you a lot of time on this one. Forget other people. Just look out for yourself. My Uncle Zoli taught me that everybody has a gun. Some people keep it up in the attic, some out in the open, some drive around with it in the glove compartment, some strap it to their sides. But everybody has one. Your job is to make sure you don't give them a bullet. That's all you have to do. Don't give them a bullet, because if you do, they'll end up shooting you with it, believe me."

"I see you've thought this through," she said.

"Absolutely, because you never know who's got a gun pointed at you. They could be sitting right next to you and you wouldn't even know it."

He paused and looked directly at her.

"You sound as if you don't trust me," she said.

"I don't."

"What have I done to deserve that?"

"You tell me."

"No, if you want to know something, you'll have to come out and ask me."

"Okay, then, have you ever been to Philadelphia?"

"Excuse me?"

"You know, William Penn, the City of Brotherly Love."

"No, I've never been there or anywhere else in the States, although I'd love to go. Chamba said he would take me someday, but now that might not happen."

"And you don't know anybody there?"

"How would I?"

"You meet a lot of people in the travel business, don't you?"

"Of course I do, but the only people I've met from there are Chamba and his friends from Penn State University. Is that close?"

"No, not really."

"Leave her alone, would you?"CJ interrupted, his voice muffled by the droning of the bus. "She doesn't know anything about Updike or the firm."

"Hey, I'm just doing my diligence."

"No, you're not. You're being a jackass."

"Diligence?" Mia asked.

"You know, gathering information."

"Well, if it's information you want, I can tell you plenty about my family. I've been thinking about my father lately, so maybe you can help me. I'm worried about him."

"All right. When it comes to figuring out family relations, I'm your guy."

She waited for a second or two and then fidgeted in her seat. He hadn't seen her nervous before, so now he was curious.

"We come from a small town, a very poor town, where a person's reputation is all he has," she began. "My father worked very hard earning his. He owns a tourist shop now in Panajachel, but he started out years ago selling clothes, toiletries, cooking utensils, and toys from a wooden cart that he used to haul around from town to town. I remember the day he came home with a small, used pickup. It was red with a spare tire in the back. He was so proud of it. He took me aside and told me it was from all the money he and my brothers had saved by working hard. He said that one day he would open a shop, one with bright lights and windows, and he did. But he didn't want me to work like that, because he said I was smart and should go to the university."

"So you went?"

"Yes, I studied accounting at the Universidad de San Carlos, but my grandfather thought it was wrong to educate girls. He was a *zahorín*, which is a priest who performs the rituals of the old religion, and he and my father were constantly fighting."

"About what?"

"My father thought burning copal and lighting candles were superstitions that didn't mean anything or have any benefit for the family, so he rejected them. But my grandfather took it as a rejection of him, especially since my father wouldn't learn how to make *metates*, those hollowed-out rocks used to grind cornmeal for tortillas. You've seen them. So now they haven't spoken to each other in years. You know how men are."

"I can imagine."

"I don't know why I'm telling you all this," she said. "I guess it's been bothering me. I try not to think about it, but it's no use."

"I don't mind," he told her, taken not so much by the story but her sincerity and the fact that Jacinta stared at her in admiration. He could have been wrong about her; probably *was* wrong about her, and that bothered him.

"So, do you have any advice?"

He looked out the window just as they passed a roadside stand with a naked boy holding up a *garrobo* for the tourists. He had seen them cut open these female lizards, remove the string of eggs for consommé, and sew them back up again.

"I don't think so, Mia. Maybe just leave them alone and let them come around when they're ready."

"But it makes me sad."

"Welcome to Planeta Ricardo," he said.

"Speaking of which, why don't you tell me something about you?"

"*Me?* Not on your life. I'm no good at sharing. You wouldn't find it very interesting, anyway. I'm full of a lot of repressed anger and emotional detachment and crap like that."

"Who told you that?"

"Everybody."

"I'd love to hear it, anyway," she said.

"Why?"

She didn't answer right away but instead played with Jacinta's hair. The dog snorted, smearing Richard's knee. "I want to find out everything I can about you, that's why," she said finally.

"You writing a book?"

"Maybe."

"Well, what do you want to know?" he said, wiping his knee with his bare hand.

"Let's start with how long."

"I believe you've already seen it."

"Were you married?" she said, ignoring him and handing him a tissue. Where she got the tissue he couldn't say, but he appreciated it.

"The bathroom," she said almost immediately.

"Oh, right."

"So?"

"Well, let's see. It was long enough to lose everything in the divorce and curse the ground she walks on."

"Children?"

"No."

"Why not?"

"I don't know."

"You don't know?"

"We both had careers."

"What do you do?"

"I'm a lawyer, but probably not much longer."

"And your wife?"

"Ex, please."

"Ex-wife?"

"You're not going to believe this, but she wanted to be a travel agent. Started taking courses at a community college and had me invest all kinds of money in it. She was really into it for a while, but then she got sidetracked."

Mia looked at him without saying a word, but she didn't have to. He felt enough humiliation for both of them. "It was this guy who was a writer but ended up being just another snorkeler."

"A what?"

"A snorkeler, one of those poisonous snakes that prey on women who wander off the beaten path."

"Oh, you mean the coral snake," she said as if it were perfectly normal. "I didn't know they had them in the States."

"Coral snake?"

"Yes, they're ugly, venomous things that eat the flowers of mimosa trees, but sometimes they just kiss the flowers, leaving their spit on the petal. They say that if you smell the flower or the spit drips on you from above, you'll die."

"That makes perfect sense to me. He was the coral snake and my wife was the flower: beautiful to behold, lethal to touch."

"Ex," Mia reminded him.

"Ex."

"So what was her name?"

"Her name?"

"Yes."

He breathed in and answered, "Katherine."

"Then the only other question I have for you, Richard, is this: did you give Katherine a reason to become a snake handler?"

"You make it sound like it was my fault."

"Wasn't it?"

"Hell, no, and I'll prove it to you."

Just then a tour guide in a bird blouse and straw hat stood up and addressed the Aussies on the bus micro- phone. He hadn't noticed her before, but, given the fact that he was already agitated, he decided he didn't like her. She was having trouble with the connection, so the first part of her speech was garbled, but then it kicked in with a high-pitched, electrical squeal.

"—and that's how we were able to contact Father Pecorino, the dean of the business school in Belmopan, who assures us that the visit is back on and that they are anxious to have us work with their students. However, we'll be there for two days instead of three, as originally planned. We leave on Friday for Belize City and the islands."

"Oh, the islands," a woman nearby cooed.

"Yes, but remember we have the inventors' convention to attend. That's the culmination of our trip."

"What if we want to stay on?" a man in a yellow *guayabera* asked.

"Our departure from Belize airport is not until next Tuesday, so those of you who want to stay with the students can do so. We can come back for you Tuesday morning."

"What's the name again?"

"The Peter Claver Business School, run by the Jesuits."

Then the tour guide went on about a wonderful new program in which retired business executives worked with poor students in a "mutually beneficial educational experience designed in the tradition of Jesuit spirituality." Peter Claver was founded by Italian Jesuits during the British Honduras period and was moved to Belmopan after Hurricane Hattie destroyed Belize City in 1961, when the capital was also moved to avoid the threat of another hurricane. The school's logo, designed by Pecorino himself, came from the name of the street where the school was located, South Ring Road, and was, not surprisingly, a ring. Richard started to laugh but suddenly felt stinging all over his feet and ankles. Soon, it became death by ten thousand pinpricks, and it wouldn't go away no matter how hard he rubbed his ankles with his bark soles.

"Holy mother of——!"

He leapt out of the seat past Mia, Jacinta, and CJ, and landed in the aisle, ripping off his sandals and scratching his feet until they were raw. The tour guide stopped mid-sentence with the microphone to her mouth. The Aussies turned their heads, astonished, and stared at him. Their heads popped up above the line of seats and stuck out in the aisle like prairie dogs, but he couldn't have cared less. He was being burned alive from his toes all the way up his shins.

"Niguas!" Mia yelled, jumping up and asking for rubbing alcohol.

Three people reached into their travel bags and produced various sized bottles of rubbing alcohol, which she poured into her hands and rubbed on his feet. He found out later that *niguas* are vicious little fleas that burrow into your skin and "dan una gran picazón," according to Mia, which meant that they sting like wasps and won't let you do anything but sit, scratch, and suffer. So, he sat there scratching himself in the aisle as she rubbed his feet the same way she cared for him in his dream, when she wiped cold chicken grease from his lips with her long black hair. Her fingers were smooth but firm and, quite honestly, arousing. He was getting an erection.

"You give great feet," he told her.

"It's from walking around barefoot," she said.

"It's the curse of Guatemala."

"All you have to do is keep the sandals on."

"But they're just as bad. I've got blisters already."

"Yes, I see that. You're a real tenderfoot."

The Aussies, who surrounded them by now, laughed out loud. One of them with a salon tan and radioactive teeth offered Richard a drink from his flask. It was chilled rum, which tasted rich and smooth and burnt the lining of his stomach.

"It's Cuban, mate," the man said, winking.

Mia finished her work, the fleas fled, and the Aussies befriended them, passing around *pupusas* with gobs of cold butter, candied papaya, and a thermos of rum. He still couldn't figure out why no one had to go to the bathroom. The woman who raised her hand earlier recognized Mia and pointed to her mole, but, after a brief discussion, they decided that anybody traveling with a little girl in a pink dress and a three-legged dog couldn't possibly be a *bandido*. Then they bitched about the Australian government's lack of support for small business owners in the form of low-interest loans, tax write-offs, and protection from "all that crap coming out of Malaysia." When Richard tried out Mia's story on them about radical environmentalists, they fell in love with them and decided to smuggle them across the border at Melchor de Mencos, which Richard thought was one of the Wise Men, but what the hell did he know? This was easier than expected, since the border patrol waved them through without bothering to board the bus. The best part was watching a fully clothed Speedo and the FBI at the checkpoint, searching every car and truck destined for Belize. It looked as if all of the Adventurers were on hand, including a reed of a guy working two cell phones who must have been Disney Dude. Richard looked for Babushka Girl as they passed through the gate into Belize, recalling her dimple and bright eyes with fondness, but she was nowhere to be found.

The strange thing in all of this was that Mia kept quiet, not doing anything to alert the authorities or turn them in. He wasn't sure what to make of that but decided that he wouldn't change his opinion of her just yet. He noticed Wayne recording their crossing with cool detachment, his head no doubt filled with visions of an independent film festival and a champagne reception with a chocolate fountain in his honor. Give me the bright lights! Give me fame! Gimme, gimme, gimme!

It didn't take long for hope to die as Richard looked out the window and saw desolation in every direction. They were traveling east on the Western Highway, and outside lay an expanse of nothingness, a flat, gray marsh that unfolded around them for miles. There were mountains behind them in Guatemala, huge granite sentinels guarding the way back to a life that, although spinning out of control, was familiar. He didn't expect to feel this way. Maybe it was the swamp, the isolation, the people who didn't look Mayan at all but African and Creole, stiffly British but Caribbean. Richard had been obsessed with getting out of Guatemala, reacting not only to his mother's advice but his own sense of impending doom. They would never have gotten a fair trial in Guatemala City, but now that they had waltzed across the border with the post 9-11 world watching, he was depressed. He knew he was being stupidly sentimental, longing for a past that never existed, but the past was his personal myth, his reason for living, his motive for getting up in the morning and shaving with a single blade razor, badger brush, and silver soap dish. He even wore beaver fur fedoras in winter and straw hats in summer. Who did that anymore?

Still, he couldn't help himself and in no time started missing Guatemala the way he missed El Salvador, where he would wander around lost in places like Chalatenango and Suchitoto. Once, he sat with the mayor of Suchitoto at a cafe across from Santa Lucía Church drinking Pilsener, eating little *cubitos* of *queso pueblo*, and watching the sun set. He remembered the yeast smell of the beer, the amber light filling the square, and the sound of women's sandals slapping the cobblestone street as they walked by with pails of sliced fruit, steaming tortillas, and hibiscus blossoms.

Guatemala was different, a lot different. It had Mayans, jungles, and gang members assaulting buses, but it also had an entrepreneurial spirit that convinced him it was the place to be for Rubber Tree International. After all, didn't they claim to have the same adventurous spirit, "a rubber company with gumption"? But after traveling there several times, just as he was getting used to the country (used to bitching about it), the kabosh rock dropped and he was on a tour bus with a green kangaroo headed in the wrong direction. According to the tour guide, who felt the need to give bleeding heart travel updates every two minutes, Belize was inhabited by the descendants of African slaves and Carib Indians who weren't allowed to settle anywhere else, so they had to make do with this thumbnail of swampland that the Guatemalans were still threatening to invade.

"Many of the people we will see are called 'Garífuna,' the blackest of the black, and they have something in common with our own Aborigines—oppression," she said, making a valiant effort to hold back her emotions.

There was more socialist nonsense about global solidarity and economic justice and then she sat down, quite pleased with herself but apparently oblivious to the reaction of her listeners, who talked over her, shook their heads, and grumbled. Although she had described Belize as a tropical paradise filled with "orange groves, lush countryside, and orchids blooming in hardwood forests," all Richard could see were fetid swamps, backwater towns filled with pastel-colored shacks (poverty in pink was still poverty), and an occasional Mennonite with straw-colored hair, seven children, and a cartload of polished melons. They tried explaining that last one to him, but he didn't have the strength to listen. He was drunk on rum, which came around like clockwork with bags of candied papaya. God bless Australia! In his delirium, he decided never to set foot past the Mason-Dixon Line again, assuming he got the chance. That's as far south as he ever wanted to go, and this was as far from home as he ever wanted to be. That was fair, he thought.

After an hour of drinking and Mia reminding him not to scratch, they arrived at the seat of government, Belmopan, which consisted of a row of squat, "Mayan inspired" office buildings situated at the entrance of a loop, Pecorino's ring. The Peter Claver

Business School and Center for Vocational Training ("The Clav") was a cinder block building at the corner of Bliss Parade Road and South Ring Road, near the National Museum. Once there, they were greeted by the man himself, the Big Cheese, the Capo, the Cacique, the brains behind the mutually beneficial educational experience: Giuseppe Pecorino. He was about sixty-five, tall, with a long stride, peppered hair, a nose straight enough to be on Mount Rushmore, and hands large enough to carry a cannonball, which was fortunate, since there was a cannon lying on the parched lawn outside the National Assembly. He was slow moving and, from what Richard could tell, equally witted. He had overheard the Aussies discussing his inability to smell (the result of an industrial accident in his youth involving hydrochloric acid), which was a blessing in disguise the day the first-floor toilets backed up and he was able to conduct school business impervious to the stench. "No, really, I don't smell a thing." Behind him stood half a dozen Jesuits, faculty members at the school, and behind them two lines of angelic novices in short-sleeved shirts and even shorter haircuts. Richard was the last one off the bus, and, just as he stepped onto the pavement, thunder ripped overhead and rain came cascading down.

The novices rushed everyone inside to their "guest suites" on the second floor, which consisted of four cinder block rooms the color of pus and a common area with broken furniture and stained drapes. Richard and CJ got one room; Wayne and Patrick, the man with the radioactive smile, another; and Mia and Jacinta a third. The woman who couldn't wait to get to the islands was alone in the last one, having had an argument with her traveling companion, a childhood friend from Perth, over the friend's alleged stinginess with tips, but then Mia invited her to stay with her. That left the last bedroom unoccupied, and Richard thought about taking it but in the end decided it would be too anti-social, even for him. As they settled in, Mia and Maggie, her new roommate, chatted about quilts and lovers while Jacinta played with the dog, Wayne and Patrick smoked cigarettes and drank rum out of paper cups, and CJ went to phone his wife. That left Richard alone with a blue and gold Clav towel, a new bar of soap, and a hot-water shower. He didn't need to think twice.

Before showering, he bummed a cigarette off Patrick and gulped down some rum. Once in the shower, he felt so happy he cried. It was as if the hand of God had reached down and pulled him out of hell. He washed everything on him three times, just to be sure, pulling the penguin shower curtain aside every now and then to take a drag from the cigarette. At one point, the dog wandered in, sticking its nose in the stall, but then slunk away, satisfied that what it had seen wasn't worth barking at. When he was as wrinkled as beef jerky, he dried himself, wrapped the towel as tightly as he could around his waist, and plodded back to his room. He was so loose that the only thing holding him together was the towel. He barely had enough strength to fall back on the bed, arms spread out crucifixion style. CJ was waiting for him with a drink in his hand.

"Did you have a nice time?" CJ asked.

"Are you kidding? I didn't want to get out. Where'd you get the drink?"

"Downstairs. It's Happy Hour."

"Happy Hour?"

"What did you expect? They're Jesuits. Come on, get dressed. Patrick left clothes for us to change into."

CJ was wearing a white *guayabera* and handed Richard a purple one, which he put on, not caring what he looked like. Then they headed downstairs to the dining hall.

"I asked Christine to meet with Updike to find out what the hell is going on," CJ said to him on the way.

"What do you think he's going to tell her that he hasn't told us?"

"Probably nothing, but I want them to know that we know what's going on and that we're not taking this lying down."

"That's exactly how we're taking it. And no offense, CJ, but sending your wife isn't going to change anything."

"Maybe not, but we already talked about it and she's going."

"Well, as long as she's there, see if she can find out anything about Eckstrom. In the meantime, I'll keep an eye on Mia. I don't understand why she hasn't made her move yet."

"I don't understand why you haven't made *your* move yet," CJ said.

"What do you mean?"

"You've had your eye on her from the beginning, haven't you?"

"It's that obvious?"

"Maybe not if you're dead."

"Look, that's all over with. Besides, there's no time for a jungle romance while we're still in the jungle."

"If you say so."

"I say so... Anything else?"

"I asked Christine to wire us cash once we get to Belize City."

"Good, we'll need it. Now, let's have some fun."

The dining hall had a note on the door that said, "Through this Door Pass the World's Greatest Students." Below the note was Pecorino's Ring, in the middle of which someone had written "UP THE CLAV!" in blue and gold marker. Richard went straight to the bar, which was a cafeteria table wrapped in crepe paper and staffed by two students, one of whom wore a Rastafarian t-shirt; the other, "Kiss Me, I'm Irish." He ordered a martini, dry, two olives. Neither one knew how to make it, so he directed them. He was used to ice being a *problema* in this part of the universe, but these guys didn't even have gin. In the end, he walked away with a cup of strawberry flavored vodka, a dash of cooking sherry, and a slice of dill pickle. He wasn't going to bitch about it, though, not after a shower, smoke, and drink: the Trifecta of traveling. He didn't care if the roof caved in. Of course, his luck being what it was, as he walked around to the music of somebody called "Smash Mouth" (Wayne's CD and exactly what he'd like to do to him), it did cave in.

Pecorino cornered him to say how delighted he was to have visitors from the States, especially a documentary filmmaker and a corporate attorney who was going to address the group after dinner on the role of small business in the developing world.

"Small business?"

"Yes, that's what they tell me," Pecorino said. "Unless you've prepared something else. Just say the word. We're very flexible here."

"Let me think about it."

"Whatever you like. I think this is a wonderful opportunity for our community to hear from an expert on globalization. It's a surprise, too. I had no idea you were coming. In fact, this is fortuitous, because we have a special treat for our guests."

"Yes, fortuitous."

"The students have been working on it for a month now under the direction of Felix Twist, our new artist-in-residence."

Pecorino paused, waiting for Richard to be impressed beyond words, but the guy's name sounded like one of his father's hand tools. Richard mumbled something about not knowing art but recognizing it when he saw it, and the importance of being in a residence, especially when it rains.

"I'll bring him over. Would you excuse me for a moment?" Pecorino asked.

"Certainly."

As soon as he left, Richard joined CJ, who was pinned down in a conversation with Patrick, who was telling him that he was a retired dentist who "dabbled in latex." Richard listened at a safe distance, swirling the pickle in his cup, but then Pecorino & Twist came back and started blathering about historical materialism and German philosophy. He tried to ignore them, but it didn't work.

"I'm sorry, what did you say?"

Twist couldn't have been more than five-and-a-half feet tall with wavy red hair down to his shoulders, a matching goatee, and eyes like a rat. He wore a silk scarf and smelled of patchouli oil.

"Cravat," Twist insisted, fingering the scarf. "It's called a cravat."

"I see."

"Anyway, I'm the Hegel expert here on campus, and the point I was making is that once you learn to crack the code, as it were, the rest of his dialectic, while still fundamentally obtuse, becomes accessible even to the average scholar. I believe it's all in the transcending moment he referred to as 'das Aufheben.'"

"Das what?"

"Das Aufheben."

"You teach Hegel in a business school?"

"Well, not exactly, although it's my main area of interest. I teach theatre and dramatic arts. Our goal is to empower students, through artistic expression and training, to critically appropriate God in everything they do."

"That's our tradition," Pecorino added proudly, bouncing on the balls of his feet.

"Funny, that's just what Father Flaherty said," Richard told them.

"You know him?"

"Yes, we met not that long ago, but he talked mainly about critically appropriating King Kong."

"Well, this really is fortuitous, because he's here tonight. He's spending the night before driving back to El Zapote."

Richard choked, spraying a mouthful of vodka onto Pecorino, who reared back, startled, and poked his nose with his thumb. Twist, who had been staring at Richard's sandals with a penetrating, dialectical gaze, as it were, offered his cravat.

"Never mind that!" Pecorino snapped. "Just get the dancing started."

"At once," Twist replied, going to the front of the room and raising his voice. "Everyone, may I have your attention? May I have your attention, please? The Peter Claver Business School and Center for Vocational Training— the Clav, as we like to call it—would like to welcome all of you to Belize with an exhibition of folk song and dance featuring our students. We hope you enjoy the performance, and we thank you for your commitment to the future of this economically troubled yet spiritually vibrant part of the globe. We hope that you are transformed by what you see here tonight and that you return to your home countries committed to work even harder for the greater glory of God and the liberation of all the oppressed."

He bowed dramatically, the Aussies clapped dutifully, and the lights went out. Immediately, two lines of dancers burst through the swinging doors of the kitchen: scantily clad women and bare-chested men. The men beat drums, carried torches, and chanted in baritone. The women danced gracefully, pirouetting and prancing as if in a Caribbean version of Swan Lake (Swan Lagoon?). Each had a black orchid that she presented to a dinner guest. Then the two lines merged, the dancers touching each other provocatively in what was called a "punta rock," probably because the punta was pretty obvious. This went on until Twist gave two clicks on a hand-held clicker, which Richard thought had gone out with filmstrips.

On cue, the women formed an inner circle, the men an outer one, and they swayed in opposite directions as a blue banner with a gold ring was lowered from the ceiling. When it got into position above their heads, a reggae version of Johnny Cash's "Ring of Fire" came on, and the men rushed to the middle of the circle. They held up their torches and spun around at the words "and the flames reached higher," and the women pointed down at the floor with each chorus of "down, down, down....the ring of fire, the ring of fire." The twirling lasted until the song finally ended and the lights came back on. The guests roared with delight, many stamping their feet and whistling. Richard watched the scene in disbelief even after rum, strawberry vodka, sherry, a shower, and Vicodin. He hadn't been this medicated since college.

"Incredible," he said.

"Yes, isn't it wonderful?" Maggie agreed.

"Fucking awesome!" Wayne yelled.

"Right."

The conversation at dinner, which didn't come soon enough, was filled with hymns of praise for that God of Geist, Felix Twist, choreographer extraordinaire. When Richard said that it certainly bore his stamp, "Twisted, you might say," people at his table frowned and ignored him. He went back to eating silently and playing with the pickle in his cup.

"Don't worry, I heard the runt got into trouble for running for provincial," Patrick whispered, leaning across the table toward Richard.

"What did you say?"

"Twist—the bloke's so up on himself they had to banish him to Belize until he learns some manners. At least that's the word on him. He's more puffed up than an adder on juice, mate, believe you me."

"I'm not sure what any of that means, but I have to agree," Richard said.

He looked over at Twist, who resembled a mongoose more than an adder, but what did he know? The runt, as Patrick called him, sat next to Pecorino, who was regaling Mia with stories of his time at the Jesuit university in Guatemala City ("The Guat"?), where he taught information systems technology to undergraduates majoring in, of all things, information systems technology. Apparently, it was a match made in heaven.

"So, you see, it worked out quite nicely," Pecorino said, touching Mia's forearm with his slimy fingers.

Richard did not like that, which surprised him. After all, there was nothing to be jealous about; they weren't even dating. Before he could think about it, CJ interrupted, asking for one of the Melamine serving bowls filled with crab stew that a waiter had just set on their table. He had been stuffing himself with stale French bread and little tabs of frozen butter in silver wrappers while waiting for dinner.

"It was the phone call," he explained. "I feel much better now that I got through. I was worried about the girls."

"Well, don't start celebrating. We're not out of the jungle yet, especially if Flaherty starts talking."

"Have you seen him?"

"No, but he's around here somewhere. I can feel it."

"Listen, if you two are in a tight spot, maybe I can help," Patrick offered. "I might be able to do something about those nasty environmentalists. As a matter of fact, why don't you both come with me tomorrow morning?"

"Where to?"

"I'm going to the islands ahead of everyone else for the inventors' convention sponsored by Rubber Tree International. They're introducing a new product that has so many applications you can't keep up with it. It's got to do with—"

"What did you say?"

"I'm going to the islands for a convention sponsored by—"

"Rubber Tree International?"

"That's right. See, they make this rubber mat that prevents feeding bowls from sliding across the floor or some bloody thing like that. Everybody's talking about it. It's supposed to be the next thing to revolutionize domestic life. I guess the point is then you can spend more time having a naughty with the cook."

Richard stared at him, paralyzed, and he could feel his body slipping underwater again just as it had at other horrific times in his life, the most recent being when he had been abandoned on the beach by the woman he had pledged everything to, which was ironic since that was exactly what she got—everything. He was sinking now, bubbling, gurgling, flailing away in slow motion, his movements heavy and labored.

"Pet Mat?"

"Yes, that's right. That's exactly right. You've heard of it?"

"Heard of it? I invented it!"

He didn't have the strength for anything else, not for reaching for his cocktail, falling face first into the crab stew, or even swallowing his spit. In fact, he was pretty sure he didn't have any spit. The life force was draining out of him slowly, inexorably, and soon he would be past the point of no return. Death would have been welcome, but then, in a final act of cruelty on the part of the universe, he was denied even that by a barrage of tone deaf questions that exploded like distant artillery: what, where, when, why, what if I wanted to use Pet Mat in dental technology, can you tell us about the suction cup design that prevents feeding bowls from sliding across any surface, so what happened, did you lose the patent or something, why are you at The Clav, are you all right, you don't look well, why don't you answer, hey, would you pass the crab stew again, I'm still hungry.

"I have no fucking idea! I don't know!"

Still, they persisted, and he wasn't sure that he had actually said anything; his voice shrill, shallow, feeble.

"Really, I have no idea," he repeated. "None at all."

"Oh," Patrick said finally, disappointed. "I see."

They left him alone, but before he could recover the torture continued. It was show time. Pecorino introduced him in a long-winded speech that recounted the odd string of fortuities that had brought them all together and then described in painstaking detail the strategic plan the Board of Directors had approved for making The Clav "the best business and vocational school in all of Belize." In addition to aggressive fundraising, they planned an internship program with a ball bearing company in Rockford, Illinois, an AM radio station whose signal would reach "all the way to Dangriga," and an e-newsletter entitled *Building a Better Belize* that would be read by all of the decision-makers whose decisions really mattered. According to Patrick, since the Clav was the *only* business school in Belize, they stood a fair chance of achieving their goal.

"And I mean *fair*," he insisted.

When Pecorino finished his speech to the Roman senate, Richard shuffled to the podium with a golden ring that had been dragged out for the occasion. Wayne recorded his talk from a nearby tabletop, reminding him of those Nazi cameramen on the back of flatbed trucks panning the prisoners. He stood at the podium without looking up and ran his fingers along the edge of the wood, up and down, back and forth, trying to braid strands of thought into a coherent pattern. When he finally looked up, he saw Fr. Flaherty dressed in a priest's collar sitting in a forest of black faces and white grins. The priest smiled, which Richard took as a positive sign, since there were no police in the room and Pecorino didn't seem to be aware of anything amiss, although that was probably his natural look. Even so, Richard knew it was too late: the hordes had emerged from the *stalag* and the chase was over. They had captured their man. They could now boil the colorless flesh from his bones and add it to the stew, stirring in Old Bay seasoning. He had been destroyed by a conspiracy of greed, stupidity, and vice that was not nice, not at all.

Then, in a flash of inspiration, he decided to tell these people just that, since they—with all of their smiling, dancing, and black orchids—were next to be added to the stew. It was simply a matter of time.

"Vice is not nice," he stammered. Then, with impeccable elegance, "Badness does not lead to gladness but sadness."

They stared at him.

"And virtue is not supposed to hurt you...like a ring of fire, where the flames climb higher. ..and higher."

Open-mouthed staring now. A distant cough.

"You see, all of you, all of you people, students and tourists and teachers and priests, you are supposed to be...true...blue...."

He paused, waiting for a word to come, for poetry, for the Seventh Cavalry, but there was nothing. A drop of sweat raced down his face, which he patted with a black orchid. It was clear to him now: he was losing his mind. In the silence, he could hear the tiny motor in Wayne's camera whirring. *God, don't leave me like this,* he prayed; *don't leave me hanging here like an imbecile. . .a goddamned imbecile.*

"And gold!" a student shouted back.

"What?"

"Gold!"

"Yes, blue and gold," Richard answered excitedly, unable to contain himself. "That's it! Blue and gold!"

"And that ain't old," another yelled.

"No, it's bold," someone else added.

"As it was foretold."

"From the beginning, when we was winning."

"—the battle for freedom, freedom."

"Hmm, hmm. . .let freedom ring."

"Let it ring, sweet freedom."

"Oh, yeah. . .like a ring of fire!"

"A ring of fire!"

"The sweet sound of freedom!"

"The sound of ringing!"

"Ring, ring, ring!"

"Ring, ring like a telephone call from God, cause we got freedom now, brother! We got freedom now! In season and out, in the fire and out, we got freedom now!"

And as he stood there he saw a miracle happen. The students, the poorest of the poor and blackest of the black, started to sway, rhyming words, clapping hands, beating drums, and singing reggae Johnny Cash. The Aussies joined in, and even Pecorino waved his hands, yelling, "I told you we were flexible!" And Richard knew that what he was watching was a miracle, truly the hand of God reaching down to ring his bell.

In the midst of the singing and ringing, the dancing and gyrating, Twist rushed to the podium to say how enormously inventive this was, how wonderfully creative and transcendental, how relational, how inculturated, how thoroughly divine.

"After all, it's all about community—and *Aufheben.*"

Richard wanted to tell him to shut the fuck up, but his throat was too dry and he was crying now, moaning. Eventually, it became a wail. He was embarrassed at first, but then he realized that something else had happened. He wasn't afraid anymore. How could he be? At that moment he feared no man. There he was in the middle of his life in the middle of failure in the middle of a school cafeteria in the middle of fucking Belmopan. The odd thing was that, as the drumming got louder, he began to taste blood. He was sure of it. Then he, too, started to sway.

It was supposed to be his *Aufheben*, his transcending moment, his chance to overcome divorce, homelessness, being passed up for promotion, never fulfilling the promise of those childhood years that he remembered so fondly—or was it all a delusion?—when they would choose sides for war games and go marauding around the neighborhood like a pack of wild dogs, gathering chestnuts to throw at one other. Remarkably, he could hit a kid square in the chest at fifty feet (they even measured it once), so they nicknamed him "Sniper," which only added to his reputation for coolness and sneaky fastness. When his mother found out, she was scandalized and went around to all of his friends' to ask if anyone had been seriously injured. No one had, of course, although he was never invited back for dinner after that. Still, this was supposed to be his redeeming moment, his ultimate act of revenge that would prove beyond a reasonable doubt that he was not a schmuck, putz, or also-ran but good at something, anything, even if it meant rubber suction cups stuck to the bottom of a fucking pet dish. It came out of his personal suffering, which lent it a legitimacy that he had never experienced before. It had come from *him*, snatched from the jaws of mediocrity. For so long he had felt obligated to make amends for familial mediocrity, first his uncle's, then his father's, and now his own. This was an act of defiance against a genetic determinism that had doomed the Mercurius family from the very start. So, it was also an act of life, wasn't it? Sure it was. It had to be.

There were defining moments in the past when he had had a flash of true genius or a flush of testicular fortitude. There hadn't been many, granted, but the ones that occurred were unforgettable. The most recent was standing in the kitchen with his friend's carving knife, humming "Three Blind Mice" and watching the decrepit dog watching him back, eye to eye, nerve to nerve, twitch to twitch. Richard raised the knife and that's when it hit him—not the twin of a rotten mango but a beatific vision of—all things—*Pet Mat!*

"Think of it!" he had told his friend, Richard Macy, whose apartment he was sharing during the divorce. "Just think of the possibilities!"

He had sought solace from the onetime friend who had introduced him to Katherine through the medium of blood sport on ice, which could not have been more appropriate. Either through kindness or guilt, Macy had taken him in once things started unraveling, which was enough to allay any suspicions Richard had that something had been going on between them. To make a point once during lunch, he had asked Katherine which Dick she preferred, but she simply rolled her eyes in that way that humiliated him and continued eating her grilled salmon. That's when he realized that she didn't just eat the salmon, she *was* the salmon: cold, aloof, expensive, and thoroughly out of his league, or so he thought. He recalled the smudge of tartar on her lower lip, not unlike the foam from a latte, which had given him an erection, and the tip of the linen napkin that she used to daub her lip with, slowly, tenderly, more for herself and the waiter who had been watching from a distance of two tables than for him.

"Think of it," he had said. "A rubber mat that you put the pet dish on to prevent it from sliding across the floor. That way you won't get water all over the floor and the dog doesn't have to push the bowl halfway across the kitchen."

"*What?*"

"You know, a mat."

"A mat?"

"A rubber mat with suction cups that stick to the floor to hold the feeding bowl in place. It can come in all sizes to fit the bowl. You don't have to buy another bowl, move the bowl to another spot on the floor, or do anything other than put it down, press the cups, and set the bowl on top. It's like goddamn magic!"

"When did you come up with this?"

"Today. I called in sick and spent the day drawing designs."

He showed Macy the designs he had sketched on a roll of butcher paper in the kitchen. The trick, he had discovered, was not the cups but the spaces in between, which restricted the number of cups in any given area. He had to calculate the ratio of space to cups in such a way that there would be enough cups to hold a bowl of water in place within the dimensions of any given feeding bowl. It wasn't easy, so when he got tired of that he outlined a business plan for the fledgling company, settling on the name "Pet Mat." He had thought about naming it after the terrier, but "Zoe Foods" sounded too pretentious. He was so excited he had even given Zoe a can of kidney beans he had found in the pantry, which gave the dog gas.

"We're going to be rich," he had told it, elated, from a distance.

Ironically, those were also the parting words of his father to his mother on what turned out to be his last sales call. His father had been convinced that the people at Allegheny Airways were impressed with his variable and wanted to discuss how it could fit into their marketing plan. He was so confident that he had asked Richard to go along. They left Kornél playing gin rummy at the dining room table with his mother, who had the day off because of the veterans, "God bless them every one." It was a late October afternoon with a slate sky and eddies of leaves and candy wrappers whipped up by the wind. They walked all the way to the subway station at North Broad, rode to the airport, and waited in a glass-enclosed room until five o'clock, when the secretary announced that they were closing and Richard and his father would have to leave. She had been nice enough, serving them coffee with powdered milk and sugar in Styrofoam cups that tasted like mud and Danish cookies from a large tin, but now it was time to go. She was eager to head home, since the airline had decided that the most patriotic thing it could do for the veterans was to remain open on the new date and observe Veterans Day on the old date in November (as confusing as that was), and now she wanted to leave.

"Oh, and watch the elevator doors," she warned. "They've been sticking lately."

Richard's father crossed into the elevator without saying a word, which wasn't like him, since he had always been courteous even if eccentric. Richard turned to look at the woman for the last time. She had short, brown hair combed in a wave that made her head look like a pot roast, a beige and black dress (the official colors of the airline), and a white blouse with a big bow. She wore a sterling company pin that read "AA," and he could smell her perfume, which was not like the rose and gardenia scents of his mother's friends but a blend of salt water and sand reminiscent of their summer vacations on Long Beach Island. He even thought he smelled Coppertone as she handed him his coffee. He was spellbound and imagined living with her near Barnegat Lighthouse, their days filled with muddy coffee and semen as they made love in the dunes; her hair pressed with reeds and her dress wrinkled with the imprint of his warm body.

"What do you want, Richard?" his father asked after waiting for the elevator doors to close, which took four or five presses of the button.

"Sorry?"

"We could take the train back home, visit your uncle, or have dinner at Fred's Diner. What will it be?"

"Fred's," he answered, eager to make the outing last as long as possible, even if it meant greasy spoons and crusty bottles of ketchup.

Later in the diner, after they had settled into a bulging red booth with gold buttons, his father said, "So, what do you want?"

"I don't know."

"Richard, what do you want?"

"I don't know, dad."

Only now was he able to answer the question; not just about what he wanted but what would be (apologies to Doris Day). Both were as plain as the mole on Mia's face. Sure, he wanted revenge as much as the next guy, being a red-blooded American male, but he had known for a while now that he wasn't the next guy. Revenge was just the beginning of a permanent and decisive *Aufheben* in his life; what he had in mind was far more audacious. It wasn't about going back to right a wrong or undo an injustice. That was for people who expected life to be fair and whined all day long when it wasn't. He wasn't into that. He wanted what everyone else wanted; that is, everyone honest enough to admit the truth and not pretend to love the pile of horse manure that life dumped on them.

What was that? A second chance, another shot, a do-over, a mulligan, that's what. He didn't want to salvage the wreckage of this stupid life, even if that were possible. He wanted a brand new one. He wanted to crawl back into his mother's dried out womb and come out again. And he would get it right this time. He would be a better son, lover, employee at Central Penn Printing, because he would take the job that his father had left when his uncle begged him to come work for him as an apprentice. Or he would work with his father, helping him as a patent attorney. Or maybe he wouldn't become an attorney at all. The only reason he had chosen law was that it provided a lucrative career that required no introspection, which was what he had been looking for all along. It certainly beat staring at Petri dishes or actuarial tables all day. It was as if they were still living in the Middle Ages, when you had to go into law, the military, or the church. Pick a card, son, any card. He hadn't picked as much as forfeited, which he was still doing. The problem was that he wasn't a kid anymore.

"Time's up," his father announced, peering at him over a laminated menu with permanent chili stains.

"Have you made up your mind?"

"Sure, dad," he said, lying.

Nothing was really the same after that. His father's descent was slow, being neither moral nor intellectual but spiritual, a deadening of the soul until he couldn't even come out of his room. That was the last time they did anything together, and Richard could still taste his tuna melt, coleslaw, and vanilla malt (precursor to the latte), although he had not ordered them since. He hadn't been in a greasy spoon, either, unless you counted the *pupuserías* he and CJ frequented in El Salvador, which reminded him to have his stool tested when he got back; assuming he got back and could produce something solid enough to smear into a vial. Ever since that day he had been on his own, left to his own devices in a world that, according to his mother, "made about as much sense as testicles on a telephone," which was why he had worked so hard in law school. It had given him something to do and a reason not to dwell on it. The legal profession was going to pay the bills and give him the status that had eluded the rest of the family since the thirties, when his mother's family, tailors by trade, had two fitting rooms on Gábor Street with five seamstresses on the payroll.

"Think of it," he had said to himself as he poured over the designs and decided on Rittenhouse Square as the location of Pet Mat's headquarters: a chance to make up for years of demeaning work and an even more demeaning marriage during which he had wandered around aimlessly as if living somebody else's life. But whose? Certainly not his own. He couldn't remember the last time he actually felt comfortable in his own wingtips. Not his father's, who had died cold and alone in a sloped room on the third floor, nor his mother's, who moved to a gated community in Atlantic

City and joined a Kino club for seniors. Not his brother's, who was in the professional care of strangers, most of whom came from squalid towns in the Philippines. And certainly not Katherine's, the woman with the glacial stare who began tacking up psychic "No Trespassing" signs the moment he met her, which should have been a clue but somehow wasn't. So whose life had he been living? The awful truth was that he did not know. Macy's reaction, which was less than stellar, only made things worse.

"Well, I don't know. It seems pretty strange, Richard," he said, looking at him out of the corner of his eye as he drank a microbrew with a silver foil label.

"You don't think it will work?"

"Think it will work? I think you have better things to do with your time than designing doggie mats."

"Like what?"

"Finding another place to live."

Every so often, the offender became the offended, even a master offender like Richard. He didn't like it, of course, but it came with the territory. He had learned to accept it and move on, which was exactly what he did the next morning. To cite his mother again, "You don't have to connect too many dots for me to get the picture." And here was the picture: Macy had stolen the drawings and gone to Rubber Tree behind his back. How else could this have happened?

At first, he had suspected Macy of throwing them out before leaving for work the next morning, because there wasn't a scrap to be found anywhere in the apartment, and he had searched everywhere, from Macy's underwear draw (was that Katherine's earring?) to the pantry where the dog food was kept. How Macy ended up at Rubber Tree was another story, although he figured that might work in his favor, assuming he could come up with a plan before getting whacked or arrested. They still hadn't identified the hit man, and Flaherty might decide to turn them in whenever God ordered him to do so. So there wasn't a lot of time to act, but for the first time in his life, Richard wasn't running away from something; he was running toward something: revenge, the new "R" word. This revenge would be sweet, swift, and oh so satisfying.

Excited by the prospect of revenge and unable to sleep, he snuck out of his room in the middle of the night and went to the computer lab on the first floor. He did some investigating on the Internet and came across an article that solved the mystery.

Richard Macy had married one Beatrice Updike, daughter of a senior partner at the Philadelphia law firm of Spinelli, Carter, Updike & Minx by the name of Lucien Freud Updike. The couple had honeymooned in Belize and returned to their new home in Bala Cynwyd just three months ago! The Tudor style home was a wedding gift from the bride's father, who had chosen the architectural firm of Schmidt & Mauser to design a home that would reflect the couple's "eclectic lifestyle," which included horseback riding, brunches, and fundraisers for Christian orphanages in Kenya. The bride was an ardent admirer of Isak Dinesen and knew everything there was to know about the Kikuyu, coffee, and orphans. The article included a photo of the happy couple embracing in a cheesy valentine arbor with horses in the background. Beatrice, not exactly a debutante, had pearls in her hair strung together with what looked like seaweed; Macy, himself graying at the temples, wore pinstriped coattails and an ascot. Once again, Richard hadn't seen this coming. He hadn't done his diligence. Hadn't done any diligence, actually. He had been set up, swindled, hoodwinked, stabbed in the back, and double-lacrossed by a guy who was supposed to be his friend and another who was supposed to be his mentor. If this kept up, pretty soon there would be no one left to trust, which would confirm just about everything he had ever thought about everyone.

Then, sitting back and glaring at the computer screen, he had another insight. He decided that, just like the Brioni overcoat, enough was enough. This time he would go for the jugular. He would travel with Patrick to the islands—*oh, the islands*—and hold the groom's head under water until the gurgling stopped, which would make him a Water Warrior after all. He felt certain that Macy would be at Pet Mat's grand debut, since its "inventor" would want to tell everyone the story of its creation and reap the love and admiration due him. Not only was the plan elegant in its simplicity, but if he could make Macy's death look like an act of reprisal perpetrated by *Planeta Libre*, then he would have pulled off the perfect crime (but for a white Bronco and parasitic legal team). He might even be able to escape with CJ, who was an innocent bystander in all of this, which was why he wanted to make sure that his next phone call to his wife wouldn't be through smudged Plexiglas. He owed his friend that much. He owed himself that much. He owed Richard Macy that much, the prick.

Back to bed again in his cinder block room, dreaming of him and Katherine arriving at Hôtel du Soleil for a soiree hosted by Saul and Daphne, a dark woman with stringy hair and a Chechnyan accent, something like Natasha of Rocky & Bullwinkle fame, although without the cigarette holder. She shuffles around the marble lobby in fuzzy slippers, chomping baby carrots dipped in ranch dressing and asking if anyone has baggage to check. Everyone raises their hands. As more guests arrive, he and Katherine get split up, and before long he realizes that she has gone for a car ride. Something tells him that this is not going to end well. He waits for her at the bar, but she does not come back. Guests come and go, and the party lasts all night long. He stays at the bar, sipping bourbon with a twist and eating peanut butter out of the jar with his finger. Most of the revelers are elsewhere and only a few are with him at the bar. He speaks to none of them, although he can overhear them gossiping. At dawn, the few remaining guests put their overcoats on and leave. Then Saul enters wearing a black apron and sweeping the floor. The hotel is a mess of dirty plates, glasses, crumpled cocktail napkins, rancid alcohol, and stale smoke. Saul doesn't speak but concentrates on his work.

"Do you know where my wife is?" Richard asks him.

"A man shouldn't have to ask that," Saul says without looking up.

"Well I am. Where is she?"

"With friends from college, I think."

"Where'd they go?"

"Arkansas."

"What's in Arkansas?"

"Hope."

"Is that supposed to be funny?"

"No, it's not funny. It can't be. I'm dead, you know."

"Look, it wasn't me, it was the olives," Richard tells him, scooping one more finger of peanut butter into his mouth before going after Katherine.

Richard leaves the hotel and finds himself not in Arkansas but Pennsylvania in autumn. Behind the kitchen where the shed used to be is an old church with a sign that reads, "United Methodist Church," but the sign is rotted and the "U" is split in half, dangling. It starts raining, so he stands under the eaves and watches the rainfall. Katherine comes back and he can hear her inside the kitchen asking about him, where has he gone and is he all right. He sees right through her phony concern and keeps walking down the driveway that they raced on in the Fury to escape the *policía*. Now, he is escaping her. Saul tells her that she just missed him, so she runs after him, waving her arms and pleading with him to stop. She wears a bright blue raincoat with a hood that matches her eyes, and he realizes how stupid he has been falling for this femme fatale, this sinister Blue Riding Hood.

"Where have you been?" he asks as she catches up to him.

"Philadelphia."

"Liar."

"It's true."

"Pants on fire."

"I went with my study group to another party and we played the chin game."

"You mean by the hair of my chinny-chin-chin?"

"No, we passed oranges from one person to another using our chins," she explains, mimicking the motion.

"Is that all?"

"I kissed the boys."

"And made them cry?"

She doesn't answer but stares at him with those sapphire eyes that match her hood, looking every bit like a Siamese cat cowering in the rain.

"Why are you even here?" he asks, annoyed.

"You invited me."

"And you betrayed me."

"Don't be so melodramatic. We're all adults here."

Richard walks into the forest up a winding road lined with liquidambar trees that twists at a sharp angle to the left. She follows him. Rain gushes down the gullies of the road, and, since there is no place to walk, he has to tread through the runoff. People are commuting to work in the direction of the hotel. He sees a woman driving with a small dog on her lap. He takes out a maroon baseball cap that he had in his pocket and throws it at the car. The cap misses and falls into the gully on the opposite side of the road. He waits for an opening in the traffic to retrieve the cap, but when he gets there, it is gone. He suspects that another woman walking by has stolen it. He pulls out a white one and puts it on his head. He crosses back to Katherine, upset that he lost the maroon cap but then discovers that it was in his pocket all along.

"What do you make of that?" he asks her.

"Not much. You made the whole thing up."

"What do you mean?"

"It's all in your head."

"How do you know that?"

"It's none of your business."

"Tell me."

She shakes her head.

"I'll do that thing you like," he offers, drawing her close to him.

"What thing?"

"You know."

"God, you're disgusting."

"Come on, we'll go for lattes afterward. There'll be plenty of foam."

"I doubt it," she says, ridiculing him. "You haven't got the steam."

Katherine, Queen of the Bon Mot Low Blow, strikes again. He ventures deeper into the forest, which is ablaze in orange liquidambar trees and strewn with the spindly fruit they called "itchy balls." Unlike chestnuts, these were too light to be used as projectiles but proved more than adequate for torture. They would fill an adversary's pants with them and roll him around the ground until he cried uncle. He picks up a handful and throws them at Katherine, who is now a Siamese cat, but she dodges them easily. Then he remembered the cat she owned when they first met. It had a nasty habit of peeing in the same spot on the living room carpet every morning, which was under the retro-modern Paltrona Frau loveseat. He told her the cat did it to punish her for being left out all night, since it was as spoiled and petty as it was fat and ugly. Katherine scoffed at the idea, but he said he knew revenge.

"It's instinctual," he had said.

"For you, maybe, but not Mister Bo Jangles. He's above that."

"I'm telling you, you're being punished."

"Nonsense," she replied, holding the cat up to her face and snuggling with it in a way that made him jealous. "Mister Jangles *loves* me."

"It would eat you if it had the chance."

"So would you, Richard."

True, but even she would have to admit that he had the distinct advantage of not peeing on the carpet or shedding fur that drifted in and out of their lives like dandelion down, finding its way into bars of French soap and the sugar bowl. He dreamt of drowning the cat in the toilet but discovered that its head was too big after measuring it one day with a shoestring. Then he thought about carving it up. It hadn't come to that only because an *Inquirer* delivery truck beat him to it, crushing its head as it dashed across the street one morning on its way home, its bladder laden with hot urine. He convinced Katherine not to get another cat out of respect for Jangles' memory.

"I didn't know you cared that much," she had said.

"Are you kidding? Anything that's important to you is important to me, my love."

It was still early enough in the relationship to fool her, or so he thought. Had he known that she was about to pull an even larger sack of not-so-virgin wool over his eyes, he would have been Jack-Be-Nimble, Jack-Be-Quick and jumped out of her life forever.

"Big talk," the Siamese cat says.

"Believe me, it's true."

"You really would have left me?"

"No."

"I didn't think so, but why lie about it?"

"I don't know."

"I think you do."

"Piss off," he tells her.

"Oh, sure, very mature."

He wanders off in circles through the forest until he sees Jacinta standing by a tamarindo tree. As he gets close, she points to a house across a meadow. She takes him by the hand and leads him there, but the ground gets softer and softer until his feet sink and his shoes—fashionable, Cole Haan sneakers—are soaked. The house has a sign that says "Magister" and nearby Mayans huddle around a fire. He smells the familiar smoke and asks them about it, but before they answer Jacinta points to a book in the foyer, where there is a large bowl of mangoes and a jaguar roaming around. They have to write their intentions in the book or the jaguar will devour them.

"What are you going to write?" she asks.

"I don't know. Something out of the ordinary, I guess."

"How wonderful," she says.

"You really think so?"

"Oh, yes."

He scribbles something in Mayan graffiti that he doesn't understand, and the jaguar lets them pass. They descend a staircase to the basement, where Flaherty waits for them with the Fury, which has been tuned, lubed, and washed for his escape. He asks what escape, and the priest points out a window to the meadow, which is not a meadow anymore but a swamp filled with cypress trees, Spanish moss, and canoe-size crocodiles. A sheet of green algae covers the water, out of which emerge sun-glassed FBI agents, the Three Witches of Tikal, two naked teams of Adventurers, an army of archaeologists, a Cuban baseball team named "The Habaneros," and the "Three Richards." When he asks about this last group, which he thinks has something to do with Italian opera, Flaherty tells him they come from the time he was waiting to be seen for a panic attack and there were two men in the doctor's office ahead of him, both named Richard. In order to be seen first, he impersonated the first Richard, who turned out to be an Iraqi combat veteran in a wheelchair with a failing kidney. They ushered him in but then had to switch charts upon discovering the error. By then it was too late. He was already in Examination Room Two in a blue smock and black socks with his legs dangling from the table. Then, on his way out, he chided the nursing staff for being incompetent. He wanted to show them how stupid their insistence on first names was and that informality breeds contempt, even if it meant acting like an asshole, which is why Flaherty says they are after him.

"Can you blame them?" Flaherty asks.

"Are you kidding? I blame everyone."

"But yourself."

"Of course."

Suddenly, a burst of wind nearly rips the roof off the house. It comes from an Apache helicopter that Macy and Updike are flying directly overhead. There is a 30-millimeter machine gun mounted on the side that they fire across the roof, which sounds like reindeer stampeding in stilettos. Wayne hangs out of the helicopter, filming the attack and shouting maniacally: "Now Dasher, now Dancer, on Prancer and Vixen!"

"Well, there's no time like the past," Flaherty says, pressing a remote control button to open a door to a tunnel.

"Right."

Richard jumps into the Fury and races down the tunnel. It is such a tight fit that he smashes all of the lights but finally reaches the center of the earth, where there is the muffled quiet of winter. Snow falls gently and the trees have turned to dark pine and evergreen, and the heavy scent of balsam clings to the cold air. He sits in the silence, having forgotten the feel of winter. Then he gets out and walks up to a gold lamé handbag hanging from a tree branch. He pulls it down, brushes off the snow, and opens it. Inside is an inscription scratched in jaguar blood with a pine needle that reads, "Hell hath no fury like destiny reborn."

"I knew it!" he shouts. "I knew it!"

"What does it mean?" CJ asks, appearing from the other side of the tree.

"Where did you come from?"

"I've been here all along. You didn't see me."

"It means we're going to claim our birthright."

"Our?"

"You're in this, too," Richard tells him.

"I just want to go home."

The sound of machine gun fire erupts at the entrance to the tunnel, and he realizes that Flaherty and Jacinta have just been executed.

"It's too late for that," he tells CJ.

"So what will we do?"

"You heard Cane Lady."

"Revenge?"

"With little to no mercy."

"When do we start?"

"First thing in the morning. Be there at seven sharp."

Richard leaves CJ and walks down the sharp-angled road back to the hotel. There is not a car in sight, so he walks in the middle of the road with his hands in his pockets, avoiding the runoff on either side.

"That's what a Water Warrior is supposed to do," he says to himself. "Avoid the runoff at all costs."

The next morning, Richard gorged himself on plantains, beans, and runny eggs that helped his hangover but kept him on the toilet for the better part of an hour. CJ and Mia tried to talk him out of murder while Patrick talked the Eco-Australia bus driver into taking all of them to the airport outside of Belize City for the trip to the islands. During the ride, Patrick serenaded them with "Believe Me if All Those Endearing Young Charms" and "When You and I Were Young, Maggie," which made Maggie cry mercilessly, and then "Oh, Danny, Boy," which made Richard cry mercilessly, especially when he hit the high A and his voice warbled for what seemed like the other part of the hour. It even made the dog howl. That's when Patrick confessed to being a tenor in a barbershop quartet called "The Sweeny Todds." Since Wayne remembered to charge the camera overnight, being incredibly responsible, they were treated to reruns of the performance ad nauseam. With a straight face, Richard suggested that Patrick get an agent and book Branson as soon as possible, which Patrick considered doing, since he knew a friend of a friend who took tennis lessons from another friend of a friend who had dated the sister of the wife of Andy Williams.

"Small world," Richard said.

Once in Belize City, the driver announced a sudden change of plans. He couldn't take them to the airport after all, which was about ten miles from the bus terminal, because the brakes felt spongy and he couldn't risk death or dismemberment, insurance premiums being what they were. So he parked the bus and went searching for a mechanic, leaving Richard, CJ, Mia, Wayne, Patrick, Maggie, Jacinta, and the dog on their own. To cheer everyone up, Patrick went to a travel agency across the street and paid for all of their flights on Amber Air. He also reserved three rooms at "The Great Kiskadee Resort & Conference Centre."

"We'll be staying on Ambergris Caye, Belize's largest island," he told them, handing out brochures and the plane tickets.

"I thought Belize *was* an island," Richard said.

"Oh, no, the islands are the best part of Belize, believe you me. And I swear on my mother's grave that the Kiss is one of the finest resorts in the country. It's owned by a native, a Creole by the name of Fats Cahona, who is the only bloke capable of competing with the multinational chains.

He runs a first-rate operation."

"Fats?"

"Cahona."

"Friend of yours?"

"As sure as I'm standing here. We met three years ago at a dinner party at the British High Commission Office. They were looking for investors in the conference center, and I was more than happy to do my part, especially since I needed a place to hide my latex profits. I had the highest return ever that year from my shares in latex companies." "No rubber checks there," Richard said.

"Exactly. Fats used to be Belize's finance minister until they caught him in a Ponzi scheme, and then that was that."

"He went to prison?"

"Are you kidding? This ain't Washington, mate."

"He's a lucky man."

"That's why they call him 'Fats.'"

"You know, this would make a great background piece to my movie. Mind if I interview you on camera?" Wayne interrupted.

"Sure thing," Patrick said. "Just make sure you get my best side."

So now Wayne's documentary had become a movie. Not wanting any part of it, Richard crossed the street to a park and sat down on a bench. Jacinta followed along with the dog, which sniffed the grass and pissed on all the trash cans. The great advantage of having three legs, as Richard saw it, was that it did away with the need to lift the hind leg. Who knew, it might even become an evolutionary adaptation. Quite impressive, he thought. He sat back and watched the boats glittering in the harbor and the terminal bustling across the street, but after a while he noticed that Jacinta and the dog had disappeared. He found them on the other side of a bandstand with two Mayan women and their children, who were preparing lunch over a fire. The familiar smell of Mayan smoke filled the air. Richard asked about it and they said, poker-faced, "Ocote."

"Ocote?"

"Ocote."

"Ocote," he repeated helplessly.

Then one of them handed him a piece of pine kindling, and there it was: the smell that had been haunting him for weeks. It wasn't from dirt, smog, sweat, diesel, or unwashed feet after all. It was this resinous wood that smelled like a church after a morning Mass when the priest blew out the candles and shuffled back to his rectory for a breakfast of warm tortillas and eggs. But there was something else, too, something he couldn't put his finger on. What was it? Peat moss, eucalyptus, single-malt scotch? Maybe it was all of these, which he found fascinating. He must have looked strange, because the children were staring at him now, not sure what to make of him. You could never tell with a gringo. How would they react if he ate it, he wondered? He put it up to his mouth and they giggled. Then he sniffed it from end to end as if getting ready to smoke it, and they broke into laughter. Then the oldest kid in black basketball sneakers with holes, pointed behind him. Richard turned around to see Mia and CJ approaching.

"We think we've figured it out," CJ said coming up to him, breathless.

"Figured what out?"

"How to get back home."

"I thought we were blaming the *Planeta* people."

"Not anymore. Patrick told us that Fats knows a guy who can get us fake travel visas to the States."

"As what?"

"Cultural attachés to the Belizean embassy."

"They have an embassy?"

"I guess so."

"No joke?"

CJ shook his head.

"But I'm wearing bark sandals and a shirt that makes me look like an eggplant. How are we going to pass ourselves off as cultural anything?"

"We'll buy new clothes on the island."

"This is easier than blaming guerillas?" Richard asked doubtfully.

"Maybe not, but it's faster. The guy happens to be at the resort right now, so Patrick said we can work out the details once we get there."

"Details? You mean like what he wants in exchange for all this?"

"Patrick has a pretty good idea about that, too."

Richard looked over at Mia, who had her hair pinned up, revealing a slender neck that seemed to glow in the bright light of the harbor.

"What does he want?"

"He says that *chicle* is making a comeback, so he wants a Rubber Tree processing plant in Belize and all the labor contracts for its construction."

"*Chicle* is making a comeback—the guy actually said that?"

"Yeah."

Richard couldn't help but smile. As a Mercurius, he knew that things never worked out for the best. Empirical evidence supported this, since events in his life often imploded no matter how prepared he had been. In fact, there was an inverse relationship between expectation and result, with the end turning out to be the opposite of what he had hoped for. Once he had accepted this, he was able to live his life with what might be described as Irish pessimism minus the whiskey, although he never turned down pear-flavored Hungarian brandy, *pálinka*. Now, however, he would have to revise his cosmology, update his theory of revenge, pay special attention to the string theory of the universe, because heavenly violins were playing his song. Or, maybe the law of averages was finally working out in his favor and this was the break he had been waiting for. It was bound to happen. After all, a room full of chimpanzees with typewriters will eventually smear their feces on the wall, and some moron in a beret will come along and declare it art.

"*Chicle* is making a comeback! This is incredible. If the guy wants the construction contracts, fine. It won't cost us a dime, and by the time he figures out that there aren't any contracts, we'll be long gone."

"So this is going to work? We're finally going home?" CJ asked excitedly.

"You can count on it."

"You've said that before."

"I've said a lot of things before."

Despite his arthritis, CJ did a little dance that delighted the children, and while everyone watched him, Richard checked out Mia, who looked beautiful in the sunlight. He kept it to himself, though, since he had noticed her noticing him noticing her. They even did it during the cab ride to the airport, which they took as soon as Wayne finished his interview. They made the trip in record time, the driver imitating Steve McQueen the instant he spotted Wayne's video camera, but then the flight was delayed two hours at the gate due to "technical difficulties." Apparently, the propeller wasn't turning, which, technically, would have made things very difficult. That gave CJ time to check on the money his wife had sent.

Meanwhile, Wayne's girlfriend, Heather, met them at the airport with four suitcases of trendy (and probably slutty) summer wear and proceeded to throw a hissy fit with the woman at the ticket counter, who tried to explain weight limits and vertical lift to her, although Heather appeared to be knowledgeable in both. After a scene worthy of "The Adventurers," they promised to put two suitcases on the next flight, which did not placate Wayne's Asian Barbie in the least, since she threatened to write to the chairman of Amber Air, who was probably on the runway with jumper cables.

The ticket agent, who was also their gate attendant, wore a blue scarf with red pinstripes and an "AA" pin on her collar. This unnerved Richard so much that he kept sniffing the piece of ocote that he taken from the Mayan women in the park. That's when he remembered that airports have bars and bars have gin and gin has been blessed by God. He said adios to the group, and, after getting lost twice and stopped by camouflaged soldiers with thick boots and M-16s, found the only bar on their side of airport security: a speckled Formica lunch counter with a neon sign that blinked, "Alberto's." As he looked at the wall behind the bar he thought he must have died and gone to distillery heaven. It was filled with every liquor imaginable and decorated with Christmas lights, garlands, tinsel, plastic peppers, voodoo dolls, model airplanes, Belikin beer bottles, colored beads, hand-held fans, Playmate calendars, Chinese dragons, rhinestone cat clocks, tiki torches (again, with the tiki torches), clay Mayan figurines with pencil-length erections, fat Elvis photos, balsa wood airplanes, a blow-up Godzilla, votive candles, an enormous bleeding crucifix that looked like something from a Mel Gibson movie, a Yankee baseball pennant from the

1978 World Series, and an electric train that went around all of this, whistling and puffing smoke.

Richard didn't know where to look and so ended up looking everywhere. Then the owner, a short man smoking a cigar and wearing a gold *guayabera*, came out and asked gruffly what he wanted to drink.

"M-m-martini," Richard faltered, overwhelmed.

"Martini what?"

"Martini, *please?*"

The man looked him over once, twice, from his *Abenteurer* cap to his purple *guayabera* and bark sandals and said, "No, how do you want it?"

Richard hesitated.

"The martini," the man repeated.

"You can do that?"

"I'll make it any way you want, but you have to tell me how you want it."

Richard's mouth started to water and sweat ran down his back. This was the answer to the prayers he ought to have been saying.

"Really?"

The man raised his eyebrows, which were uneven and the thickest Richard had ever seen, and nodded.

"All right, then. I'll have a double martini, up, dry, no, extra dry, no, the driest you can make it, ten to one Junípero Serra gin, with two anchovy stuffed olives, no, three. Right, three. I mean, what the hell, I've got a lot to celebrate. Then, before you pour it—please listen very carefully, this is important, extremely important—before you pour it, lace the glass with the finest coat of Triple Sec you can manage. Just a trickle, really, no more than a taste, a hint, a smidgen, a skosh to balance the brine of the anchovies. And make it as cold as you can, no, colder than that, the coldest martini in the world. I want to shiver with frost."

"Shiver with frost?"

"I'm a little excited."

"Is that all?"

"Let me think....I believe so, yes."

Alberto studied him, blew a smoke ring, reflected on the ring, and disappeared behind his wall of kitsch. Exhausted, Richard made his way to one of the stools at the Formica counter but then shot back up in a panic.

"Oh, my God, I forgot to tell you. Please make it *stirred, stirred*, not shaken! I'm not some goddamned British agent!"

Normally, he wouldn't have expected anything to come of this, but if his ship really were cruising into port (was that calypso music he heard?), then maybe Alberto would come through. The last time he had sipped a real martini in that Gatsby way of his was at the Houston airport, when a waiter in a black velvet vest and matching bowtie served the drink on a sterling tray, handling it as delicately as if it were nitroglycerine. It didn't get any better than that, yet he was hoping it might. This dwarf of a man and his kaleidoscope bar were so outrageous that they must have been heaven-sent, like some court jester or shaman with a magical potion, root juice, to make him numb to everything and everyone else around him. Now, *that* would be nice. Would it have sexual-enhancing properties, too? Maybe that was just too much to ask.

When it finally arrived on a plastic Coca Cola tray from the fifties, it was so wonderful that he cried all over again. Alberto had made it beyond specifications to perfection, right down to the trickle of Triple, and, although it was a tad sweeter than Richard preferred, it was so good that he thought about not getting on the plane. After two of them, he didn't even care about the propeller. He sat there, listening to Alberto talk about how he was a Dominican cabbie from the Bronx who had come down five years earlier to visit his son, a marine biologist on a graduate fellowship, and decided to stay. His current wife, the third Mrs. Alberto Plotón, was a native Garífuna who tended the bar in the morning, turning all the electrical devices on and lighting the tiki torches. Alberto plied him with

Turkish cigarettes and Swiss chocolate, which Richard devoured gratefully before buying even more to celebrate his escape from jail and imminent return to it. He wasn't sure how long he was at the bar, but it was long enough for CJ to come back, unsuccessful in his quest for money, and Mia to have to come and pry him from the stool. By then, he had smeared chocolate all over his chin, which was numb.

The flight lasted all of twenty-five minutes, which was just enough time for Heather to adjust her seat belt and primp her hair. She had to sit as far away from the dog as possible, which was difficult in an eight-passenger Cessna. Richard wanted to shove her out the door but decided to save his strength for Pet Mat Armageddon. Besides, there was a notice in the cockpit that said, "Notice: Do Not Touch Anything," so, being an officer of the court, he obeyed. Their jaunt over crystalline, shark-infested waters was deafening but uneventful, and he played flight attendant by handing out packs of cigarettes and bars of chocolate to everyone. Heather had a fit over both (one was morally offensive; the other bad for her skin, although he couldn't tell which was which). However, the pilot, a lanky Texan who had flown close-air support in Fallujah, was most grateful. Wayne recorded everything, including their "deplaning," into a dilapidated hut with an aluminum roof that served as Amber Air's terminal. Richard asked if it was a hub but got no response from the hefty Garífuna woman who welcomed them with a tray overflowing with tropical fruit and big black breasts. She, too, wore a blue scarf with red pinstripes, although the "AA" was conspicuously absent.

The ride to the resort was even worse than the flight. They were crammed into two souped-up golf carts and driven at NASCAR speed past dive shops, souvenir stands, and "The Laughing Gull Bar & Grill" to the resort, which was only a ten-minute walk from the airport. From what Richard could tell, just about everything in San Pedro was a ten-minute walk from the airport. Before he knew it, they rounded a bend in the palm-tree lined road and there it was, towering over them like a magnificent Mormon temple: the blinding white façade of The Great Kiskadee Resort & Conference Centre; guest parking to the right, valet parking ahead, deliveries in the rear. As they sped around the circular driveway, one of Heather's suitcases went flying off the cart but was retrieved by a Mayan groundskeeper in a dark uniform and baseball cap working a turbo leaf blower.

"This is it!" Richard yelled, stumbling out of the cart and falling on his face, his head still buzzing from the flight.

The groundskeeper helped him up, and Richard noticed that he had a gold nametag that said "Augustin Chok: The Great Kiss." While everyone checked in, Richard stayed outside with the dog, dazzled by this white palace, this tropical Matterhorn, this three-story mansion of windows, porticoes, Jamaican palm trees, and breezeways attended to by an industrious army of Choks. There were gardeners, bellhops, shuttle drivers, mechanics, maids, and security personnel in maroon sports coats yelling at each other on walkie-talkies in Creole. Everywhere, Choks were busy clipping, snipping, trimming, and leaf blowing everything in sight. It was such an amazing place that Richard had to force himself to remember why he had come here in the first place: the drowning death of his onetime friend and betrayer of all his dreams, no matter how ludicrous those dreams may have been.

"And who's to say what's ludicrous?" his mother asked through a crackling walkie-talkie from the tarred roof of the resort.

"That's right, mom," he answered, shading his eyes and looking up.

"So things are going better for you?" she asked, waving to him.

"A little. The martinis helped."

"They always do, Richard. Just make sure you stick to the plan."

"No sweat."

"That's my boy. Keep your eye on the ball."

"I will."

"I'm a big Phillies fan, you know. Connie Mack all the way."

"Sure, I know."

"Remember the reason for the season."

"There's no way I'll forget it, Scout's honor."

"Good to hear. I'm proud of you. Well, I've going down to the beach now, so I'll check back with you later. Over and out, Richard."

"Over and out, mom."

———

"At high noon, when other birds of Ambergris Caye have escaped from the heat into corners and pockets of shade, the Great Kiskadee (*Pitangus sulphuratus*), a member of the flycatcher family found from the American plains all the way south to Argentina, will perch on an electrical line or telephone pole and delight listeners below with its resplendent pattern of song, which resembles the French expression, *Qu'est-ce que dit?* or 'What do you say?' It has a black mask around its eyes, not unlike Zorro's, and a full-throated, bright yellow chest. Its diet consists of insects, bees, grasshoppers, lizards, mice, and frogs, as well as berries from the island's varied flora. For this reason, the Great Kiskadee is said to be an anomaly in the flycatcher family."

Richard paused and looked up from the brochure he had found in their room. "Did you hear that? An anomaly."

CJ was trimming his toenails over a wastepaper basket at the edge of the bed. Occasionally, a clipping shot into the air like shrapnel and hit the closet door. He grunted without looking up and continued clipping.

They were in the "Jacques Cousteau Room," which had a watercolor painting of the famous beaked Frenchman above the bed. Somebody with an overactive thyroid had decided that each floor should have a different underwater color, ranging from iodine reds to coral whites and marine blues. Their room was done in the latter, with an aqua blue, queen-size bed, an aqua blue sofa, two aqua blue, wicker chairs, and a 1500-watt hairdryer in the bathroom, aqua blue enamel. Louvered doors opened onto a balcony above the beach, which was as blinding as the resort itself. While the others settled into their rooms, Richard and CJ had bought clothes in the gift shop and then came back to their room to change. When CJ finished grooming, they followed the signs to the beach through "Shark Alley," which was a hallway lined with black and white photos of Hollywood celebrities with bloody sharks of all sizes hanging upside down from hooks, past meeting rooms with names like Turneffe Island and Lighthouse Reef.

Outside at the cabaña, they bought two bottles of Belikin beer, collected their beach towels, and settled in a spot in the hot sand between a British family with two children, not of equal height, and four buxom college students from Wisconsin (he overheard them talking about cheese and utters, although the utters could have just been his imagination) in various neon-colored strings and not much else. When they began smearing each other with coconut oil—rubbing, massaging, caressing—Richard went down to the water to cool off.

The water was warm—*das Wasser war warm*—clear, and not crowded, although little kids still played at the water's edge and boogie boarders splashed around in the surf. He swam away from them, just far enough out so that he couldn't touch the bottom. Swimming parallel to the shore, all the pressure in his back and shoulders melted away. It was a wonderful feeling, swimming freely like this, weightless, concentrating on nothing but his body in the salt water. He swam back and forth twice before tiring out and paddling back to the beach. By then, the sun had begun its slow descent in the west, forming a halo around the Great Kiss, which shimmered above the water like a mirage. He swam toward it, passing a woman on a rubber raft. Seagulls cried mournfully overhead, and he thought how easy their lives were. He would love nothing more than to hang above the beach like that and watch the world below without ever coming down. But to do that he would have to give up on revenge, which right now was the only thing keeping him alive. So, he couldn't possibly *not* drown Macy in this sparkling sea with the golden glow. It was his destiny.

He reached the waves curling up on the beach and collapsed just past them in the sand. Reggae music throbbed on a boombox and teenagers chased a Frisbee nearby. He pressed his toes into the sand and noticed that his feet, wrinkled and raw, had stopped bleeding. He sat back and took a deep breath. Finally, things were starting to go his way. He even thought about whistling. Well, thought about it but wasn't serious. Whistling wasn't one of the things he did, not even as a kid, since he had had a problem with stuttering. Funny, but he hadn't thought about that in a long time, years. Misery can dredge up the oldest, most forlorn memories. Not that he had any other kind; they seemed to parallel his dreams. But that was all in the past. No more suffering, no more misery, no more Mister Loser. Right now, the sun was shining, the water was lapping, and tropical breezes were caressing his skin. What could be better than this?

"Richard?"

He looked up, shielding his eyes from the sun, to see the silhouette of a large man holding a boogie board.

"Richard Mercurius?"

Normally, he hated answering a question with a question, but the voice didn't sound like Agent Brad or Speedo or Flaherty or anyone else like that.

"Yes?"

The silhouette stuck a hand out for him to shake, which he did, rising at the same time and trying to recognize the face now coming into view. The man was young, good-looking, with broad shoulders and surfer hair.

"It's Nick," he said, flashing a smile.

"Who?"

"Nick Negroponte."

"Sonofabitch."

"Yeah, no kidding. I never expected to find you here, either. I was getting out of the water and thought, isn't that the guy who just swam by me? It looks like Richard, and, sure enough, it was.... So, what are you doing here, vacationing?"

"What?"

"You're on vacation?"

"Yes, uh, no. I mean, I'm down here on business and decided to take a couple of days off to enjoy the beach."

"It sure is wonderful, isn't it?"

"Oh, it's beautiful...really...so, I guess you're on vacation, too."

"Well, like you, yes and no. We're down here to relax, but I'm also doing some research for my next novel. So I guess you could say we're combining business with pleasure."

"Business with pleasure, right."

Nick smiled again and Richard nodded stupidly. His hair was lighter than he remembered, longer, too. The fact that he had said "we" had not escaped him.

"Katherine's here, of course. Would you like to see her?"

"*What?*"

"Katherine. She's up at the restaurant. You know how much she loves oysters on the half shell and Bloody Marys. You can't keep her away from them."

Richard stammered something about oysters and libido and then stared stupidly again. He thought about excusing himself to take another swim, this time far out to sea, maybe even right off the edge of the map.

"She'd love to see you," Nick said, pressing the point.

"Really?"

"Sure. Why don't you come up?"

"No, I couldn't."

"Come on. It'll be fun."

"*Fun?*"

He made it sound as if they'd be playing Wiffle Ball and eating ice cream sandwiches with the other kids at the resort.

"What do you say? We're just up there at the outdoor restaurant overlooking the water. It's a beautiful view.'"

Richard hesitated as Nick stood there smiling, waiting, waiting, smiling.

"All right, but let me put my shirt and sandals on first. Then I'll meet you up there."

"Terrific."

And then, just as suddenly as he appeared, Nick Negroponte, the guy who had ruined his life and usurped his place in bed, turned his back and walked away, revealing a tattoo on his right shoulder that looked an awful lot like the mermaids on the fountain in Antigua. Richard couldn't tell if the fingers were in the same nippled position, but he wondered whether it was supposed to be Katherine the Oyster Eater. He wondered, too, what the hell he was doing. This wasn't like him or anyone else in his bloodline. Instead of treating these two the way they deserved to be treated—like child molesters—he had just signed up for a repeat performance of Atlantic City without so much as a, "No, thanks, I'd rather stick my head in the oven." What was the next line in the brochure, the one he had not read aloud?

The coral snake, found throughout the region and highly venomous, is a feared predator of the Kiskadee, which makes every attempt to avoid anything that even resembles that snake's characteristic bands of red, yellow, and black.

That meant, of course, that he didn't have the sense of a goddamned bird. Somehow, he understood this but still couldn't stop himself from lying to CJ when he got back to his towel. It was the longing, the obsession, the infatuation with a woman who had sliced his kidneys out and slurped them down whole. How in God's name did he ever get to that point, and what kept him there?

"Uh, I forgot my cap," he told CJ feebly. "I'm going up to the room to get it. I won't be gone long."

CJ sat on his towel without saying a word, watching him with a suspicious look as he walked away.

"Richard?"

"Yeah?"

"The room's that way."

"Oh, right."

He had to trudge back up the beach, past the cabaña, across the patio, and into the lobby. Once there, he went out the opposite door and across the bar to the restaurant, pretending the entire time that he knew exactly where he was going. By the time he reached the restaurant, he had lost his nerve and started to turn around, but it was too late. Nick had spotted him through a trellis of purple bougainvillea and was waving him over.

"Glad you came," Nick said, rising from his chair to greet him.

He wore a white linen shirt unbuttoned halfway to show off his tanned pectorals. Richard moved cautiously, by starts and stops, more like a chickadee than a kiskadee.

"Katherine went up to the gift shop for some postcards. She'll be back in a minute. Please, have a seat."

As Richard sat down, he noticed the familiar lamé handbag in the chair next to his. Even in her absence, Katherine had to make her presence felt, but that was Katherine for you. Who else brings a three thousand dollar handbag to the beach? He was so nervous that when the cocktail waitress came over, he ordered something from the menu that embarrassed him.

"Don't worry. You'll like it," Nick reassured him. "What could go wrong with a drink called a Blow Job?"

"Right."

"Just don't throw it back the way the kids do. Sip it."

He imagined Nick and Katherine in bed in their coral-colored bedroom, checking off all the drinks on the menu. He turned away in disgust and saw plastic parrots hanging in silver hoops from the ceiling. Calypso music was playing at the bar, and the bartender wore a bright red shirt with yellow birds on it. He felt as if he might throw up.

"Richard?"

"Yes."

"Are you all right?"

"Oh, sure. I was just thinking how strange it is to run into you down here."

Nick shrugged it off and took a sip of his drink, a mojito, which looked like a patch of sod mixed with Sprite and a dirty lime in a twenty-ounce plastic tumbler.

"So, you're working on another novel?" Richard asked, trying to make conversation. "That must be exciting."

"It's a living," Nick said dryly.

"Care to tell me about it?"

"No, I don't want to bore you."

"No, seriously, I'd like to hear it. You've probably expanded your theme of suburban malaise by now."

"Actually, that's old news. I'm exploring new territory, *sexual* territory."

"Like a Blow Job?"

"It's much deeper than that, but, to tell you the truth, I'm not sure you're ready to hear it. It's not exactly a conventional story and certainly not something you talk about casually."

"Listen, Nick, I think we're beyond casual at this point, don't you? Besides, after what I've been through, I'm ready for anything."

"Are you sure?"

"Hit me with your best shot, snorkeler."

"Is that what you call me?"

"Only when I'm feeling resentful."

Nick looked at him, unsure, and then said, "All right. It's the story of a couple on vacation at a Caribbean resort whose relationship has deteriorated to the point where they are only able to experience intimacy through the sexual torture and mutilation of unsuspecting tourists they capture and enslave in the basement of the resort. They are aided in this by one of the resort's personnel, who records their 'sessions' on a security camera and then sells the tapes to a local porno producer for profit."

He paused here and, without the slightest trace of emotion, added, "It's an ill-fated attempt at redemption through acts of evil that lead the characters to utter destruction. I would characterize it as rather bleak."

"I see."

"It's called, 'The Last Resort.'"

"I can see why," Richard said.

"I told you it was different."

"You sure did."

Luckily, the waitress returned with his drink, which had a layer of froth on top that he slurped as slowly as possible.

"Tell me, did you get an advance for it?" he asked finally.

"Of course I did. I never do anything without an advance. My agent makes sure of that."

"Such a deal, right?"

"Right."

And such a freak, Richard thought. Katherine, too. She wasn't buying postcards. She was probably downstairs cleaning toe screws, adjusting the rack, and tidying the place up for the camera. These two were made for each other.

"So, are you still working at that community college?" Richard asked, wiping his mouth with a cocktail napkin that said, "Kiss Me."

"No, I have a new appointment at Ursinus College in Collegeville."

"Is that right? Congratulations."

Nick nodded as if he didn't care either way and, in an act eerily reminiscent of Richard's dream, pulled an Ursinus College baseball cap out of his pocket and put it on. It still had the price tag and bore the college's Reformation colors of red, gold, and black.

"Holy shit!" Richard blurted out.

"What?"

"The coral snake. Those are its colors."

"You know about the coral snake?" Nick asked, surprised.

"Of course I do, why?"

"Well, it just so happens that the wife in my novel wears red, gold, and black leather made from the skin of the coral snake. I've had to do some reading up on it. I just thought it was ironic that Ursinus had the same colors."

"Ironic isn't the word for it, believe me."

"All right, then, fortuitous."

"That's even worse," Richard said. "By the way, you weren't bitten doing your research, were you?"

"Oh, no, I'm very careful."

"I bet you are. Katherine can help you with that, you know. She's a snake handler from way back."

"I don't know what you mean."

"Sure you do. You know exactly what I mean."

"No, really, I—"

Before Nick could finish, a couple he had befriended came up to their table. The guy was thin and sleazy; the woman short and squat with a face like cheap porcelain and a hairdo that had been epoxied in place. It had loops and curls and a prom-like kitsch beyond anything Richard had seen. She held a dog the breed of which sounded like *lapis lazuli* and whined about it having "separation anxiety." Like its owner, it, too, had loops and curls and a nose like a Black Crow. They pulled up a couple of wicker chairs and introduced themselves. Ted and Glenda (third marriage for him, second for her) were animal lovers from Anaheim who had made millions selling marketing ideas to failing businesses to help them rebound. They were the ones who came up with the idea of sticking coupons to the covers of phone directories with little wads of glue. Now, they had a brand new idea called "Mart," which Ted had to explain three times before Richard finally got it.

"Now let me see if I understand this," Richard said, not trying to hide his disdain. "Whatever business somebody happens to be in, if they add 'Mart' to the name, all of a sudden sales will increase and their business will turn around faster than you can say...*qu'est-ce que dit?*"

Ted stared at him.

"I got it from the hotel brochure...Just tell me how it works."

"That's the funny thing. I don't know myself, but our research bears it out. If a company wants to increase sales, it could happen immediately. I've seen sales increase twenty, thirty percent in one quarter. For companies trying to avoid bankruptcy, it will help them in six months' time. And if a company has been running deficits for more quarters than you'd find at the laundromat, it will make them profitable again in no more than two years."

"Two years?"

"That may not be faster than whatever you said there about kissing cousins, but it's pretty damn fast, wouldn't you say?"

"No, that's not fast, Ted, that's a miracle. You should bottle it and sell it to General Motors."

"I would, but we're all booked up, aren't we honey? You wouldn't believe it, but we practically had to sneak away to come on this vacation. Right now, we're working with an automotive parts company called 'Parts-Mart,' a standardized test preparation service called 'Smart-Mart,' and, our favorite, a modern art franchise called 'Mart-Mart.'"

"Mart Mart?"

"They specialize in neon landscapes and things done on velvet, you know, like Elvis. We plan on investing in it and expanding the business throughout the Inland Empire."

Richard sat back, thought for a moment, and said, "You know, Ted, that's great, truly, but I've got an even better idea for you. This one you're going to love."

"Wonderful, let's hear it."

"You should open a gastrointestinal consulting practice and call it...'Fart-Mart.'"

Ted choked and looked at Nick, who frowned at Richard.

"Actually, we're here for the convention," Ted explained in a serious voice. "We're looking into starting a pet business ourselves. There's a new invention we want to check out. What's that thing called, dear?"

He snapped his fingers, trying to get a quick response, but it only made the dog snarl.

"You're upsetting Ginger," Glenda complained.

"Well, what's it called?"

"Pet Mat," she answered, calming the dog.

"Yeah, that's right. It's supposed to—"

"Keep feeding bowls from sliding across the floor so you don't butcher your goddamned friend's terrier with a German carving knife?" Richard said.

They stared at him as if he were out of medication, which he was, and sat at the table in silence. Nick adjusted his cap to keep the price tag from hitting him in the face. Richard decided to leave before his blood boiled and he did something that would get him arrested before having a chance to strangle Macy and get arrested. Katherine had not returned and the sun was nearly down, casting a pearl white sheen across the sky.

"Well, my work here is done," he declared, downing his drink. "Glenda, you really ought to give Ted a Blow Job. They're terrific."

As he exited, Wayne entered with Heather, who had a pair of pudding cup breasts held in place with a sort of sling and legs exposed to her inner thighs. Richard thought she also had that freshly ravaged look about her.

"You know, Wayne, now that I've met Heather, you don't have to hand her over to me and CJ for sexual favors. Consider the deal done."

He walked away before anyone had a chance to react. Then he heard Heather yelling at Wayne, Glenda yelling at Ted, and the sweet chiming of calypso music in the background. His job done, it was now time to head off for greener pastures, fairer climes, and distant shores, where he could cry his heart out in true country music fashion. As incredible as it seemed, it had happened all over again. He had been jilted by the same woman, abandoned and, just like before, by the sea, by the sea, by the beautiful sea, you and me, you and me, oh how happy we'll be. And then he realized that he was never going to be happy, never. It wasn't possible. Not ever again.

"Let's have some steel guitar and twang," he said sadly as he crossed back to the lobby. "Hit it, boys!"

She broke my heart, the little tart, amid the surf and sun.
Now I'm alone, all on my own, not having any fun.
What's even worse, I must confess, is feeling like a clown.
She got me good, Blue Riding Hood, the second time around.

It wasn't as if he needed a pretext to make things worse; they just naturally occurred that way, sort of like Flaherty's ability to see into his soul. Richard's gift was to take whatever he was handed and make it worse. He had been blessed that way from the beginning. This took the form of screwing things up by trying to make them better, to *improve* upon them, or the proverbial not being able to leave well enough alone. This time, however, it was simple forgetfulness. He left his key in the room, so he had to go to the front desk to ask for another, which meant going down Shark Alley again with its bloody hoists and joists to the lobby, which was deserted. It was already too late in the afternoon to go to the beach but still too early for dinner, so most guests were in their rooms watching reruns of "Magnum PI," yelling at their sun-burnt kids, or in the shower cleaning sand out of their white marble heinies in preparation for hotel sex.

"Name, sir?" the clerk asked.

"It's room two fourteen," Richard said.

"Yes, sir, but I still need confirmation. What name is the room reserved under?"

It occurred to Richard that he didn't know Patrick's last name or even if Patrick had registered them. CJ could have done it using an alias, which could have been anything.

"Uh, I don't know," he said.

"Sir?"

"Mercurius."

"I'm sorry. What was that?"

"Mercurius, like the planet."

"Could you spell that, please."

As Richard spelled it, the clerk flailed away at his computer, attacked it, really—click, click, click, pause, click, click, click, longer pause, puzzled look—and shook his head.

"I'm sorry, sir, but that's not the name we have on file. Perhaps you registered under your partner's name."

"Partner?"

"We don't like to inquire about such things, but we do need confirmation. Perhaps you registered under his name."

"Yes, you know, that's right. That's probably what happened. Why didn't I think of that? I'll just go ask him and be right back."

He started to back away in what his mother referred to as a "slow exit," but one of the marooned security guards sniffed trouble and came scurrying over.

"Sir, did you lose your key?"

The man had the face of a bulldog with sad eyes and sagging jowls.

"Yes, yes, I did. That must be what happened. It's in my room. I don't know what I was thinking. The funny thing about it is, you leave your room and you think you have everything—sunscreen, towel, umbrella, flip-flops, beach ball—only to discover that you forgot the most important thing of all, the room key. Funny, isn't it? I bet you see that kind of thing all the time."

"Sir?"

"I bet you see that all the time."

The man stared at him without speaking, which made Richard even more nervous, so he shifted his weight back and forth and continued.

"You know, people getting locked out of their rooms for one reason or another, most often having to do with forgetfulness, or because they're worried about a coworker back at the office screwing them over while they're on vacation, or they're wondering why they never said anything to the waiter the night before about the grilled lobster, because now they're about to vomit, or they're thinking about that woman in the bar with languid eyes and legs as long as a drink of water giving them the once over. You know, just the usual stuff people think about."

The guard looked at the clerk and then said something to him in that local patois. Immediately, another guard rushed over with a walkie-talkie in hand, and they escorted Richard to an office off the lobby.

"I want my own bunk," he told them as they led him away.

They smiled agreeably and made him lie down on a couch with his feet elevated. From what he could gather, they thought he was the victim of sunstroke or some mental disability beyond their capacity to diagnose and treat.

"Not sure what to make of me?" he asked.

"We're just trying to find out who you are. Please stay here with your feet up. We're going to talk to our supervisor."

As soon as they left, Richard got up, checked the hallway, and walked in the opposite direction past the first floor guest rooms, which were the color of pink sea anemones. He passed an ice machine in a corner and decided to cool himself off by putting his head in the metal bin and breathing the cold vapor. If he could get back to his room without being seen, all he would have to do would be to steer clear of the guards or disguise himself as one of the jellyfish lampshades that were all over the resort. Then he would wait in hiding for Macy. How about that for a plan?

"Sir, is there a problem?"

He pulled his head out, banging it on the top of the bin, to see yet another member of the Chok brigade in the hallway staring at him. This one wore a gold jacket with a nametag that said "Teodoro Ack."

"No, I just lost my contact. It'll turn up, I'm sure. There's nothing to worry about."

"Is there anything I can do?"

"No, thank you."

But then Richard thought for a moment and decided that another drink was in order. One was simply not enough.

"Actually, I'm in the mood for a Blow Job," he said.

Teodoro didn't move. Richard cleared his throat and added, "The drink, I mean. You can get me one from the bar, can't you?"

"I believe so, sir."

"All right, then, bring me one frothy Blow Job."

"Right away sir. Would you like it here?"

"Here, there, anywhere, it doesn't matter... Wait, on second thought, bring it to me over there, would you?"

He pointed to the doors at the far end of the hall, which opened onto a patio with a wooden bench under a huge palm tree.

"And if you make it quick, I'll give you a five-dollar tip."

"Yes sir."

Teodoro left and Richard went to the patio to sit with his favorite obsession. Running into Katherine (actually, *not* running into her) should have been declared unconstitutional on the basis of excessive cruelty, but what could he do? It seemed it was meant to be, which was something he had never really understood, or liked. Most people used "meant to be" as an escape from whatever problems they were facing, but he saw it as the lazy man's guide to a shallow life. That started to change as he sat there waiting for his drink and watching seagulls jockeying for position above the water. It was certainly no coincidence that Nick and Katherine were here, just as it was no coincidence that the address of the Kiss was 1961 Cahona Boulevard, which, in addition to being the year Hurricane Hattie hit the Belizean coast, was the year JFK was sworn into office and Richard was born. Then there was the number itself,

"1961," which was one of those rare numbers composed of three or more integers that looked the same upside down as right-side up. He wasn't a superstitious man, but, good God, what could be more telling than that? He was finally connecting all of the dots, and for the first time in his life, he seemed to be in the right place at the right time for the right purpose.

"How comforting is that?" he said, grinning. "Then maybe *I* can kill two birds with one mango, Macy and Katherine."

When Teodoro Ack returned, he paid for the drink, tip included, and strolled around the patio. There were lounge chairs, umbrellas, and tables spread around the beach. He noticed a dog with three legs sniffing clumps of seaweed and discarded beer bottles. Then he saw Jacinta, who sat half buried in the sand eating, oddly enough, an ice cream sandwich. Next to her sat Mia in a red lounge chair, reading a paperback and chewing a piece of licorice. She wore a green and white striped bikini and straw hat with a wide brim. He was immediately aroused.

"It's a little late to be reading, isn't it?" he asked, approaching her.

"And it's a little early to be drinking, isn't it?" she answered without looking up.

"Are you kidding? I'm going to make this part of my daily routine."

"Good for you."

"Is there something wrong?" he asked.

"No, not at all. Why do you ask?"

"I don't know. You seem mad at me."

She didn't respond but turned a page and continued reading.

"Look, Mia, I have something to tell you... I've been wrong about you all along. You're not the enemy, which means I owe you an apology."

"What made you change your mind?"

"I've been thinking about the past few days, and I finally realized that I made things more complicated than they really are."

She smiled.

"You're not surprised?"

"No, I've known it all along. I've also been talking to CJ, and he told me everything. It seems you have no secrets anymore, Richard."

"That's great."

"It's not so bad," she said.

"Maybe not, but I feel like a heel."

"Because you thought I was trying to have you arrested? Richard, if I wanted you arrested, why would I help you escape from jail?"

"I never said it made sense."

"No, it doesn't, and I thought Americans were all about common sense."

"Not all of us," he said. "So, do you forgive me?'

"Not all of you," she answered.

He had to admit that running into her was no coincidence, either. Still, not being a superstitious man, he had to go through the sequence just to be sure. It went something like this: had he remembered his room key, he would not have been stopped by the security guard. Had he not been stopped, he would not have had to escape. Not escaping, he would not have fled to this part of the resort. Not fleeing to this part of the resort, he would not have seen her, and not seeing her, he would not have bent down to kiss her, which was exactly what he did, both to her amazement and his; the Kahlua and licorice blending sweetly on their lips. Mia's were soft and wet, his thin and dry, being Magyar, but also because he was nervous leaning into her and didn't know what to expect. He was right, too, for as he pressed his lips to hers, he was overcome by the memory of a summer day with Laura Fedora at Valley Forge, when their lips met for the first time and they declared their undying teenage love for one another. Laura's lips had felt cool and moist and tasted of anise, and here it was again years later and thousands of miles away.

"Hang on!" she said abruptly as he was about to declare his undying love yet again. He felt absolutely giddy. *"What?!?"*

"Give me a second. I'm almost finished. I just got to the good part."

"But—"

Mia held her licorice up to silence him, and the amazing thing was that it worked: he was silenced. What kind of woman could suspend the force of love in mid-air with a piece of candy? He would have thought only one woman capable of such an act, but lately it seemed they all had that power. Then he remembered one night when Katherine, bored to death as he was working up a sweat pleasuring her, reached down, squeezed his shoulder, and asked, "Are you done yet?" Apparently, an epic drama had started ten minutes earlier on the Ovary Channel and she was missing it. Then again, Mia's reaction might have been a good thing, since he was just about to use the "L" word, which was infinitely worse than the "R" one, because it involved a person rather than a contractual state. That is, it was relatively easy to get out of a relationship. Situations changed, people grew apart, accidents (planned and unplanned) happened. Love, however, was a function of who you were, not what you did, and he was too old not to have figured himself out yet, as he was reminded every Tuesday morning by his therapist. So he felt compelled by love to stand there and wait dutifully.

He tried to look over her shoulder, but Mia turned away and cupped her hand over the page. He cleared his throat, but she ignored him. He whistled, "Oh, Danny, Boy," but she shook her head and continued reading. Her hair was tucked under her hat, and several strands on the back of her neck waved back and forth in the breeze like a sea anemone (there was a photo in the hall). Unable to contain himself, he leaned down and ran his lips lightly over the bone at the base of her neck and through her hair. There was the slightest trace of brown sugar on her skin. Hotel shampoo? He'd have to ask housekeeping for extra bottles when they checked out.

Mia stuck an "Eco-Australia, Go Green!" bookmark in the spot and closed the book with what might be called "attitude."

"I heard," she said flatly.

"Excuse me?"

"I heard," she repeated.

"Heard what?"

"That she's here."

"Who's here?"

"Your wife."

"Look, I told you I'm not married."

"CJ followed you to the restaurant and saw everything," she said accusingly. "He was suspicious, and I don't blame him."

"But that's not what happened. I never even saw Katherine."

"How can that be?"

"I don't know. She was cleaning toe screws or something."

"You mean you weren't sitting with her?"

"That wasn't her."

"Who was it, then?"

"I don't know, some woman with a toy dog from Anaheim."

Mia glared at him, and he thought it ironic that he had to answer for a crime that he did not commit but that was entirely in keeping with his character.

"Is that why we came all the way to Belize—just so you could see her?"

"What? You've got it all wrong. I didn't even know she'd be here."

"I'm beginning to think you're a liar," she said.

"That's not fair."

"What else am I supposed to think?"

Not knowing what else to do, he offered her his drink, which she declined at first but then accepted. As she drank, he noticed that the book she was reading was none other than Negroponte's blockbuster, *Pas de Deux*, on the cover of which was a middle-aged housewife with a cigarette hanging out of her mouth wearing a grimy tutu.

"Well, what do we have here? You know, I'm beginning to think *you're* the liar," he told her, pointing to the book. "I just wanted to see what it was like," she said, trying to keep it from him.

"Why?"

"I don't know."

"You don't know why you bought the book?"

"No."

"Maybe you were thinking of taking ballet."

"Don't make fun of me," she said.

"Or maybe you have a crush on the author. Could that be it? I can get him to autograph it for you."

"Now you're being cruel," she said.

"Just tell me why you're reading it."

"I can't."

"Why not?"

"It's silly."

"The book? I believe it. The guy's a freak."

"No, my reason."

"Have you seen what my life is like? I wouldn't worry about silly."

"No?"

"Hey, I'd love nothing more than for my life to be silly. It'd be an improvement over what it is now."

She turned away to think about what he said, and the book slid off her lap in a flurry of pages to the ground. He bent down to retrieve it and noticed her feet. He had never really looked at them before, not like this, but they were magnificent. He wasn't sure what fetishes were, clinically at least, but he was well aware of an obsession he had had since childhood that took the form of an overpowering attraction to feet. Not all feet, mind you, just certain ones. Unlike other parts of the body, where imperfections and abnormalities might be arousing, the feet were entirely different, since they were the ugliest part of the body and had to be kept out of sight at all times. Mia's feet, though, were not like that.

They were in perfect harmony with her calf and the rest of her leg. Neither was there a hair on them; they were as smooth as her cheeks and of the same Arabica color. The toes were not too long, not too short, unexpectedly graceful, and fitted one against another like measuring spoons. Her arches were just right, not precipitous like the arches of high-strung, cold, or domineering women, but not too low, either, which would have made her phlegmatic. And, while she may have been many things, Mia was not phlegmatic. The inner curve of her sole, where the flesh on most people was wrinkled and pale, had neither a crease nor an unsightly blue vein. It was as smooth as sanded mahogany and perfect for nestling his lips and rubbing the tip of his nose, which he imagined doing as he waited for her answer to a question that he could not even remember. But the most wonderful thing of all and the flowering of all his fetishing were her toenails, which were polished glossy pink and contrasted the brown leather cord of her sandals that ran up from the river delta of her toes to the mound of her instep before veering off on either side of her arch. He followed the cord up and down, back and forth, in and out, until nothing remained for him but her feet: their smell, their touch, their taste. They were, in a word, exquisite.

"Richard, are you all right?"

"What?"

"Are you all right?"

"I'm fine," he answered, collapsing in the chair beside her.

"You don't look fine."

"I got a little light-headed, that's all. It happens when I bend down too fast."

"Is there anything I can do?"

"No, really."

"Are you sure?"

"Positive. Well maybe."

"What?"

"You're going to think it's strange."

"Tell me," she said.

"All right, sit back and rest your feet on my lap. I'd like to give you a foot massage like the one you gave me yesterday on the bus."

"Are you joking?"

"I never joke about feet."

She hesitated at first, looking for a sign that this was some sort of trick, but he remained as grim as a Mayan undertaker. He removed her sandals and set them down slowly, passing them close enough to his nose to inhale the sweet odor of leathered sweat and warm skin. He paused, breathless, not daring to look into her eyes. He stroked the ball of her left foot, and, if he thought he had died and gone to heaven with Laura, this sent him into rapture. If he could have swooned and gotten away with it, he would have, but he knew Mia was too smart, too savvy, too sensitive for anything like that, and he didn't want her to pull away for fear of being made fun of. Besides, he could tell that she enjoyed the massage as well as the attention. He was sure of it. After all, he had a certain intuition about women.

Mia's lips parted slightly, her calf muscles relaxed, and she sent him a smile that floated toward him like a tissue. He looked at her mole, which gave her face a certain imbalance, asymmetry, and he got aroused.

"You're a pervert, aren't you?" she asked.

The question hit him like a rotten mango. There was no denying it, of course. How could he? But if he told her the truth and she ran away, at least he wouldn't be wasting his time on Oyster Eater Número Dos. If she accepted him and understood the needs of a rather—how should he put it?—*complex* man, then maybe they had something. Maybe they could pass the time rubbing each other's feet, fleas or no fleas. At least the question made sense, being the logical progression from his father's suspicion and his ex-wife's conviction that he was not normal.

"What gave it away?" he asked.

"You mean besides your pulling your pants down every chance you get?"

"No, that would do it."

She left it at that and he waited before massaging her foot again. She giggled when he traced his index finger up and down her sole.

"So, do you want to hear about the book?" she asked demurely.

"Sure."

"All right. I thought if I read it, I'd find something out about your ex-wife."

"How did you know that Nick Negroponte is the Snorkeler?"

"CJ told me."

"But why would you be interested in Katherine?"

She didn't answer right away but looked at him as if he ought to know, which made him feel stupid for not knowing.

"I don't get it," he confessed.

"I wanted to find out why she left you," she said.

"And reading his book will tell you?"

"I didn't know where else to start."

"How about asking me?"

"You're not good at sharing, remember?"

She was right. He didn't share, which was part of the problem with Katherine; well, among five hundred and nineteen other problems. In his defense, however, he had to inform the court that he was not used to sharing and did not know how to do it without looking like an idiot. He also resisted change, which was why he still did the same things he had done twenty years earlier, apparently having learned nothing in all that time. He still set himself up for failure, still made the same errors of judgment, still thought the same confused thoughts, still expected things to turn out for the best despite the avalanche of evidence to the contrary.

"You want the truth?"

She nodded, waiting patiently.

"She married me to get even with her mother, who couldn't stand me even though I had a lot of money, and when the magic wore off she took up with the Snorkeler. She's got all the money now and, I guess, whatever magic is left. I don't think you'll find that in his book, though."

"Actually, it is."

"Oh."

"Is that all?" she asked.

"You want more?"

"No, but I was expecting a lot worse."

"Really, how worse?"

"It doesn't matter."

"No, I suppose not," he said.

The sun was melting below the horizon by now and the sea had turned charcoal gray with fringes of white surf. Far off, lights twinkled from fishing boats and scuba divers were chugging back from their day trips. Richard decided to risk everything and leaned over and kissed her feet. To his surprise, she did not run away or jump up in protest but kept them on his lap and even settled back in the chair. They sat like that in silence, a bizarre Pietá, her feet on his lap and his lips on her feet as twilight descended and Jacinta and the dog waited curiously nearby. Mia's skin was taut and warm and everything he imagined it would be except for that trace of licorice lingering on his lips, which he could taste as he licked her toes. Slowly, delicately. Combined with the salt from her sweat, it was heavenly.

He couldn't say why he did it, except that way led on to way, as Robert Frost had observed, and in the end he could not help himself. It was simply meant to be.

If the truth be told, Katherine's feet were gnarled, twisted things that looked like old driftwood or the aftermath of two trains colliding; one carrying garden claws, the other ball-peen hammers. As much as he was drawn to the rest of her, he could not stand her feet and lived in a state of perpetual anxiety from May to September at the possibility of her wanting to throw a pool party. Licking her toes not only never occurred to him, the mere thought was repulsive. On those rare occasions when she would cuddle with him on the couch or in bed, pressing her cold, calloused toes against his skin as a prelude to sex, he would recoil in disgust and pretend to have left the iron plugged in or the hose running in the yard ("There's a drought, you know!"). It was such a painful existence that he had divorced himself from it long before she divorced him. But now the second chance he had dreamt of, the mulligan, was finally here. He had Mia, a burnt version of Laura with feet as supple as an orchid, and a chance to reclaim his legacy (i.e., a rubber mat). Love and career were coming together nicely like rhythm and music. And, really, who could ask for anything more?

Richard felt like a new man, a new creation, not because of any romantic notions he had about himself and Mia, but because she hadn't judged him. That was it. She had accepted him for who he was, fetish and all, and he even spent the night on her bed, fully clothed, his body curled around hers and his instep gently filling the sole of her foot. No one else existed in all of San Pedro or at least Room 209 (not counting Jacinta and the dog, who slept in Maggie's bed). They had taken advantage of Maggie being away all night, although neither she nor Patrick was admitting anything. Privacy, "for your information, young man," wasn't dead in her neck of the woods in Perth, where people could still "stroll along the banks of Swan River without being disturbed by stickybeaks." Or was it Swan Lake and sticky buns? Anyway, the important thing was that the urgency of revenge, of holding Macy's head under water until the gurgling stopped, had vanished. Sure, he wouldn't turn Macy away if he showed up with a bucket of water and offered to dunk his own head, but that didn't seem very likely right now. Richard had a new mission: not to land in a Belizean prison, thereby shooting himself in the foot and losing both of Mia's forever.

Part of that mission was accepting the fact that he wouldn't be making up for mediocrity after all. He had come close, though, closer than anyone in his family had been in generations. And, although that may have been the very definition of mediocrity, he was sure of one thing: this change in him was not the result of licking Mia's toes, as exciting as that had been (when this was over, he would start a fetish support group called "Club Foot"). That was the catalyst but not the clincher. What really did it for him was not that she accepted him but the *idea* of her accepting him; that is, not that it *was* done but that it *could be* done. In reality, he didn't care about being accepted as much as he cared about being worthy of acceptance. It may have been splitting pubic hairs, but this distinction was as crucial to him as the one about love, because it had to do with a person's being rather than his actions. Being the vixen that she was, Katherine never fully understood this and tried to make up for her withering attacks on his person and profession with trivial acts of redemption like vacuuming cat fur out of the rug or planting irises in the yard. When he didn't respond, she would get morose and sulk for days, trying to reconcile in that cutesy wootsy way of hers by burrowing her toes under his behind as he sat reading. Yet, no matter what he did he was still a disappointment in her eyes and knew it. How many times does a person have to be told in bed that his breathing is annoying before he realizes that it isn't his breathing that's annoying but the fact that he *is* breathing?

He woke the next morning curled up on the bed, wrapped around Mia's body. You could tell a lot about a person by their feet, which was how he knew Mia was different. She differed from Katherine in a thousand and one ways, the greatest of which was that she kept coming back. She had shown up at the Magis, jumped into the Fury, ridden the bus to Belize, and, after making the All Time Fugitive Hit List, suckled him in a way that would have scandalized her saggy-breasted relatives back home. He had to trust her even though she had soured his taste for revenge with tropical sweetness. So maybe this was a sign. Maybe it was time to surrender, turn himself in, tell them the whole truth and nothing but the truth so help him Mayan God of Humiliation. It was possible now only because of her. She was sponging him off in his corner of the ring, whereas before there was nothing but bird shit, which he had stepped in for the last time.

"I swear I'll never do that again," he whispered.

But it didn't take long before he heard voices from beyond the louvered doors, from the surf outside, and the doubt began all over again. He couldn't help it.

"What did I tell you about never saying never?" Katherine said.

"I don't remember."

"Yes, you do."

"Do not."

"Richard?"

"Yes, my love?"

"Grow up."

"I am grown up."

"Then why are you obsessing like a lovesick teenager over this colored girl from the jungle in a lollipop bikini?"

"It's not an obsession," he told her.

"What is it, then—*love?*"

He hesitated. "Maybe."

"Oh, come on. You're incapable of loving anyone but yourself and that stupid career of yours, if you can call it that."

"That's not true."

"You don't even know what love is."

"No, I don't," he admitted, "but I know it makes you stop and think twice before doing anything stupid."

"Then you can't be in love, because that's all you do."

"I'm not arguing with you anymore."

"What are you going to do about it?" she snarled.

"Banish you."

"You haven't got the moxie."

"Watch me."

He was fully awake now and imagined driving with Katherine along a steep cliff. He headed into a curve and leaned over to open her door.

"Wait, aren't you forgetting something?" she demanded.

"What?"

"Your girlfriend. She's geographically undesirable."

"So are you," he told her. "Now get lost."

"You're the one who's lost, Richard, not me."

"Look, I've finally found someone who's interested in me, not in what I can do for her, and I'm not going to screw it up."

"You screw everything up."

"Not this time, dear."

"Then stay down here. Who knows? Maybe you can get a job tending bar at Alberto's, if they don't arrest you first."

"It'll be better than the life I had with you."

"Well, now you know how it feels," she said in that spiteful way of hers, looking out her window.

"So I guess I'm supposed to be sympathetic now that I understand why you cheated on me?" he asked.

"Something like that."

"Then you can do something like go to hell."

He jerked the handle and shoved her out, watching as her body rolled down the highway and flopped into a ditch like a ragdoll. It landed at the base of the alabaster monument to the war dead. The historian with the plastic daisy in his lapel shuffled over in a walker to check her pulse and pronounced her dead. Dutifully, his friends at the gift shop dug a grave and, at the *frau's* suggestion, chose a sensible granite tombstone. The interesting thing was that Richard didn't care at all and continued driving, singing with Hank on the radio about her cheatin heart and thinking about going home.

"Go on," the *frau* said to him. "You deserve it."

"You think so?"

"Of course. I'm never mistaken about these things."

"You said never."

"Who are you going to believe, *her* or me?" she asked, pointing to the fresh mound of dirt at the gravesite.

"I'm on my way," he said.

He propped himself up on an elbow and watched Mia sleeping. True, she may have looked like a bowl of chicken mole in green stripes, but to him she was beautiful. He decided to make a go of it with her and, if lucky, he would live long enough to plant a garden behind her travel agency where they would sit naked in the morning and sip lattes as the sun warmed their private parts. Why not? He would even put in a gravel path for meditative walking exercises. Spending the night with her had given him a chance to pull his head out of his ass. All he had to do was survive, which he would do no matter what, even if it meant staying in Belize and making a living writing brochures for Amber Air, which would be poetic justice. He was the kind of guy who needed a home, a family, a way to be remembered. He didn't want to be alone anymore, which reminded him of the documentary he had seen about a recluse who spent thirty-five years alone in a cabin in Alaska. Caribou came around every spring, munching.

Not so long ago, he would have given his left testicle to live like that, but now he realized it would have been a dis-aster. They would have had to airdrop coffee and gin to him every month, expensive as that was, and, with no one to bitch to or run from, he probably would have hanged himself before the gin ran out, unless the voices in his head got to him first, which would have been a distinct possibility. He was pretty sure caribou could talk, even though he had never seen one in real life.

So, were his misanthropic days behind him? Did rebirth mean that he couldn't make fun of people anymore? That would be hard. How would he be able to resist criticizing a world that thought of freedom as the inalienable right to order a double-tall, soy, extra-whip gingerbread latte? The pilot who flew them to San Pedro might have something to say about that. As for him, having been too young for Vietnam and too old for Iraq, his defense of freedom was limited to the boardroom, which, although not requiring a beach landing, certainly had its moments. The enemy wore striped suspenders and tasseled Guccis, to be sure, but they could be just as deadly. How many times had he been forced to hunker down during rocket-propelled grenade attacks and walk through minefields? He had mentioned combat pay once to Mike Spinelli at a cocktail party at his mansion on the Main Line, but the senior partner just stared at him as if he had asked to swap wives, which wouldn't have been such a bad idea now that he thought about it.

"Just kidding, Mike, hey, hey. Say, is that a Lladró?"

"Why, yes, Richard, it is..."

Then again, there was the possibility that if he remained true to the New Man, revenge might happen anyway, the unexpected byproduct of centripetal force or a sudden burst of cosmic libido. Maybe the expanding universe would turn inside out and losers would suddenly become winners. But if it did, if revenge occurred naturally, should he ignore it or pretend that it didn't matter after he had spent his whole life chasing it? And if it came when he no longer needed it, didn't that mean he had been right all along, that God was either incompetent or unimaginative? Either way, the waste of time would have been enormous. It wasn't how he wanted to end this trip, but he had already learned one important lesson: he was not in charge and never had been. So, the opportunity for revenge came when he no longer wanted it, love crashed through his living room window like a brick thrown from a passing car, and failure came home to roost on a rubber mat in his bathroom. It was ironic the same way that running into Nick but not Katherine was ironic. At least the ex was dead, and he had work to do: proving his innocence and settling down in a ramshackle shackle on Ambergris Caye, where he and Mia would dine on boiled shrimp and grouper (which he would do nightly) as fishing boats slipped into and out of the harbor, as he slipped into and out of her harbor. Misanthropy, cynicism, sarcasm, his ability to find the absurd in all things like a pig sniffing for truffles had to make room for Mercurius II, which he believed was what Alan Shepard had flown in.

"Make room or vacate, that's the deal," he whispered as he got out of bed. "And maybe even get rid of the voices."

The dog exhaled deeply, watching him the entire time as he moved about the room. It was hard to admit, but Richard knew that at his age he couldn't count on another thirty years, so he had to make use of the time he had left as wisely as possible. And the wisest way to get out of this madness was to admit that he had been wrong about everything, absolutely everything. There, he did it; he turned himself in. The clerk will now read the verdict.

————————

"Guilty."

"What?"

"Guilty," CJ repeated as Richard joined him for break-fast at the "Blue Hole Grill," the resort restaurant.

Neon lights were everywhere along with white linen jackets and calypso music. CJ wore a Hawaiian shirt with peacocks and orange shorts, blending perfectly with the surrounding décor. Richard had his *Abenteurer* cap on and a pair of photochromic, polycarbonate "eyewear" that he bought in the gift shop.

"That's what they're saying about us back at the office," CJ said. "I heard it from Christine, who went to see Updike. She said he was there with Eckstrom and they want us to turn ourselves in to the police here in Belize."

"I bet they do. They don't want any more publicity. I'm sure Updike would rather have the whole thing go away."

"They're serious, Richard."

"So am I."

"What are we going to do?"

"Well, I don't know about you, but I'm going to have breakfast."

"And then what?"

"I'll talk to Macy and see what we can work out."

"Good, no violence, though. That'll just make things worse."

"Look, I'll talk to the sonofabitch without even raising my voice. I'll tell him that if he doesn't want the whole thing to blow up in their faces, they'd better call off their goons."

"What if he calls your bluff?"

"He wouldn't dare. He knows me too well. Besides, I have an ace up my sleeve: Pet Mat. He has no idea what proof I have that Pet Mat is really mine. I could threaten legal action."

"But I thought you said you never applied for a patent."

"I didn't."

"That doesn't make sense."

"Just trust me on this."

"Do I have a choice?"

"Not really."

Richard went to the buffet table, in the center of which was an ice sculpture of a smiling kiskadee that had started to melt and looked like a penguin. He returned with a tray loaded with corn-flakes, banana pancakes in orange syrup (*pancakes d'orange*), boiled sausages, a bowl of mixed fruit and yogurt, and two glasses of papaya-lime juice with stringy pulp. He felt much better and had so little churning in his stomach that he thought about sending a note to the horse doctor. He just needed a knock-knock joke that rhymed with Vicodin.

"Worked up an appetite?" CJ asked, grinning.

"Never mind that. Before I talk to Macy we should meet with this Fats guy so we can get you on a plane out of here."

"*Me?*"

"That's right."

"What about you?"

"I'm not going. This is my last stop, CJ."

"When the hell did you decide that?"

"About ten minutes ago. I know what it looks like, but I haven't lost my mind. I just figure there's nothing left for me back there, so why not try something new?"

"Something new? Richard, we're not talking about shaving cream."

"I'd call this a pretty close shave."

"Sure, make jokes. This is serious. You're not safe here, you know. You can still get busted anytime."

"I know that, which is why I'm having a little chat with Macy."

"You're sure about this?"

"Never been surer. I'm going to start a new life here with Mia."

CJ stared at him with a mixture of frustration and disbelief. "Tell me, does Mia know about this new life of yours?"

"No. We still have a lot to talk about."

"Unbelievable."

"Don't worry, I'll help you get out. You have my word."

Richard dug into his pancakes (the syrup was slightly tart, like Mia), when Patrick and an enormous guy showed up at the hostess station. CJ waved them over, and, after the introductions, Fats Cahona excused himself, returning from the buffet table with a tray filled with sliced watermelon, nothing more. He tucked a corner of the tablecloth into the collar of his shirt, which had barbeque stains and what looked like moth holes, and exclaimed in a booming voice, "In this heat, I used to think heaven was a watermelon!"

"That's all right. I used to think hell was a fairytale," Richard muttered.

"What's that?"

"Nothing."

Then Fats dove in, attacking the watermelon and talking about how he had already chosen a site for the rubber factory, which sounded even more ludicrous coming from him. Richard couldn't take his eyes off his fingers, which looked like fat cigars, and his pinkie ring, which was solid gold with a heart-shaped ruby.

"Yeah, about that, there's been a slight change of plans, Fats," Richard said. "You don't mind if I call you Fats, do you?"

"No, not at all. That's how everyone on the island knows me, even all of Belize," he answered, spreading his arms.

"The truth is, we're in trouble with the authorities, and CJ has to leave the country as soon as possible."

"I already know that, Mister Richard, which is why I have decided to postpone doing business with you. You see, I want to see the outcome of your efforts to clear your name. As a businessman, I'm sure you can appreciate that. But as a courtesy to Mister Patrick here, I will put you in touch with someone who can get your friend on a flight to Chetumal Bay in Mexico. Of course, there's some risk involved."

"Risk?"

"Nothing major, more of an inconvenience, really. Let's just say the pilot won't be filing a flight plan."

"I don't understand."

"Smugglers," Patrick interjected, leaning forward and tapping the side of his nose.

"But what happened to cultural attachés?" CJ asked.

"That was before I understood the full nature of your predicament," Fats said, nibbling a rind as if it were a pig knuckle. "I can't get involved personally, not at this point. I'm sure you can appreciate that, too."

CJ sat back, expressionless. Richard took another forkful of pancakes. "Seems we're destined to smuggle cocaine one way or another."

"All right, what do we have to do?" CJ asked.

"Your contact is here at the convention. We'll go over and I'll point him out to you. After that, you're on your own and I am out of it. Agreed?"

"Agreed."

"Mister Richard?"

"Sure."

Fats polished off the watermelon tout suite, wiped his mouth, and grabbed a slice of pineapple upside down cake for the walk to the Conference Centre, which was in one half of a converted airplane hangar. They had to leave the resort along an unshaded path, and by the time they arrived, Richard had broken a sweat.

"The other half of the hangar is being prepared for the ball tonight," Fats told them. "We celebrate Carnevale once a month during the summer. It's more festive that way. You should plan on attending. There'll be an orchestra, food, and plenty of beautiful women. You'll need costumes, of course."

"That's not a problem," Richard said, airing out his shirt.

"Then you may win a prize."

"Really, like what?"

"A weekend trip for two to the Mayan wonders of Tikal."

The ironies kept piling up like pistachio shells on poker night. Before Richard could respond, Fats pointed to a young Garífuna man in a yellow shirt and white pants hanging out with some other guys. His hair was braided in cornrows and he wore alligator shoes that must have cost a planeload.

"That's him," Fats said, sucking the last of the cake from his fingertips. "Good luck to you gentlemen."

"Richard, let me find out what's going on before we commit to anything. I want to meet this guy myself, all right?" CJ said.

"He's all yours."

"In the meantime, why don't you and Patrick have a look at the exhibits? See if you can find Macy. This may take a while. And don't attract any attention, would you? Try to be as inconspicuous as possible."

"You won't even know I'm here," Richard assured him.

The "Rubber Tree Inventors' Convention" was an eclectic mix of the bizarre and fantastic with more than three hundred booths from Central America and the States. These included exhibits for rubber floors, rubber walls, non-snapping rubber bands, rubber ducks, rubber stamps, rubber erasers, rubber balls that never stopped bouncing, rubber mats for playgrounds and gymnasiums, rubber heart valves, rubber bra "enhancers," self-healing latex paint in case your car got dinged by a shopping cart, water soluble urethane, reusable condoms, and a cheaper way for discarded tires to be used in the production of asphalt. This last one was from a company in Detroit whose motto was, "Where the rubber meets the road." They gave out free chocolate and buttons for signing their "Have a Salesman Contact Me" list, which Richard signed as Lucien Updike. In addition, they passed a booth lauding Charles Goodyear of tire and blimp fame and another depicting the history of vulcanization with a media presentation entitled, "Welcome to Planet Vulcan."

"What, no silicone implants?" Richard asked.

"Aisle two," the guy answered, holding his hand up and forking his fingers like Mr. Spock. "They're in between 'Baking with Bakelite' and 'Pet Mat.'"

"Pet Mat?" Patrick yelled excitedly. "Come on, let's go!"

He pulled Richard along, who resisted as best he could, past aisles five, four, and three. As they rounded the corner of aisle two, there was Richard Macy demonstrating the "amazing strength" of Pet Mat. He was heavier than Richard remembered, with pasty cheeks and sweat on his lip. He stood on a stage with red and blue bunting before an audience of enraptured dog people.

Richard drew a clear distinction between dog owners and dog people. The former were humans who happened to own pets, willingly or otherwise, and made the most of it (his case); the latter were disturbed enough to believe that their pets were not animals at all but members of the family who needed their own clothing and medical insurance. They brushed their teeth, kissed them, slept with them, paraded them around in baby strollers, and rubbed sunscreen on their genitals. He had actually seen his mother-in-law do that once. Ironically, these same people were usually nasty to children and waitresses and did not wash their hands after using the bathroom. He had seen that, too. Right now, there were about eighty of them assembled in front of the stage.

Macy lined up a dozen feeding bowls on the stage, each one on a small square of Pet Mat, and invited audience members to come forward to pour water into the bowls from pitchers on the far side of the stage.

"Go ahead, right up to the brim."

As people crowded the stage, Richard saw Ted and Glenda with their little shit of a dog, which hopped up and down, yelping. Macy handed out rubber balls to everyone but not before shamelessly plugging the exhibitor that donated them, "The Ball Barn." Each ball had an outline of a barn stenciled in silver.

"Check them out. They're on aisle five."

"Guess we missed them," Patrick whispered. "We'll have to go back."

"Now, I'd like you to pick a bowl, any bowl," Macy continued. "On my command, throw your ball at the bowl and try to spill the water. Remember, even though we didn't do anything special to the bowls—all we did was place them on the squares—Pet Mat's revolutionary design will keep them from sliding no matter how hard you throw the ball." "How is that?" somebody asked.

"Good question. Let me briefly explain the design of the suction cups before we begin the demonstration."

Macy proceeded to describe the design and how the answer to the "geometric puzzle" involving the spaces between the cups came to him in a dream. It was almost religious, he said, like an angel coming to him in his sleep.

"I'm leaving," Richard told Patrick.

"No, you can't leave now, mate, you'll miss the ball throwing. Why would you want to do that?"

"Gee, I don't know."

Patrick bent down and handed him two balls that were rolling around at their feet. Then, in one of those seemingly insignificant moments that ends up determining the rest of your life—whether it makes sense or not, but for some reason especially if it doesn't—

Richard decided enough was enough. He squeezed one of the balls and threw it at Macy.

It veered to the right of his head.

"Uh, I haven't given the signal yet, so would you please hold onto your balls?" Macy said, looking up.

The crowd erupted with laughter, and Patrick made a show of grabbing himself. Two teenage girls next to him giggled. Richard thought about the money Macy would earn from this little piece of rubber and how he didn't deserve a nickel, not because he didn't invent it (he could accept that), but because he had never suffered for it. He hadn't *earned* it. That, combined with the fact that Macy was a terrible liar and an even worse presenter, sent Richard into orbit, which was what he did with the other ball.

It whizzed past Macy's left ear.

"All right, who's throwing the balls?" Macy growled. "Someone's having fun at my expense. Come on, who is it?"

Richard crouched down behind Patrick. The only sound in the crowd was the yelping of Glenda's dog. When it finally stopped and the action resumed, he felt around the floor for a third ball. He was handed one by, of all people, Wayne, who stood there grinning like an Evil Buddha. He was chewing gum and had his video camera turned on, recording everything. Heather was with him, displaying a porn star navel ring and six inches of midriff. She rubbed her leg with Wayne's backscratcher and blew a bubble the size of a softball.

"Oh, it's you. So, how's your movie coming along?" Richard asked.

"Fine. How's my bonus coming along?"

"What?"

"You promised me a hundred bucks when we got to Belize. Well, we're in Belize, so where's my bonus?"

"You're kidding, right?"

"No, I'm not."

"Why, you little prick. You've been filming your goddamned documentary and getting a free ride all along. Now you want more money?"

"They took my car," Wayne insisted.

"You mean the one Saul gave you?"

"A deal's a deal."

"And an accomplice is an accomplice, which means you do jail time. Did you know that, asshole?"

"What?"

"You aided and abetted two fugitives."

"Oh, really?"

"Yeah, really."

"Well, let's just see about aiding and abetting. Hey everybody, listen up. See this guy here? His name is Richard Mercurius. He's a drug dealer wanted by the FBI and if you turn him in, you'll get fifty thousand dollars in reward money!"

Patrick tried his best to grab Richard from behind, but it was too late. Richard lunged at Wayne, which he had wanted to do ever since El Zapote. The two of them sprawled across the floor, knocking over people, chairs, and two potted ferns at the end of the aisle. Wayne's video camera sailed into the air and hit the ground with full force. Richard lost his cap and glasses but stood up and kept a firm grip on Wayne's throat, which was as soft and slimy as squid. He pressed harder, slowly forcing air out of his body, but then Heather jumped on his back. She whipped him with the back-scratcher and pummeled him with little fists of fury, digging her nails into his scalp. Patrick peeled her off, but not before drawing blood. She kicked at the air and shouted obscenities as Patrick held her in a bear hug three feet off the ground.

"Mercurius?" Macy yelled in disbelief from the stage. "What the hell are *you* doing here?"

"No, Macy, the question is, what are *you* doing here!" Richard screamed, out of breath and bleeding.

Macy stammered, paced back and forth, and finally called for security. Instantly, bulldog-faced security guards descended on the crowd, calling on their walkie-talkies for "Mister Muscle." But before backup could arrive, Richard picked up another ball and let loose. This time it found its target, smacking Macy in the forehead and leaving a red welt. Macy staggered backward, almost falling off the rear of the stage. Then, as if on cue, everyone else joined in and rubber balls went flying everywhere. It was as if the hangar had turned into a giant Powerball machine, and Richard had to take cover under a chair. From there, he made his way to the stage and crawled on the floor to another booth. He escaped by crawling from one booth to the next until he got to the other side of the hangar. As pandemonium reigned over in Rubber Tree Land, on the Carnevale side it was dark and cool and as peaceful as a cemetery, which, he thought, was just about right. It was just what he needed. He saw a red exit sign and left the building, rubbing spit on his wound and heading toward the beach, as far away from the Great Kiss as possible. So much for inconspicuous.

Dazed from the attack and blinded by sunlight, he stumbled along the jagged shoreline, which had pure white sand littered with sea-weed and driftwood, past bathers and children and lovers holding hands. Cumulus clouds swarmed the horizon and the sun burned directly overhead. The next hotel over, no more than a hundred yards away, was "The Royal Tern: Where One Good Stay Deserves Another." He headed for it, wanting to put as much distance as pos-sible between him and the Convention Centre, but walking in the heavy sand tired him out. He went to the water's edge, cupped the clear, warm water into his hands, and washed the cuts on his head, which stung. Then he found a spot up at the tree line. He sat down in the shade and, waving sand flies away, tried to make sense out of what had just happened. He was as confused as ever. He didn't know why he did it except that, once again, way led on to way and he couldn't help himself.

"Story of my life," he muttered.

"So that's it, then? You're giving up?" he imagined Flaherty asking from the brush behind him. He turned around and pictured the priest as a howler monkey sitting in the sand.

"You got that right."

"But didn't your mother teach you never to give up?"

"No, she taught me never to get caught."

"But you did."

"I'm aware of that, thank you."

"Through your own fault," Flaherty said.

"Yeah, my most maxima culpa."

"Well, as long as we're clear on that. I like clarity, Richard, as you might imagine. In fact, you're lucky. This could be one of those rare moments when you actually have clarity, the rest of your life being such a screw-up."

"As my friend back there would say, *whatever, dude.*"

"That's the best you can come up with? No wonder you're in such a mess. No wonder at all."

"Leave me alone."

"Leave me alone! Leave me alone!" the monkey mocked, eating a banana and throwing the peel at him.

Richard looked at the water again, where there were mangrove trees and a dock that stretched to the horizon. At the end of it sat a shed with a green, corrugated roof. Farther north, near the Royal Tern, was a jetty with a dead iguana, which drew a crowd of tourists. He couldn't believe how big it was. Then he imagined Flaherty returning with his father and Saul, the three of them standing on the jetty, studying the iguana and marveling as it turned into his own corpse.

"The spirit was willing but the flesh was weak," Flaherty said, shaking his head in disapproval and examining the body.

"It may have been weak, but it must have been tasty," Saul said. "Looks like the crabs got to him."

"He was always allergic to seafood," his father added.

"It just goes to show, you can't be too sensitive about anything. I tried telling him that, but would he listen?"

"Nope," Saul said.

"He was very sensitive but very confused," Flaherty said. "He had trouble figuring out who he was. Can you imagine that? What kind of condition do you have to be in not to know who you are, I ask you?"

"Human," Saul replied.

"Okay, I'll give you that. Jews one, Christians nothing."

The three of them carried his body on their shoulders to the tree line and buried it in the sand. Flaherty stuck a cross made out of driftwood and palm fronds at the head of the grave and tossed orchid petals over it. Saul put his autographed picture of Nicholas Sarkozy on top. Then Mister Jangles appeared, its head crushed and splattered with blood. The cat danced in worn out shoes and lifted its leg, urinating on the cross.

"Whoever heard of a cat named Mister Bo Jangles, for chrissakes?" Flaherty chided. "It's supposed to be a dog."

"It was the wife's idea," his father said.

"Well, that explains it. Whatever happened to her?"

"Up and died."

"I see."

Then the priest led them in a prayer and sat down beside Richard in the shade. He looked old and haggard.

"What's the problem?" Richard asked.

"No problem, except for the fact that you had so much potential. I really thought our talk the other day straightened you out."

"You misjudged me."

"No, I didn't. You just need more time."

"That's one thing I don't have anymore."

"True, but none of us does, no matter our age."

"Look, I couldn't help it," Richard said. "It was just too much. That kid's been pushing my buttons ever since I met him.

Then I saw Macy up there with all those balls bouncing around, and I just had to do it."

"Fate?" Flaherty asked.

"What would you have done in my place?"

"Probably the same thing."

"Really?"

"No."

"Why not?"

"Because you had a choice, that's why. You could have walked away or given him the hundred bucks."

"Sure, that's easy for you to say. You live in some fantasyland with a goddamned ark and a rollercoaster from hell. I, on the other hand, live in the real world with real people who can be real assholes. Got that?"

"Quit your whining. It's annoying in this heat. Besides, it's not a done deal yet. You can still get out of this."

"How?"

"By facing the music."

"I've already thought of that."

"No, I mean actually facing the music. Go to the ball tonight."

"What?"

"Don't miss it for the world."

"Why?"

Flaherty wouldn't answer. Instead, he patted Richard on the knee and got up. Then the three of them walked to the green shed at the end of the dock, disappearing inside, his father turning to wave before closing the door behind him.

"It didn't stick," he yelled into the wind.

"That's great, dad, just great."

His bowels were churning again. What the hell was he supposed to do when Patrick put that ball in his hand? He wound up and delivered, that's what, and, if the truth be known, it felt better than shitting in the woods. The problem was that this time he screwed himself over royally. Now, instead of having time to figure things out with Mia, he would have to scramble like a one-armed juggler. By now, Wayne must have tweeted everyone from the FBI to Disney Dude that they were at the resort. So, once again, they were one step ahead of the Pomade Patrol, except this time they were cornered. There was literally nowhere else to go. What could they do; rent a boat? There were motorboats and dinghies moored to the dock, so it would have been easy enough to steal one. He considered it until he imagined spending weeks on the open sea before drifting, scorched and lifeless, into Cuban territorial waters. Of course, they might run aground on the Cayman Islands, maybe open a tax shelter.

"So what do I do now?"

Silence, then waves and an occasional cry of laughter from kids playing at the water. There was no denying what had to be done, even though he'd most likely get screwed. But, really, what options did he have that *wouldn't* make things worse? Just this one. And, contrary to what every muscle in his body was aching to do, he wouldn't make things worse anymore. Wouldn't run, either. At this point in his life, he *couldn't* run. So he got up, brushed the sand from his pants, and headed back toward the Great Kiss, determined to find CJ and Mia. He hoped it would make a difference; what kind of difference he wasn't sure, but anything would be better than this, even jail. Actually, thinking about jail, accepting it, brought relief. At least the Great Escape would be over.

When he got back to the resort, he sat down in a lounge chair as a groundskeeper straightened out the furniture and collected trash from the night before. The man smiled politely but said nothing. Richard took that as a sign that things were normal, at least on this area of beach, which was fortunate, because he had nothing left. He was down to bone on bone; not a shred of cartilage remained. So, he managed to do the only thing a man in his condition could do.

"Got a cigarette?"

The groundskeeper, another local, took pity on him and gave him two.

"Thanks."

The man smiled and went back to work. Richard finished the first cigarette and lit the second. He looked back at the dock, the people standing at the water's edge, the water that was so clear the sea was filled with sky, and decided that, like his old man, for the first time in his life he would follow his heart. What the hell, he would go to the ball. It would be a perfectly ludicrous ending to an even more ludicrous trip. He wanted CJ and Mia to go with him, but convincing them wouldn't be easy, considering it sounded crazy.

"But everything great sounds crazy at first, doesn't it?"

He waited for an answer, but there was only silence again. He finished the second cigarette and closed his eyes. He felt better about his decision and the gamble he was taking. It just might work. It also might be the biggest mistake of his life; well, second. Okay, third. Still, he felt "cautiously optimistic," which is what they would say to clients since the subprime meltdown, but given his track record he wouldn't put money on it. Not that he had any, of course, so it really wasn't a problem. He stretched out in the chair, the sun warming his scalp, and dozed off. He was exhausted, and death would have been preferable, but it just wasn't his time yet. Maybe later.

He didn't dream or even sleep but drifted like those seagulls above the beach, but it wasn't long before he heard voices and felt the pounding of feet. As they came closer, he prepared for the worst: handcuffs, cold and heavy around his wrists, and a crowd of people.

"Once again, Richard, nice work."

"What?"

"They're still cleaning up the mess back there, you know. There's water all over, too. Maybe your mats aren't as good as you thought."

CJ stood in front of his chair with Mia, who wore the wide-brimmed hat and leather sandals from yesterday. "Hello," Richard said, staring up into the sun.

"Hello yourself," she said back.

"How are you?"

"I'm fine, but when I couldn't find you this morning, I thought something happened and you decided to run away."

"No, I'll never do that again, I promise."

"I'm glad to hear that," she said, adding, "Jacinta has been asking for you. I think she misses you."

"That's nice."

"I miss you, too."

"You do?"

He couldn't make out her face, but the brim of her hat moved up and down.

"I really hate to interrupt your little chit-chat here, but the reason he'll never run away again is he'll be behind bars in a federal prison," CJ said. "That's why we've got to make this quick. There's a plane leaving tonight, and they've agreed to take us as a favor to Fats. The guy says they have space for two, but it'll be tight."

"Two?"

"It's better that way," Mia said. "I've already talked it over with CJ. You can't stay here, and I can't keep running away anymore."

"But won't you get into trouble?"

"I'll figure something out."

"What about us?"

Without realizing it, he had just committed himself. *Us?* It was one thing to lick her toes and spend the night curled up with her in bed, but this was a whole different ballgame. Still, he didn't mind. He had to draw his line in the sand somewhere, and this was as good a place as any. There was actually sand here.

"You get your life straightened out and then come down to Antigua. You can stay with me. I have an apartment behind the travel agency," she said.

"Is there a garden?"

"Yes."

"Do you have an espresso machine?"

"No, but I can get one."

"Good, I like to have a latte every morning."

"Cut the crap, Richard," CJ said. "This place will be crawling with police in about three minutes. We've got to find somewhere to hide until the plane leaves."

"When is that?"

"After the ball."

"That's perfect. We can go to the ball in costumes, and nobody will suspect a thing."

"Okay, but where do we go in the meantime? We've got to get out of here."

Richard thought for a moment, trying not to panic, and then, inspired by his daydream, said "There."

"Where?"

"There."

"The water?"

"Just follow me."

They walked down to the water past the mangrove trees to the shed at the end of the dock, which was unlocked and filled with junk. Light pierced the walls inside and waves slapped the pilings below. It took time to adjust to the dark, but it was a perfect place to hide out. Richard worried that some fishermen might come back, but Mia assured him they would hear anyone approaching, even with the wind.

"So how about it?" she asked.

"It's perfect," he said.

"Good, I think you'll be safe here."

"All right, so now what do we do?"

"Well, you've got time, so why not make costumes for the Carnevale?"

"*Make* costumes?"

"Why not? And they have to be convincing or you might get caught. You don't want that to happen, do you?"

"She's right," CJ agreed.

"Let's see if we can find something in all this mess."

CJ and Mia started scrounging around crates and nets and spare engine parts as if they were at a garage sale.

"Why don't we just go as tourists?" Richard said, but they ignored him and continued foraging through the junk.

Mia dug through a pile and uncovered, to their astonishment, a wooden carousel horse that had been fished out of the water. It was creamy white with a golden saddle and a red bridle. A red striped pole stuck out of its neck as if it had been harpooned by barbers. With CJ's help, she set it against the wall and stood back, admiring it.

"See, there's magic here!" she exclaimed.

"There's something here," Richard said.

The whole thing sounded ridiculous, but he spent the next couple of hours sorting through propellers, gas cans, buoys, tackles, old nets, scuba gear, and discarded clothes anyway. When they finished, CJ was wearing multi-colored glass floats and a yellow rain hat that looked like something on the label of a can of tuna. Richard looked like a disco Aquaman in a loincloth, fishnet shirt, scuba fins, and a mangled face mask. He also had a broken spear to wave around like a true superhero, a gay one, but a superhero nevertheless.

"I still think we should go as Australian tourists. We're supposed to blend, you know," he told them.

"But the way to blend at Carnevale is by being as outlandish as possible," Mia said. "Besides, I think you look terrific."

"Terrific? Mia, look at me. I can't go around like this, I'll get beaten up. You've got to go back and get our clothes and whatever else you can sneak out of our room."

"But we just spent all this time on your costumes. Are you sure?"

"Positive."

"I guess I can do that."

"Talk to the police, too."

"Tell them the same story?"

"Sure, it's worth a try. We'll stay here till you get back and then we'll go to the ball together. Okay?"

"Okay."

Mia left and Richard spread an oily tarp on the floor to sleep, but the planks were too hard and his head hurt. CJ sat in a corner and stared into an opening in the floor that had a ladder that went all the way to the water. Every time he moved the glass floats tinkled.

"Richard?" he said after a while, his voice barely audible with the wind and waves. "There's something I have to tell you."

"Can't it wait?"

No answer, then tinkling.

"Wait a minute. You're not going to tell me you really had cocaine on you?"

"No, it's not that."

"Good, cause I would have drowned *you* instead of Macy. And if it's about me and Mia, you can save your breath. I don't want to hear it. I haven't decided whether to go with you or not, so let's just drop it."

"But—"

"Drop it, would you?"

Rather than argue, CJ went back to staring. Richard tried to sleep, but it was impossible. The best he could do was close his eyes and try to match his breathing to the waves. When Mia finally came back, she had a bag filled with rice, beans, tortillas, and fish from a nearby food stand. She also brought a bottle of Cuban rum and more cigarettes: gifts from Patrick. God bless him.

"I wasn't able to get to your room," she apologized. "The police are all over the resort and I had to be careful."

"Is the FBI there?"

"Yes, they wanted to hold me, but I told them I would help them find you."

"What about *Planeta Libre*? Did they believe it?"

"At first they did, but then Wayne told them the truth."

"I should have finished him off when I had the chance," Richard said. "So, I guess this is it, do or die."

"Don't be so pessimistic," Mia said. "You have to have faith."

"Faith?"

She went up and kissed him on the lips. Her mouth was warm and salty this time, not like the licorice from yesterday but not unpleasant, either. This was a different version of Mia, a salt water Mia, Aquaman's Mia. He wanted to take her up to his aqua blue room and almost said so but then thought better of it.

"I should go now," she said. "They might have followed me."

"Not before you tell me."

"Tell you what?"

"What do you think?"

"I don't know," she said, her eyes widening.

"Your costume."

"Oh, it's a surprise, but don't worry. I'm sure you'll like it."

She kissed him again and left, leaving the door open behind her. He watched her walk down the dock to the beach, shading her eyes and avoiding the stares of people in the water. When she was out of sight, he looked out at the Caribbean. Farther out, past the shallow water, he thought he saw a skiff with one white sail and three men in it. They waved and then set out to sea. He watched until they disappeared on the horizon.

───

Apparently, the same morons who came up with the phrase, "Please, Belize," to lure tourists to the islands also thought of the theme for the Carnevale, which was a fundraiser for the Ambergris Society for Alzheimer Prevention (ASAP). Richard didn't believe it at first and had to spell out the letters of each word to be sure, but there it was as large as the Hindenburg as they entered the other half of the hangar in their fishing attire, him waddling like a duck and

CJ clinking like a life-sized chandelier. There, above the stage that contained a forty-piece orchestra in white sports coats and black bowties was a banner declaring this to be "A Night to Remember."

"I couldn't make this up if I tried."

"Come on, let's go," CJ said, moving him along.

They filed past a table manned by security guards and four policemen looking very butch with badges, boots, and batons. Richard adjusted the mask and kept his eyes lowered. All eyes were on CJ, whose floats reflected the lights on the stage and the glittering silver ball above the dance floor, and Mia, who looked like a Mayan princess in feathers, beads, and a Busby Berkeley headdress. She wore pink lipstick that matched her toenails, which excited Richard so much that he tripped and fell into one of the policemen, who eyed his spear with suspicion but said nothing. Once past the checkpoint, they found a dimly-lit corner table and sat down to watch the spectacle unfold before them.

The hangar was crowded with party-goers. People were eating, drinking, dancing, and parading in their costumes, which were as lavish as any he'd seen. These included traditional Carnevale costumes from Venice and modern ones, some outlandish, some obscene. There were Harlequins, Robin Hoods, caliphs, sheiks, and sultans (the Arabic influence in Belize, no doubt), eighteenth-century aristocrats, ladies in petticoats, men in codpieces, Dickensian types in frock coats and top hats, wild-eyed shamans, greased Roman gladiators, Malaysian pirates, a guy with a chain saw, and a couple joined together like a strand of DNA. He and CJ were the only ones dressed in a maritime theme except for an oldtimer with a beard smoking a calabash pipe, who could have been either the figurehead of a ship or one of Chamba's colleagues.

They sat in silence at their table, not wanting to attract attention, when suddenly a stern looking Marie Antoinette joined them from out of nowhere. She plopped down with a thud and removed her shoe, a silver slipper, revealing what could only be described as carnage. She rubbed her toes and complained to no one in particular about some "idiot with three left feet." The bitching went on for so long that Richard decided, unwisely, to say something.

"Look, it could be worse," he told her, trying to be friendly.

"Oh, really, and how is that?"

"The idiot could be your husband."

She scowled in one of those condescending ways that reminded him of Katherine, and he noticed that she had a fake mole on her cheek larger than Mia's.

"I'm very happily divorced," she informed him, pointing to a toe ring that had been made from a gold wedding band and flexing her toes. "Not that it's any of your business."

"I'm just making conversation. You don't have to get upset."

"What?" she asked over the crowd.

"I said you don't have to get upset."

"Don't tell me what to do."

"I'm not telling you what to do."

"What do you call it, then?"

"What do I call what?"

The woman groaned.

"Look, it's just talk," he said.

"What?"

Richard tried to explain himself, but she turned away, hiding behind a rhinestone fan that matched her tinsel tiara.

"This is impossible," he said.

"What, so I'm impossible?" she shouted, fanning herself.

"Well, maybe not impossible, but you remind me of my ex-wife."

"How is that?"

"You're losing your head over nothing."

He slapped the table and burst out laughing. Indignant, Marie Antoinette rose, shoe in one hand, fan in the other. "This is what happens when you mix with riffraff," she said to CJ and Mia in all seriousness before hobbling away.

And this was what happens when you pretend the world is *not* after you. Honestly, he wasn't sure how much more he could take. Crazy people were falling out of the sky like frogs out of a tamarindo tree. Pretending they didn't exist would have been pointless, since the facts, once again, were irrefutable. He didn't make up the conspiracy with Macy and Updike, or that Macy had pulled the rubber mat out from under him, or that Updike had set him up, or that he had just been told off by a woman with mangled feet and a Bride of Frankenstein wig. These were all facts, so "paranoia" may not have been *le mot juste* for it. It had more to do with absurdity, and the grandest absurdity of all was that he was dressed like Aquaman for an Alzheimer's fundraiser in an airplane hangar in Belize and wanted for smuggling cocaine, which he had never even tried except for that one time with Katherine and her yoga instructor, a Jewish convert to Hinduism who called herself Kali Kline. He had heard that she was selling real estate limited partnerships now.

"Richard, you're drifting off again," Mia said, touching his arm.

"Am I?"

"Don't let her bother you. You're too sensitive, you know."

"So I've been told."

"Now you're mad?"

"No."

"He's always mad," CJ said. "He's either mad or clowning around. There's not much in between with Richard."

"I've got something in between for you."

"Don't get so upset," CJ said.

"Don't tell me what to do."

"Come on, boys, let's get something to eat," Mia said, grabbing Richard by the arm. "Leave the spear, though, would you?"

He was full from lunch but went anyway, careful not to trip on his fins or injure himself. Buffet tables were set up at either end of the dance floor, so they went to the one farthest from the entrance. He waited in line behind a paunchy Punchinello and filled his plate with fried chicken, stuffed jalapeños, a slice of key lime pie at least six inches high, and orange Jello with raisins that looked like insects preserved in amber. By the time they got back to their seats, the orchestra had stopped playing, the lights had come up, and a live auction—"the business part of the evening"—had begun. The auctioneer was none other than Fats Cahona, who wore a tri-cornered hat with a purple feather and performed his work with a custom gavel that he carried in a velour case. For the next hour, he auctioned a variety of items ranging from fishing trips and gourmet dinners to an aerial tour of the island on Amber Air and a visit to Hol Chan National Park, where you can feed nursing sharks or nurse feeding sharks or whatever the hell they did there. When the sharks were auctioned off, Fats turned serious and called upon an elderly woman suffering from Alzheimer's to come up to the stage to tell everyone how much their generosity meant to her. Unfortunately, the poor woman stared at the crowd without speaking, pressed her glasses to her face, and wept so loudly they had to escort her off the stage. Apparently, after looking at the partygoers assembled before her, she thought she had died and gone to hell. Richard could not have been more sympathetic.

"Before I bring out our band leader, who will entertain us with dancing till dawn, we have one more item of business," Fats announced in his deep voice.

He held up three envelopes containing prizes for The Most Original Costume, The Most Exotic Costume, and The Costume that Best Expresses the Theme of Alzheimer Awareness and Prevention. They decided not to have one for best costume, he informed everyone, since that would have encouraged competition, which he had always fought against (and won). By now, bored, Richard decided to check out the other tables. He'd seen most of them already: pirates, maids, drag queens, and clowns. There was also a Vulcan, the salesman from the exhibit booth. Then he spotted Marie Antoinette, who was still fanning herself and looking cross. She was with a bare-chested Indian in a longhaired wig and leather headband. His seemed to have normal feet.

"The prize for The Most Original Costume goes to—"

The orchestra did a drumroll and splash and Fats boomed, "DNA Double Helix!"

The excited DNA couple bounced up the steps as if in a potato sack race to claim their prize, a trip to Mayan Wonderland, or, as Richard thought of it, Parasite Paradiso. As they took their bows, he looked back at the Indian. Something about the guy seemed familiar, although he didn't know what or where he'd seen him. Richard felt certain, though, that for once he was not being paranoid and had met the guy before. He just hoped he wasn't an undercover fed.

"The judges have awarded the prize for The Most Exotic Costume at our Carnevale this evening to—"

Another drumroll and splash, at the end of which the "Sultan of Zanzibar" lumbered up to the stage in a jeweled turban and robes. This took some time, since he rivaled Fats in girth, giving Richard enough time to sneak another peek at the Indian. As he did, Marie Antoinette dropped her fan and the Indian bent down to retrieve it, revealing a mermaid tattoo on his shoulder. It was Nicky Negroponte, which meant that Marie Antoinette was none other than Katherine, *his* Katherine, the one whose name he swore never to mention again! He thought those mangled feet looked familiar! He lifted the mask to see better but it snapped back and hit him in the face.

"And the prize that is closest to our hearts, best reflecting the reason for the season, the prize for Alzheimer Awareness and Prevention goes to—"

Just when things couldn't possibly have gotten worse, they did. The lights went out and a spotlight raced around the room as the orchestra played "Flight of the Bumble Bee," landing on CJ, who froze in his chair.

The crowd exploded. The people at the next table, believing CJ to be paralyzed as well as feeble, escorted him to the stage, where he was presented with a check for one thousand Belizean dollars and a package of Forget-Me-Not seeds to be planted anywhere, anytime, at his discretion. Fats asked him to say a word on behalf of the ASAP, but CJ was so overwhelmed that he couldn't speak, which was fortunate but only elicited more sympathy and a standing ovation from the crowd, which adored their "Old Man and the Sea."

"And now, ladies and gentlemen," Fats continued, "I take great pride in introducing one of the greatest contributions of Belize to the rest of the world. We all know him as the Yiddish Garíf, the Jew with the Do, the Man of Renown, our own Sammy Brown!"

Hurriedly, Fats exited stage left as the spotlight followed a Garífuna man with a thin mustache and gelled pompadour entering stage right. He wore a white tie and tails and performed what he called the "scissor walk," swinging his arms and legs in opposite directions, which the crowd mimicked from the dance floor.

"Is everybody happy?" he yelled, grabbing the standing mike.

They shouted back, "Yes!"

"Is everybody ready?"

They waved their hands and shouted back even louder, "Yes!"

"And why is this night different from all other nights?!?"

Silence.

"You don't know?" he asked, taunting them.

"No!"

"You really don't know?"

"No!"

"Because it's time to…it's time to…time to…"

"*Cha-cha!*" they roared.

"*Cha-cha!*"

With big band flair, he led the orchestra in a cha-cha arrangement of Amilcare Ponchielli's "Dance of the Hours," inserting cha-cha-cha after every major break, to the delight of the dancers.

Richard recognized the music only because of Laura Fedora's grandfather, who used to play it so often that he had worn out the vinyl on the record, to the delight of everyone in the house. He and Laura had known it simply as "Hello Muddah, Hello Fadduh," Allan Sherman's parody from the sixties. The crowd ate it up, and when Sammy sang the ballad of the homesick Jewish kid at summer camp, replacing Camp Granada with "Camp Cahona," they went wild. Richard would have joined in the merriment, especially since the scene was surreal, but he had something else in mind.

"Would you like to dance?" he asked Mia.

"I've been waiting all night for you to ask me."

He set his spear down and led her onto the dance floor. He managed to do the steps by standing in place and shifting his weight, but any other movement was impossible in the fins. Still, he nudged Mia toward the tattooed Indian and queen. Nick and Katherine, showing off what must have cost a bundle at Arthur Murray, did three or four turns, arms interlocked, and promenaded back. They repeated it, this time Nick dipping his queen, and as he dipped her, Richard dipped Mia, whose headdress stuck in Katherine's face. Katherine spat, sputtered, and cursed as she tried to clear herself of the feathers. The two men faced each other, holding their partners above the dance floor. Nick looked down from Richard to Mia, Mia looked up from Katherine to Nick, and Richard stared at his ex-wife, pulling his face mask off and struggling to breathe at the sight of this woman who had come back from the grave, this woman he had loved and trusted and given his life to in what seemed like a world away, a parallel universe that suddenly wasn't parallel anymore, in a time that no longer counted and that was out of time, existing alongside of it in some mythic way in his own mind but no one else's.

He remembered what he was going to tell Mia now: that the disintegration of their marriage wasn't his fault and couldn't have been, for the simple reason that Katherine had always wanted *less* than he was willing to give, *less* than what was required to share a life together. She had never really wanted to get messy, which doomed them from the start. In the end, she had walked out on him, because "till death" had meant nothing to her, unless, of course, it was his death.

"*Katherine?*" he said weakly, faltering, hoping, looking for some sign of compassion. "It's me, Richard."

She pointed up at him and shrieked, "Oh, my God, it's him! He's stalking me! Quick, get me out of here!"

Sammy stopped singing just as the music swelled with *Take me home.* Then the police rushed the crowd, many of whom were drunk and oblivious to what was happening. Richard, Mia, and CJ raced to the exit, Richard ripping off his fins and grabbing his spear. It didn't escape him that this was like being chased by an army of fantasy archaeologists and that his dreams were coming true.

"Where to?" CJ asked, clinking and out of breath.

"There!" Mia said, pointing to a hallway on the other side of the exit.

As they ran through the doorway, a hand reached out and grabbed Richard from behind. He wheeled around, spear at the ready, but it turned out to be CJ's Garífuna friend.

"This way," he said, leading them down a staircase to a storeroom filled with boxes and exhibit material.

"With all of this heat, we've got to leave right away," he told them, checking the staircase every few seconds.

"So, what do we do?" CJ asked.

"You know the dock between the Kiss and the Royal Tern?"

"With the green shed? That's where we've been hiding out."

"That's the one. Meet me there in twenty minutes. We'll take a boat to the plane and fly out from there."

"From the water?"

"It's a seaplane. We use it all the time, got it?"

CJ nodded.

"There's an exit on the other side of this room, over there. You can get out that way. Just make sure the two of you are at the dock in twenty minutes. Otherwise, we'll leave without you."

He looked over at Mia as he left, repeating for emphasis, "*Two of you.* That's all there's room for."

As soon as they could, they snuck out of the storeroom, moving in and out of the shadows. Guests were spilling out of the hangar onto the beach, where police and security personnel were gathering. They went north toward the Royal Tern and then doubled back along the water. By the time they reached the dock, they were out of breath and nearly out of time. They clambered up the dock, past the mangrove trees, and ran as fast as they could to the shed, but someone walking along the water spotted them and shouted for the police. Within seconds, whistles were blowing and what seemed like the entire Belizean Defense Force came down upon them.

"I can't do it anymore," Mia said out of breath.

Richard picked her up and hoisted her onto his back, following CJ, who was having trouble with the floats. They were halfway there when the police reached the dock.

"Come on, we can do this!" Richard yelled.

They made it to the shed just ahead of the police, who pounded on the door with their flashlights and batons, ordering them to surrender on pain of something or other (Richard couldn't make it out but imagined the possibilities). Frantically, they piled junk against the door, including the harpooned horse. Meanwhile, CJ announced that the boat had arrived and was waiting below.

"Where?"

"Down that ladder to the water."

"All right, Mia, you go first," Richard said, taking her by the arm. "We'll hold them off until you're safe."

She descended the ladder, ruffling a few feathers, and disappeared into the darkness. "Okay, CJ, now you."

CJ looked down at the water, hesitated, and then stood back.

"Come on, what are you waiting for?"

"I've been thinking a lot about it, Richard, and I can't."

"What?"

"I can't do it."

"Sure you can. You just go down that ladder to the boat. Now hurry, that door won't last much longer!"

"No, you don't understand. I have to stay here, and so do you."

"What are you talking about?"

CJ looked down, curling his bottom lip. Richard tried to read his face but couldn't figure out what was going on. He had never seen CJ like this before.

"What are you talking about?"

And then, suddenly, he knew. Reality finally caught up with his dreams. He had been betrayed again, except this time it was worse than Pet Mat, worse than Katherine, worse than his father and that last sales call. He was so stunned he wasn't sure what he felt, but he knew that from this moment on he could never be sure about anything anymore.

"It's you, isn't it? You're the hit man."

"There really is no hit man, but, yeah, I'm the guy...How did you know?"

"I didn't know until now. So, all this time you've been acting?"

"No, not the whole time. I wasn't supposed to get busted in Antigua. I hadn't even gotten around to planting the cocaine when they came for me. I was so nervous I almost wet myself. That's why I called Mia."

"You mean that was just a coincidence? She's not in on it?"

"That's what I've been trying to tell you all along."

"So why are you doing this?"

CJ cleared his throat and the banging grew louder. It sounded as if they would smash through the door any second.

"They made me promise, Richard. Updike said he'd fire me and turn me over to the police. I already have a record, you know, so I can't let that happen. He even threatened Christine when she met with him."

"They caught you with dope at work, didn't they?"

CJ shrugged. "With you it was fish, with me it was weed. What's worse, this was the second time it happened."

"How much?"

"A little."

"How much is a little?"

"A lot."

"What did I tell you about that?"

"I couldn't help it."

"I understand that, believe me I do," Richard said, shaking his head, "but did you have to sell me out?"

CJ shuffled, clinking.

"So what happens now?" Richard asked.

"I'm supposed to make sure you don't escape again. They said once you're back in jail, I'm off the hook."

"You don't believe that, do you? You think they're going to let you leave here and go back to Philadelphia? Think about it, CJ. They'll dump your ass the minute you're arrested. It's the perfect setup and you're the perfect patsy."

"I'm not going to get arrested," CJ insisted. "It's all been worked out, the whole thing. I'm sorry, Richard."

"Not half as sorry as I am."

Richard shoved him backward as hard as he could into the opening down the ladder. There was a crash of floats, groans, and a distant splash. Then the police rushed in, storming the rampart of wooden horse and fishing gear and falling over each other like the Keystone Cops. Richard swung back and forth at them with his spear, holding them at bay long enough for the boat to buzz off into the night. It was his final act of defiance and the last sound he heard before the crack of a baton against his head.

He is certain this is a dream, because he is in a ballroom of white Carrera marble, waltzing toward a mahogany bar filled from floor to ceiling with mirrors. Mia is there, chat ting with the third Mrs. Alberto Plotón and sipping a martini so cold it breathes. She is taller than he remembers and wears a white gown with a headdress of red, gold, and black feathers. Alberto's wife, a plump Garífuna woman with a gap in her teeth, has adjusted the lights and lit copal in a ceremonial bowl on the bar. The smoke curls upward, reminding him of everything he loves and hates about this place, but mainly that it is not Pennsylvania. There are no proper woods here, just jungle and marshland and stinking, fetid humidity. It's the perfect place for a real estate developer with a tax problem. He keeps it to himself, since they are enjoying the evening and he doesn't want to ruin it for her. This requires tremendous self-control, since ruining things is one of his gifts. After all, didn't Katherine call him "The Ruinator?"

Alberto's wife, a part-time dance instructor, takes them onto the dance floor and shows him how to lead his partner by pushing his hips toward the floor. She has to show him several times, since he is not used to it and moves unevenly.

"Normally, I go one step forward and two back," he tells her. "We've been doing it that way in my family for generations."

"I understand that, but this is different," she says. "You move forward by going down, spiraling down like a corkscrew."

"I've been spiraling down since high school."

"Yes, that's true, but now you've lost your frame. You have to keep your frame, or you'll have no way of making her follow you. She won't know where you want to go."

"She knows where I want to go."

"And where is that, honey, second base, rounding third?"

"Home."

Richard laughs and twirls Mia around the room away from Alberto's wife, but no matter how hard he tries or where they go, they end up returning to the same spot.

"Did you have a nice trip, honey?" she asks once they come back.

"Delightful," he answers.

"Then you may be ready."

"For what?"

"The truth."

"I've never been ready for that. Just ask anyone."

"Don't listen to him," Alberto interrupts from behind the bar, puffing on his cigar. "He's lying. That's what he does best."

"Do not."

"Do."

The music starts up again, played by the Sammy Brown Orchestra dressed in sequined tuxedos. Each musician sits behind a music stand with the initials "SOB" written in large cursive letters on the front.

"Somebody at the factory screwed up," the trombone player explains, "but we were able to get them at a discount."

"You're pulling my leg, right?"

"No, it's the truth."

"Sammy doesn't mind?"

"Hell no. He says it gets his name out there."

Richard leads Mia away from them, his patent leather shoes shining so brightly he can see himself. He has always taken pride in his appearance, especially his shoes. They say something about the man who wears them, so he makes sure his are polished and resoled regularly. You can never be too careful, especially in this business, where a scuff here, a smudge there can make all the difference. Mia wears blue Ferragamo pumps, but when he asks her to take them off to show him her feet, she hops onto a carousel with the harpooned horse, which whispers secrets in her ear. He would be jealous except that this is Mia and not the Queen of the Oyster Eaters, so he is not worried. To pass the time, he walks around the carousel, noting each type of animal to ride, and comes across a paunchy Punchinello on a swan bench eating a liverwurst sandwich and slurping espresso from a thermos. His shoes are off and his feet, covered in dirty socks with holes, rest on the bench opposite him. His hat is off, too, revealing a tuft of dark, greasy hair. Richard feels sorry for the swan that has to bear him and says so. Paunch smiles demonically with liverwurst smeared all over his teeth, and Richard rushes back to Mia so disgusted that he loses count of the animals.

"So, are you going to tell me what the horse said?" he asks her, helping her down from the carousel.

"I'll tell you later."

"When?"

"When you find your frame."

"But I've got it, I swear."

"Then show me."

The shine on his shoes has brought back his confidence, so he holds her in dance position and they waltz around the room.

"So, what did it say?" he asks again. "It must have told you a thing or two or three."

"The big secret is no secret at all."

"So what is it?"

"I came on this trip because I love you."

"You don't say?" he says, crisscrossing behind her in a scissor pattern and touching his toes. He is hopeful that this will lead to sex, the big nasty.

"And how did that happen?"

"I don't know. I think it's because you make me laugh."

"If I had known that, I wouldn't have tried so hard."

"You were trying?"

"Ever since I met you."

"That's a little scary," she says.

"Tell me about it."

He draws her into his arms and dips her. As they finish, they find themselves once again back at the bar. There doesn't seem to be anything he can do about it.

"It's like water in a bathtub, isn't it?" Alberto's wife says glee-fully. "No matter where it starts, sooner or later it ends up at the drain."

"You're the drain?"

"There's no escape, honey."

"Maybe not for me, but for Mia there is."

"Ah, that's what I like to hear," Alberto shouts from the bar. "Ain't love bland?"

"Leave these two alone," the wife scolds. "Can't you see they're homesick?"

Alberto chews on his cigar, pushing it from one side of his mouth to the other. Then he strokes his tremendous eyebrows and says, "Well, I know what that's like, what with being a refugee in Hungary and all that."

"You were never in Hungary."

"Honduras, then. You know those Hondurans."

She looks at him sternly.

"I know it started with an H."

"So does my headache."

Suddenly, they transform from Alberto and his wife into Richard's parents. His father has been mixing drinks behind the bar so as not to mingle with the guests and upset them with conspiracy theories, the latest of which is that he was set up by the airlines and Iraqi oil interests.

"I have it on the highest authority," he claims.

"God told you?" Richard's mother asks.

"A little lower."

"Barack Obama?"

"Like any good cook, I can't reveal my source."

"I don't believe you," she says.

"It's perfectly believable."

"Sure, if you've had a lobotomy."

Richard wants to get away before things get out of hand, even though the waiters are now serving crab canapés straight from the oven and the champagne was bottled by hand and turned a quarter rotation every four months. He takes Mia by full rotation to a balcony overlooking the sea, where they breathe the moist night air and watch moonlight shimmering on the water. In the distance, there is a skiff with a white sail and three men huddled in it. It's the same skiff from before, but it is too far out to call or even signal, and he does not want to detract from their time together. He feels calm when he is with her, which is no small feat for a Mercurius.

"My people are nervous and paranoid," he explains. "We sleep with one eye open or, as my uncle did, with a snub-nose thirty-eight. My mother chastised him for it, saying that if he ever shot himself in his sleep, he would become the first accidental suicide. But I do not want to be an accidental anything, let alone suicide."

"Then why don't we stick together?" Mia says.

"I've been waiting for you to ask me."

"Are you making fun of me again?"

"Not at all."

"Good, because it's unseemly for a gentleman."

"All right, I promise never to make fun of you again. I promise not to drop my pants. I will keep them on at all times, along with my shorts, shoes, and bowtie, which I tied myself this evening in less than twenty minutes."

"You want a medal?" she asks.

"That would be nice."

"What kind?"

"Valor, second class."

"Second class?"

"I can't commit all the way. You know how men are."

Offended, Mia jumps down to the beach below, her feathers providing a soft landing, and walks at a brisk pace along the water. Since he cannot fly, he slides across the ballroom floor, down the marble staircase, and onto the beach after her, avoiding his parents and the troublesome trombone player, who has convinced himself that they are the best of friends and hits Richard up for bus fare to the Kutztown Folk Festival every chance he gets. By the time he gets there, however, Mia has moved onto the cliffs at Surfers' Bay, where breakers crash against the sandstone wall and craggy beach. It is a dangerous place to be, but she refuses to budge.

"That's not fair, Richard. I said that about my father and grandfather, who still aren't speaking to each other."

"I'm sorry. I couldn't help it."

"You can't help a lot of things."

"That's true."

He feels ashamed again, although he doesn't understand how family members not speaking could be a bad thing. He stands on the cliff with the waves thundering below, wondering when they can go back to the safety of the ballroom or at least the parking lot across the street, where there are signs that say "SB Parking." Someone has scribbled an O between the S and B on each sign in black marker. He waits for Mia to say something, anything, but she has grown quiet. He looks at his now scuffed shoes and wipes spray (ambergris?) from his face. When she continues her silence, he smokes a cigarette. He doesn't know what to tell her except that instinct got the better of him and he sabotaged himself.

"But I also did it for a higher purpose," he tells her.

"You see, sarcasm requires complete devotion, which is what most people don't understand, but you do. You have patience beyond your years, which allows you to put up with behavior that falls short of mine."

"You get that from a fortune cookie or something?"

He shakes his head.

"But you said falls short?"

"That's right."

"Why not falls long?"

"I don't understand."

"You know, falls long, like Niagara."

"What are you saying?"

She raises the hem of her gown, which is now a wedding dress with brocade and pearls, and shows off her bare feet in the moonlight. Her toenails are luminous pink, and he can't take his eyes off them, which is unfortunate, because he is unaware that she is inching them toward the cliff. She does it so innocently that he is caught off guard. "It's a different kind of dance," she explains. "In this one, you move forward by going down, spiraling down like a corkscrew."

"You mean I'm screwed?"

"You'll have to trust me on this."

"I'm not going."

"Sure, you are. We both are."

"But——"

"It's the only way out, Richard."

"Out of what?"

"Your life."

She steps off the cliff as calmly as if she were stepping onto an elevator, clutching his bowtie as they rush headlong toward the rocks below. He would love nothing more than to pause the action right now and rewrite the script, but it is too late. He can't believe this is an improvement over his life with Katherine. She stranded him on the beach after teasing him with oysters and Bloody Mary mix, which was bad enough, but now Mia is about to bury his head in the sand, literally. He considers telling her that he never thought her capable of such a thing, but the last thing he wants is to come across like Cane Lady. However, after thinking it over, he decides to trust her and throw himself headlong, as it were, into a new life.

"If that's not love, I don't know what is," he yells into her ear as the salt air whistles past both of them.

"What?"

"If that's not love—never mind."

"What?"

"If that's mud, my shoes will get ruined."

"Stop worrying," she shouts back in free-fall. "I'll take you into town to buy another pair, gun smoke, I promise."

"Oh, that would be nice," he says, satisfied, as he touches the top of his head, the last time he will feel his skull intact.

"Look, there's the drain. I can make out the holes," she says confidently. "And there's your therapist. He just checked his watch and is waiting for us. We're late."

"Story of my life," he says.

"Well, that's about to change."

"Can we just get this over with?"

"As you wish."

———

This time, he didn't have to ask. He knew he wasn't dead even though he wished he were, because he could feel air flowing into and out of his lungs as he lay motionless on a bed that smelled of kerosene. He opened his eyes and looked around as far as possible, but all he could see was a pink blur. He focused, painfully, and a flower came into view. It had been cut and put in a paper cup of water on a rickety table across the room, which was a jail cell. The cell was a small room in a drab, wooden house that, from the noise and commotion in the outer hall, must have served as the San Pedro police station, post office, shore patrol headquarters, and tourist information bureau. You could probably get your palm read, too. The flower provided the only color in the room, and it reminded him of Mia: her toes, her hair, the back of her neck, those leather straps caressing her feet. He had no idea how long he had been there, and he wasn't even sure what had happened. He couldn't remember much except for the sound of that crack, clear and solid like a Ted Williams homerun with an ash bat.

"Hibiscus," a voice whispered from across the room. Richard looked in the direction of the voice and recognized the policeman he had tripped into at the ball.

"Hibiscus," he repeated. "It's a pink hibiscus. I think it's called a 'lipstick hibiscus.' I noticed you staring at it."

Richard tried to speak but nothing came out. He waited, gathered his strength, and tried again but got the same result. That's when he realized that his head was throbbing.

"Don't try to talk," the policeman said. "You've got a nasty bump on the head. It'll go away, but you have to rest for a while."

He reached up and felt a bandage wrapped tight around his head. The spot where he had been hit was moist. He must have gotten a concussion, probably cracked his skull. He made a mental note to file a lawsuit and assemble a legal team. He'd own the whole island before this was over, including the Great Kiss, which Fats could kiss goodbye.

"You're supposed to keep that on. The inspector and doctor said they'd be back this afternoon to check the wound."

"How long have I been here?"

"Two days."

"*Two days?*"

The policeman smiled. "I'm afraid so."

"Just me?"

The man nodded.

"What about my friends?"

"Friends? Ah, yes, I remember them when you came to the Carnevale, especially that woman with the feathers. That was a wonderful costume. We all loved it, I tell you. I'm not sure they're your friends, though, not when they left you like that. But, if you must know, they either got away, in which case we will find them, or they drowned in the sea and their bodies will wash up before too long. It is inevitable."

The policeman stood there, waiting to see what kind of reaction this got. Richard wasn't sure himself.

"Drowned?" he asked, confused.

"It happens from time to time, although things like that never get publicized. It's bad for the tourist business, you know."

His mind raced with the possibility that CJ and Mia may not have made it, that they actually may have drowned, but then he calmed down and thought it through. He had heard the boat take off, even with the pounding at the door. Sure, CJ's drug dude could have panicked and left them in the water, but then the police would have picked them up. If they had drowned, it would have been right there at the dock, which was almost impossible, especially dressed in feathers and floats. And with the temperature of the water, they could have lasted all night. The only reason they weren't in custody right now was that they were vacationing somewhere on the beach in Mexico. He was sure of it. What other reason could there possibly be?

"I may not have much experience with interrogations, but I can tell when a cop is playing me," he told the policeman.

"Well, I can tell you honestly that I am not playing you and this is not a game. I have to say that you are in a fine mess, a very fine mess."

"I've heard that before."

"No doubt, but this time it is very bad. You resisted arrest and injured two constables with your weapon, which is a very serious offense. They had to get tetanus shots."

"Weapon?"

"Your spear, of course. I also hear you are a kidnapper and drug smuggler."

"That's a lot of hype. Did you find any drugs?"

"No, I don't believe so."

"Then you can't believe everything you hear."

"Yes, but even if it's half true..."

"I'll get a lethal injection?"

"No, but your life will most assuredly be ruined."

Richard smiled and the officer went back to his reports. He lay there, studying the wooden rafters above as they baked in the sun and listening to the wind weaving through the eaves. He was getting used to the sordid side of life by now. It beat tee time and Excel, that was for sure. In what may have been the final irony of this trip, he realized that his jailer was absolutely right: he was in a mess, but at least it was *his* mess; not Alberto's, Alberto's wife's, Katherine's, CJ's or anyone else's who had somehow wormed their way out of the psychic woodwork into his consciousness. It belonged to him and him alone, which meant that he finally had an identity, finally had an answer for his therapist, the guy at the bottom of the cliff who needled him about finding the "real Mercurius." He knew who he was, no thanks to Dr. Fraud. It was him lying here in a jail cell with a cracked head and nothing to show for a life time spent busting his ass so that others less talented could take summer vacations on cruise ships. Being wanted for more felonies than a Washington lobbyist didn't count, either. That wasn't what he had in mind when he went to law school. He was now the same age as his father when they had taken that ride to the airport. It had turned out to be his father's final humiliation, but was it possible that he had gotten something out of it? Had his father learned anything at all? Richard had certainly gotten something out of this trip besides *e-coli*. He wasn't going to chase delusions from his past anymore. That was over and done with, itself a thing of the past.

"And that's something, isn't it?"

Of course it was, and he had Mia to thank for it. Who would have guessed? Mia of the jailbreak, Mia of the majestic Magis, Mia of the twinkle toes hibiscus. She was out there somewhere, waiting for him or maybe planning his jailbreak. She could show up early one morning with her mole and an angel food cake, and they'd become the next Bonnie and Clyde, Caribbean style. They might even have their poster put up at the jail. After all they'd been through, he'd rather have the outlaw life anyway. So maybe this trip wasn't going to end in a header off the broadcast deck after all, despite how it looked right now, despite the black hole that Katherine had been in his life.

He checked the lipstick hibiscus again and started humming *Take me home, I hate Cahona*. If he had to admit the truth (at this point what was the use of lying?), he wanted to go home. That's all he had ever really wanted from the time he sat in rectal misery on that park bench in Antigua. Then, somewhere on the roof he heard a bird chirping a light, high-pitched, airy *Qu'est-ce que dit,* which he finally figured out was French for "you'll need a good lawyer, *mon ami.*" That's what he had been trying to tell CJ all along.

.